# Silver Moon

## Over 100
## Great Novels
## of
## Erotic Domination

If you like one you will probably like the rest

New Titles Every Month

All titles in print are now available from:

**www.adultbookshops.com**

If you want to be on our confidential mailing list for our Readers' Club Magazine (with extracts from past and forthcoming titles) write to:

### SILVER MOON READER SERVICES

Shadowline Publishing Ltd
No 2 Granary House
Ropery Road
Gainsborough
DN21 2NS
United Kingdom

telephone: 01427 611697
Fax: 01427 611776

### NEW AUTHORS WELCOME

Please send submissions to
Silver Moon Books
PO Box 5663
Nottingham
NG3 6PJ

Silver Moon is an imprint of Shadowline Publishing Ltd
First published 2000 Silver Moon Books
ISBN 1-897809-67-0
© 2000, 2007 Sean O'Kane & Falconer Bridges

# Tales from the Lodge

By

## Sean O'Kane
&
## Falconer Bridges

ALSO BY SEAN O'KANE
TAMING THE BRAT
CHURCH OF CHAINS
THE STORY OF EMMA
INTO THE ARENA
THE GLADIATOR
THE PRIZE
SLAVE'S HONOUR
LAST SLAVE STANDING
SLAVEMAKER

ALSO BY FALCONER BRIDGES
THE BROTHERHOOD
THE DAUGHTERS OF DESADE (FEMDOM)
THE PIT OF PAIN
SLAVES OF THE BLOODLINE (FEMDOM)

All characters in this book are fictitious, and any resemblance to real persons, living or dead, is purely coincidental.

THIS IS FICTION - IN REAL LIFE ALWAYS PRACTISE SAFE SEX!

# Contents

## Lolli
Falconer Bridges

## Rosa
Sean O'Kane

## Melinda
Sean O'Kane

## Caroline
Sean O'Kane

## Marie-Helene
Falconer Bridges

## Brat
Sean O'Kane

# LOLLI

by Falconer Bridges

"I think she's in the Common room," Alan Masterson told me as he led me along the magnificent first floor corridor in the west wing of The Lodge; probably the most exclusive and discreet club in the country. He pushed open a heavy, oak panelled door and ushered me in. I found myself in a long, high ceilinged room, four tall sash windows were spaced out down one wall and the afternoon sun flooded in on richly upholstered and luxurious chairs and sofas. On the walls were many portraits in oils and in between them, where you might have expected to see crossed halberds and muskets in a fine old house like this were tasteful arrangements of whips and canes. There were examples of virtually every possible type. And tucked away round the edges of the room were frames, bars and benches on which were arranged all the restraints and chains one could wish for.

I registered all this in a quick glance which also told me that the room was empty apart from an elegantly dressed, tall, dark haired man lounging casually against the arm of one of the sofas. He waved at us a little distractedly, and I couldn't blame him because kneeling in front of him was a dark haired girl in a long, blue satin dress. Her back was towards me and the low cut of the dress revealed the marks of what must have been a fairly recent beating. Her head was moving slowly and rhythmically backwards and forwards at the height of his waist. With something of a shock I realised that she had his penis in her mouth.

"That's Lolli," Alan said, "watch her. She's a real artist."

My initial embarrassment was quite overcome by the two men's casual acceptance of what was going on. But then, this was The Lodge, I reminded myself.

So I followed Alan over to another sofa which gave us a

side view of Lolli at work and we settled down to watch. He was right; Lolli was indeed an artist at fellatio. Her pretty mouth moved slowly and lovingly up and down the thick rod of the man's sex. Every now and then she would take her mouth off it completely and allow her tongue to lap lasciviously across the engorged glans that stood, huge and shiny in front of her face. And she didn't just lick, she put her tongue right out and made sure the man she was pleasuring could see exactly how carefully she was caressing him. When she went fully down on him I couldn't help noticing that she managed to fit in an extraordinary amount of the rigid shaft. After a few minutes we heard a small gasp from the man and his hand came down to rest on the back of her head. At once her head ducked down towards the hand which held the base of his sex and as he bucked his hips forwards as the spasms of his orgasm ran through him she took every drop without even swallowing, she obviously had the knack of opening her throat completely to whichever man wanted to use it.

Although she must have seen us from the corner of her eye she took plenty of time about making sure she licked the man clean of every last trace of sperm before tucking the softening cock back into his trousers. The man waved casually to us once more and left while Lolli got to her feet and came over to us, only to kneel down once more after carefully raising her skirts and then settling back on her heels.

"This is Lolli," Alan said getting up and preparing to leave. "No-one will want this room till after dinner so you've got plenty of time," he told me, and then turned back to Lolli. "I shall expect to hear that you've looked after our guest properly Lolli."

"Yes Master," she said.

Alan left the room and I looked at Lolli. She was very attractive, full breasted and with dark hair falling in waves round her face, framing a soft and sensual mouth and dark eyes which sparkled with intelligence.

I took out my notepad and prepared to start the interview, but I was finding it difficult to put out of my mind the scene I had just witnessed.

"Well… Lolli," I began, "is it… I mean… How did you get that nickname?"

She laughed immediately, a pleasant musical laugh.

"No it's not because of that! Although I am reckoned to be pretty good! I'll tell you why…"

It was an experiment. And she was part of it. Girls at one of the most diehard traditional boys' public schools? My God no! The Colonel Blimps were adamant; it wouldn't do at all.

But it did do and the Blimps lost the argument. However they did gain one major victory. They were insistent that discipline was the purpose of a good school. Iron discipline, in turn to be learnt, endured and respected and girls must not be allowed to threaten tradition. So it was decided that in the matters of obedience, and correction, all would be equal. The wenches were to be treated no differently to the young gentlemen and there was to be no deference to their femininity. If a thrashing was called for then a thrashing they would receive, the only reservation being that in their case no corporal punishment could be administered by a prefect.

No, the task of administering punishment to pupils of the non-male gender, that's how they put it, had to be vested in more responsible hands. But there weren't too many responsible hands that wanted the assignment. And so the onus for ensuring discipline was maintained at the highest level amongst the girls fell mainly upon the shoulders of one particular master. The girls were all terrified of him and Lolli in particular looked upon him as some kind of horrid ogre. The sight of him striding along the corridors with his robe flowing made her knees tremble.

In the event he was her housemaster and he treated his duties with extreme seriousness. Punishment was meticulous and strict. Lolli steered well clear of trouble and avoided his clutches only to be thrown into the lion's den by a shit of a prefect, who for no apparent reason had it in for her.

Talking in assembly, that was her crime apparently. The prefect hauled her out of the congregation, humiliated her in front of the whole school and put her on report. The consequence was never in doubt; it was an automatic six lashes of the strap. From then on she had to work very hard to avoid the trips down the echoing corridors to stand outside his study and await punishment. But for the most part she managed as well as any of the other girls and boys. And that was really the point because however cruel and unfair, it was the same for all of them. They all lived with the same cruelties and injustices; and the same certainties.

But then it all changed for her.

The same prefect who had had it in for her all along got her for having taken a short cut on a cross-country run. Again she was hauled out in assembly and put on report. But this time it was too much. A few weeks past her sixteenth birthday and made to bend over again like a little kid? She wasn't going to take it any more. She raced back to her dormitory and pulled on four more pairs of knickers before reporting to the Housemaster's study.

As usual matron was there to see the rules adhered to, but on that occasion she was dismissed and Lolli was alone with him for the first time. And it came as something of a shock to her to find that he wasn't really old. He made her bend over his desk, pressing her budding breasts flat against the surface, her hands stretched out and grasping the edges. By the fifth form, short pleated skirts had replaced shorts and she felt the material ride up her long thighs. He made her stand on tiptoe to push her buttocks up further and she knew that if she were naked her virgin sex would be pushing back towards him. And at that moment the dread she had been feeling evaporated to be replaced by a strange tingling feeling. It was anticipation.

But on his part, what should have been a tight little bottom thrust up for punishment was blatantly padded and he spotted immediately that she was trying to cheat.

His voice was cold. Controlled.

"I am not often called upon to strap fifth form girls," he said, "but even I can see that you are attempting to avoid your full punishment. Now stand up and remove the extra knickers or whatever they are."

Bright red with humiliation but still tingling in the pit of her stomach, she stood up, slowly hitched up her skirt and wriggled each pair of knickers down and stepped out of them. All that was left was the briefest pair of satin ones that matron would allow.

"Ah...Humbert... Humbert..." She heard him whisper as she smoothed the skirt down and resumed the punishment position.

And then he beat her, administering the lashes with much greater severity than ever before; the penalty for trying to cheat, she learned later.

As she knelt at my feet, Lolli's overpowering sexual presence was prompting a stirring of activity in my own loins. I found my thoughts distractingly running over Alan's parting instruction to her, hoping against hope that looking after me 'properly' might include the same consideration she'd been showing to the man on our entrance into the common room. That she did, after the conclusion of her tale, go on to provide me with one of my most potent sexual experiences remains a vivid memory. Her tongue, her lips and her throat all combined to bring me to a shattering orgasm, relegating any acts of fellatio before or since to an almost banal level of amateurism. The wonders of her own, very special oral talents, spoiled me forever.

"When I think about it now," she said, "I can't believe I was so stupid. But I'm glad I was. If I hadn't been, he would never have leathered me so hard and I would never have experienced the joys of submission, bondage and correction.

It stings, it hurts, sometimes it bleeds, but the pain that comes with the thwack of the cane or the slash of the whip is Heaven."

But then it was a new experience. She'd felt something other than discomfort, but exactly what emotions had been aroused in her she didn't know. And apart from that, who was Humbert Humbert? The other girls were as baffled as she was. What had he been talking about? The prefect cleared up that mystery the next time he put her on report and after that Lolita became required reading in the dorm after lights out. Her friends took to calling her Lolli and 'nymphette' seemed to be the buzzword amongst the prefect and his cronies every time she came across them.

She was quite proud.

She had many encounters with the housemaster after that, but he never beat her with such severity again. In fact he never spoke to her, except to discuss her academic progress or to comment on the reason why her rebellious nature resulted in so many referrals to him for corrective discipline. Even though by now she was committing every and all punishable offences just to get close to him, every beating was administered with clinical adherence to the school guidelines. After that one time the matron was always there to witness the absolute propriety of the enactment of the sentence, and she hated that. It felt like an intrusion on something very private.

She herself was never happy because all she cared about was him but it seemed that in his eyes she was just another rebellious teenager. And it went on like that right up until her eighteenth birthday.

She was still there, at the school. Her father was still abroad and so she had nowhere to go. She'd done well and was up for Oxford. Her father had a long distance chat with the Head and sent him a pretty hefty cheque to use in any manner he saw fit and so it was agreed between them that she could remain on campus throughout the summer break.

So there she was one night, taking stock of herself and posing in front of her mirror. Not bad, she thought. Pretty fair boobs, hat peg nipples, a good backside and a mouth no man with a serviceable rod could possibly refuse. And then out of the blue the summons arrived. He wanted to see her.

That threw her. She'd spent years pining for his attention but secretly she'd long given up hope that she might one day become more than just an errant schoolgirl in his thoughts. What was she to do? Now the opportunity had come she wasn't going to miss out, that was for sure. She thought it over for about two seconds and then pulled out the suitcase that she'd packed ready for college. She opened the lid and took out the short silken sheath she'd bought with the cash her daddy had telegraphed as a salve to his conscience. That dress was a statement. It said that she was grown up, sophisticated and alluring and its purpose was to make her the Belle of the Freshers' Ball. Now it was going to have a different destiny.

It wasn't cold but all the same she was trembling as she knocked on his door. She heard footsteps approaching and then the door swung open. Beyond the door the room was dimly lit. There was music: Roxy Music. 'Slave to love' it was, and that music itself signalled that here was a very different man from the crusty denizen of the classroom. A fleeting thought whisked through her mind that maybe the song was intended to convey some sort of message. He beckoned her inside and his private rooms were like nothing that she could have imagined; intimate, tastefully decorated and not at all the lair of a soulless bachelor. And as for him, now devoid of his schoolmasterly trappings, he was as maturely rugged as in the portrait she'd painted in her imagination: a dinner jacketed sophisticate who exuded all the sex appeal she had ever dreamed of. He closed the door behind her and ushered her in by placing a hand on the small of her back. Lolli shivered at the touch, hot shivers, then shivered more as his hand slipped down to rest very softly, but somehow possessively, on her hip.

A table was set with two places. Candles flickered, wine flowed and the food was prepared by Aphrodite herself. He was charming, eloquent and above all, although he was firmly in control of the proceedings there was no condescension; he treated her as an adult. She was swept by an elated, triumphal gratification that he should see her as a desirable woman and she determined to play her part to the full. All thoughts of the schoolroom were banished, no longer tutor and pupil; they were now seducer and willing victim. His conversation flowed along with the wine and she fell ever more deeply under his spell as his words wove patterns of magic into the fabric of her impressionable, eager young heart.

It seemed an eternity before the dinner was over and they finally rose from the table. This was the moment she'd been longing for, the fulfilment of her dreams and he didn't have to lead her to the bedroom, she couldn't wait.

She was in a hurry. All those frustrating years of yearning piled themselves into a mountain of urgency. She started to throw off her dress but he caught her arm and slipping the silken fabric back over her shoulders he motioned her into stillness. He held her at arm's length and spent several agonizing moments devouring her body with hungry eyes. He slid his palms over her hips and down her thighs, following the lines of her suspenders until he reached the lace tops of her stockings. The silkiness of the material allowed him to feel everything as if there was no barrier between his hands and her yielding flesh. He explored the ridge where stocking gave way to naked thigh and then his hands slipped around to caress her bottom. Sensitive fingers traced the perimeter of her French knickers and after working their way back lingered on the mound of Venus, gently probing her womanhood.

She was in a frenzy of arousal. She couldn't help herself

and pushed herself against him. A stinging slap came from nowhere, reddening her cheek. Then he gently pushed her back to arm's length. She learned quickly. She was to submit to his desires only and must make no moves herself. Any sexual release she craved could only come with his express permission. She tried to stay calm. Again he caressed her intimately and despite herself she shivered in delight as he found her proud nipples and cupped her breasts.

"How long have you waited for this moment Lolli?" he asked.

She was both surprised and thrilled that he'd addressed her by her nickname, the name she'd been endowed with because of that incident in his study all those years before. He must have heard it whispered furtively around the corridors but she wondered if he'd ever connected its origin to his own lips.

"Forever," she whispered as a shiver of anticipation flowed downwards from her shoulders, rolled over her eager breasts, tingled down her spine and after lingering over the soft insides of her thighs, surged into the ever-moistening depths of her vagina.

She was devoured by lust, the hunger in her soaking sex was unendurable and unable to control herself she reached out for him.

He threw her grasping arms aside and roughly spun her around.

"No! Do nothing until I instruct you," he ordered. "You must learn obedience."

A slap, much harder than the first, exploded on to her thinly protected bottom causing her to gasp in an involuntary exhalation. And then another. And another. Tears welled into her eyes, not just tears of pain but tears of euphoria. At last her dreams were coming true, she was suffering at his hands, enduring correction as she'd imagined it so many times. He turned her around to face him again and taking several steps backwards stood surveying her once more.

Her knickers were drenched now and it took all her self-control to stop herself from putting her own hand down to massage her hard little clitoris. He was aroused too, that was obvious from the impressive bulge that was straining his trousers. She wanted the cock that was throbbing inside that tent, she wanted it desperately and she couldn't tear her eyes away from it. He looked down to view the object of her attention.

"Insolence will not be tolerated," he snapped, "didn't you learn anything in the classroom?"

In firm tones he told her that voyeurism was his prerogative, his alone to enjoy and savour. She was never to display any emotion, curiosity or reaction to his personal physical state. In view of her disrespect, punishment was called for.

"Is that not so?" he questioned.

She was incapable of answering. A hurricane of need raged through her entire being, turning the pools of love juice lubricating the slit of her sex into a raging turmoil of molten lust which left her weak kneed and helpless.

"Answer girl!"

"Y... yes," She stammered out weakly.

"Speak up," he ordered. "Let me hear you. And it's still Sir, or do I have to punish you for forgetting that too?"

"No," she bleated.

His fury increased.

"What!" he bellowed.

"I mean yes," she sobbed in frustration.

He stepped forward, lifted the hem of her dress and smacked her smartly across the expanse of milky thigh that lay exposed between the tops of her stockings and the lacy edges of her soaking gusset. A cherry red impression of his open palm flashed over her yielding flesh and burned itself into her skin.

"Yes what?" he roared.

"Yes, Sir," she managed to croak out through lips that

were still trembling from the impact of his stinging slap.

"Make up your mind," he ordered, "or is that as wet as your crotch? First it's yes, then no and then yes again."

She tried to explain that yes, she deserved to be punished for her insolence and that no, he did not need to correct her for failing to address him in the correct manner, unless of course he considered her lapse sufficiently serious to warrant chastisement. He replied that he found her explanation lacking in conviction and that in the circumstance a sound thrashing was his only possible response. Her own response was a marked hardening of her nipples and an almost crippling spasm in the inner muscles of her vagina. It was unbearable, almost more than she could endure but she knew she had to control her reactions or risk turning him away.

He pushed her firmly down into a sitting position on the bed and, after instructing her to stay where she was and keep silent, walked over to an elaborate old seaman's trunk that lay against one wall. He heaved open the heavy lid and levered it upwards. She was unable to see into the dark interior of the chest and as he plunged his hand inside she could only wonder what instruments of agony lay hidden in its depths. He fiddled around for a few moments and then seemingly satisfied, he withdrew his arm and turned to face her. She saw that in his right hand he clutched a thin cane. He took the tip of the cane in his other hand and flexed it into a tight bow before swishing it cuttingly through the air in a whirlwind of slashes.

This was going to hurt, she knew it. This was going to introduce her to the ecstasy of exquisite pain and submission and there wasn't a nerve in her body that wasn't raging in anticipation. She'd touched herself up and masturbated herself into a frenzy time and again just reliving those relatively minor teacher and pupil floggings in her mind and now the real thing loomed. Her whole belly was on fire and an ocean of foam couldn't have put out the flames. Her prayers were about to be answered.

One entire wall of the bedroom was mirrored from floor to ceiling, although it wasn't until he slid one of the panels aside that she realised it was actually a giant fitted wardrobe. He stepped inside, pulled out a high four legged stool and slid the panel back into position so that the wall once again appeared to be one seamless expanse of mirror. He carefully positioned the stool a couple of feet from his reflection and when he was satisfied that it was in perfect alignment he returned his attention to her. She shuddered at his gaze. Her heart thudded, her breasts felt full and tight and her sex lips quivered. She was panic-stricken; in her state of arousal the slightest stimulation would thrust her over the edge. He leant forward and pulled her from the bed. As she rose she caught sight of the patch of dampness that had leaked from between her open lips, soaked her knickers, sodden the back of her dress and had marked the bed covers. She despaired; there was no way she was going to get through this without climaxing.

She sobbed. He mistook her tears for fear of punishment, not for the fear of failure they actually were.

"Pull yourself together girl," he rasped. "This is for your own good, you'll thank me for it when it's all over."

When it's all over! She could have ravaged him there and then. Leapt on him, plunged his wonderful swollen cock deep into the roiling tube of her vagina and sucked every ounce of his seed from his body. Never had her obedience been tested to such limits.

"Over here," he said, "in front of the stool."

She did as he bade; noticing that the seat was deeply padded and the front two legs had leather wrist straps fastened about half way down their length.

"Now, bend over the seat," he ordered, and once again she responded to his command.

He pushed her stomach flat down to the padding and looped a thick belt under the seat and up over the small of her back, buckling it not too tightly, so that she could raise her buttocks a few inches but could not escape from its confines. Her breasts hung lush and full over the opposite edge of the padding and she prayed that his hands would not brush against her tingling nipples as he leant over to secure her wrists. His slightest touch would have spelt disaster; she'd have come off with all the power of an earthquake. To have come that far and then fallen at the final hurdle was a humiliation she couldn't contemplate. This was one battle she was determined not to lose.

He stepped backwards and commanded her to turn her head towards the mirror. She did as she was told, although as she was strapped to the stool her head hung halfway to the floor and locks of her hair fell across her eyes partly obscuring her vision. It was exceedingly uncomfortable and her neck strained to support her head in such an awkward position. Instinctively she tried to straighten up but was constrained both by the thick belt wound around her back and the straps that held her wrists. She yelped in pain as a slap from nowhere stung her taut bottom, and through tearful eyes, in the mirror she could see the satin softness of her dress clinging to her backside where his palm had struck.

"Did I give you permission to move?" he asked, and without awaiting a reply answered his own question. "No, I did not. Any further misdemeanours will result in stricter retribution. Do only as I order, is that understood?"

She understood alright. She was striving with all her being to obey without reaction but it was all so hard. She was desperate to meet his standards, his conditions, but she couldn't stand it, she wanted him to shag her. *NOW!*

She bit hard on her lip, drawing blood as she fought to bring her wayward emotions back into line. He ordered her to keep looking in the mirror and whisked the hair away from eyes so that she could see clearly. She watched as his own eyes roamed over her projecting rear, taking in every feature and contour. The stool was of such a height that although the heels of her shoes were skyscraper high she was forced to stand on tip toes and although this again caused her discomfort, she was thrilled to see the angle at which this necessarily tilted her rear towards his gaze. Behind her, the hem of her dress was rucked up over the tops of her stockings and she shuddered as he slipped his hands between the inside of her thighs and caressed them. He took great care not to allow his fingers to graze her dripping sex. Her knickers were plastered to her slit and the juice trickling down her thighs had given him sufficient warning of the precarious state of her arousal. He was not going to risk any premature orgasm.

He withdrew his hands, took the hem of her dress in his fingers and flicked it up over her bottom, revealing the whole expanse of her thighs and the white stockings that clung to them. Her knickers were so wet that they'd become transparent and his eyes stayed glued on the leaking labials to which they were clinging. He hooked his thumbs over the ribboned edges of her knickers and slowly eased them down over her hips. The smooth satin slid easily past the tops of her stockings and down to her knees but no further. He didn't take them off but left them hanging for a moment and then bending down to place his palms on the insides of her calves he pushed her legs apart until they were wide enough to stretch the fabric tight.

He stood back and admired his handiwork. In the mirror she could see, in profile, the proud moons of her buttocks jutting upwards from the stool, framed between the upper band of the suspender belt around her waist and the suspender straps themselves. He frowned, something wasn't right. It was the suspenders; they were in the way and might obstruct the proper application of the cane. He stuck a finger under the middle of the belt and tugging it upwards disengaged the hooks and then, after unclipping her stocking tops he pulled the entire belt from where it now lay trapped between her stomach and the padding of the stool. The stockings were essential though and he made no attempt to remove them. It was lucky, she thought, that despite the belt she was wearing hold ups.

She was finding it increasingly difficult to remain on tiptoe and fidgeted uncomfortably. She saw him catch her movement and braced herself for the inevitable punishment. It did not come. Instead he once more slid the mirror aside, entered the wardrobe and stepped out carrying two wedge shaped wooden blocks. He slipped these beneath the heels of her shoes, instantly giving her the support she needed to remain positioned according to his desires. He was satisfied, and with one final glance at her now glaringly exposed sex, he stepped over to the bed where he'd carefully and almost ritually laid the cane. Once again flexing the cane in his hands he positioned himself behind her, and half in dread half in excitement she steeled herself for the forthcoming onslaught.

"Remember madam," he said, "no reaction and no blubbering; this is not the schoolroom. And don't take your eyes away from the mirror, it's my duty to ensure that you see as well as feel every stroke. Now, are you ready to take your punishment?"

She managed to squeak out a reply in the affirmative but in the mirror she saw her body shudder visibly as he laid the cane across her buttocks, selecting a site for the first stroke. She was hungry for the feel of that first slash and whether or not his coolness and slow method of procedure were designed to inflame her passions she couldn't say, but the tension was driving her senses into overload.

"Six strokes, as always," he said, "but you will find this somewhat different from what you've experienced until now."

And with no further ado he lifted his arm high and dealt her a stinging, swingeing slash that catapulted an uncontrollable scream of pain from her shocked lips. She gasped, blinking back the tears and her stomach sagged on to the supporting surface of the padding. Her heart sank, she'd failed. Her first test and she'd flunked it, the flash of agony had been so much greater than she'd expected.

So, it was over.

And then, surprise of surprises.

"That outburst, my disobedient young lady, will cost you another six strokes later. Discipline must be maintained. Prepare yourself."

She couldn't believe it. He was giving her another chance to prove herself. She put up her defences and now knowing what was coming she suffered the next stroke without crying out. Each succeeding stroke, though no less agonising, stoked a rising tide of arousal that matched the pain in its intensity. When he was done both her buttocks were fiery plains of torment. He'd laid three strokes across each one and the mirror displayed vividly the parallel weals that flashed out from the tender abused flesh of the single moon facing it.

He laid the cane back on the bed and resumed his stance behind her. He took off his jacket and the image of the trouser bursting erection that she saw captured in the silvered glass took her breath away. She'd never seen his cock of course, but she knew it would be magnificent and there it was, imprisoned in his pants. She was crazed with lust. Her nipples were diamond hard studs of desire, her breasts strained against the constraints of her dress and the lips of her sex peeled even wider open in spontaneous waves of expectation. Via the mirror his eyes fixed hers. She was hot, flushed and erupting with frustration. And she was still bound to the stool, immobile and helpless.

He reached for his zip and very slowly began pulling it down. She watched, open-mouthed as he freed his straining manhood and prised it clear of his underpants.

Do dreams come true?

One look at that glorious dick told her that they did and her eyes devoured every inch of its thickly veined shaft. He looped his palm around it and, loose gripped, ran his fist backwards and forwards over his bulbous bell end. He moved closer to her straining rear and pointed it straight at her lusting hole.

"You want this, don't you?" he demanded.

Oh God, did she!

"Yes," she blurted out. He waited expectantly.

"You're not making a very good start, my girl," he said. "At the moment your report reads 'Must do better'."

Christ, she'd done it again.

"Yes Sir," she blurted out in what was practically a shout.

"That's better. Now, keep your eyes on the mirror," he ordered.

Almost insane with need she obeyed his instruction and was horrified to see him take a step backwards.

"Naughty girls don't get their goodies," he said. "Naughty girls require discipline. And you're a naughty girl aren't you?"

She strangled on her reply. She knew she should agree, that things would go badly for her if she didn't, but she was delirious with lust. She was a tart. She had to have him.

"NO!" she cried. "Don't leave me. Fuck me Sir... Fuck me please!"

His eyes turned to steel and he addressed her coldly.

"We have further to go than I imagined," he said and gripped his penis as if to return it to its lair. He stopped in mid action, seemingly having changed his mind. "No, on second thoughts, part of the punishment for your inexcusable insolence shall be to observe exactly what it is that you have placed in jeopardy."

Once again he brought the engorged and shiny glans close to her twitching and grasping sex lips, but not close enough to touch. In disbelief she watched as he began slowly stroking and caressing his shaft along its entire length. He was masturbating! He really was going to leave her unfulfilled. Gradually, with unhurried motions he increased the length of the strokes. Even she could smell the musky odour of her own arousal as her sex exuded desperate need, but he resisted the summons and instead of plunging his gorgeous manhood into the welcoming depths of her vagina he carried on. Faster and faster in perfect rhythm the strokes intensified.

An elephant could have fucked her at that moment and she would have welcomed its gargantuan proportions, but no such relief was at hand. Wide-eyed and open mouthed she watched as the strokes became a frenzy. His eyes never left the glistening pink gash of her dripping sex which strained back towards him until at last he clasped both fists around his jerking manhood and directed the stream of his ejaculation straight onto her gushing hole.

She was devastated. Sobbing uncontrollably in frustration she dropped her eyes from the mirror. Almost instantaneously she felt his still throbbing weapon slap up against the weals on her backside as he leapt forward, grabbed a fistful of her hair and jerked her head back upwards. She was to keep on watching, he had not given her permission to stop. She had committed yet another punishable offence. He untangled his fingers from her hair as her neck took over the support of her head and she saw herself in the mirror. She was a mess. Her eyes were puffy and red rimmed, black streams of mascara ran down her cheeks, the stripes on her buttocks were livid and sticky trails of semen dripped from the swollen lips of her sex. She'd wanted that thick fluid pumped deep inside her, smashing down the walls of her womb and there it was collecting in puddles on the already soaked surface of her knickers.

This was a punishment far greater than she could bear.

"There's always a salve for physical pain but mental torment is the cruellest form of torture," he told her. "And there will be no release for you until you learn obedience, which for the time being means remaining as you are whilst I consider the next step in your tuition." He did however allow her to drop her head and peering backwards between six legs she watched him tuck his softening sex back into his trousers and leave the room.

It seemed like an eternity had passed before she heard him come back. Although her legs and her back were aching and protesting violently against the intermittent cramps that gripped them, she had not moved an iota during his absence. She was learning, and although her emotions had calmed somewhat she was still crazed with need for him to take her. But she wasn't about to foul up again. She'd had her eyes closed and opened them to see him approaching her carrying a bowl and a towel. He laid the towel across her back and put the bowl down on top of it, instructing her not to move; if so much as one drop of water was spilled there'd be extra punishment. He lifted a sponge from the bowl and after wringing it out carefully cleaned his emission and her love juice from the insides of her thighs and towelled them dry. He didn't touch her sex though, he knew how aroused she'd been and he was going to stretch the agony of her frustration to its limits. He moved around to the front of the stool and once again raising her head by clasping her hair he sponged her face. He told her he could deal with a disobedient girl, but not a dirty one and now that she was a little more presentable he could carry on with her education.

Carrying the bowl he left the room, returning almost immediately, empty handed. He picked up the cane and stalked the room, whipping and slashing the air. And there it came again. She couldn't stop it. Just the sight of him and the cane in action was enough to kick-start the engine of her desire. Her nipples stiffened and once again she felt the moist heat of wanting spread up from between her legs. She shuddered and then cursed inwardly. He'd seen. She felt the springiness in the cane as he laid it lightly on her rear.

"Come, come girl. Self control remember?" he said and in a lightning move pulled back his arm and with a single stroke lashed her smartly across the backs of both her tender white thighs. The breath rushed from her lips but she didn't scream. He gave her a moment and then whipped another cutting lash from on high to twin up with the first. She gasped again and although tears welled into her eyes she managed to remain silent.

"Very good," he said, "A Plus, for effort."

The blows had stung like the devil but the glow radiating from the livid raised weals was as nothing to the glow of satisfaction that flushed through her body. At last she'd passed a test, only a small one but it was enough to give her hope and strengthen her resolve. She determined to meet every demand he made of her, to take her punishment and to be the most obedient pupil possible.

Her dress was still pulled up over her buttocks, the enticing entrance to her sex staring him straight in the eyes. He bent forward and for one heart-stopping minute she imagined that he was about to fasten his lips to her glistening slit. No such luck! He reached down and after telling her to close her legs he slipped her knickers down and lifting each foot in turn slipped them off. They fell to the floor and inserting the tip of the cane into their elasticated waist he lifted them into the air. Flying like a pennant from the thin willow, he transported the soaking silk over her back and then, slipping them from the cane, he bunched the knickers in his hands and fed them to her, pressing them against her face. A wide lace edged knicker leg covered her eyes and her nose was buried in the sopping gusset. The smell of sex was overpowering, his sperm and her love juice mixed into a cocktail of intoxicating eroticism. She puckered her lips and sucked in the fabric. Bliss. Whether he liked it or not, she'd finally got something she wanted: his sperm in her mouth.

He whisked the underwear off her face. She was apprehensive but his demeanour was unchanged and he did not admonish her or threaten additional punishment. Instead he stood in front of her and trawling two fingers along the inside of the knickers' gusset scooped up the sticky juice still clinging there, he pushed the fingers into her mouth ordered her to suck it off. She worked on his fingers as though they were his cock, licking, sucking and sliding them over her tongue. She wanted him to know what pleasure lay in store should he decide to fuck her mouth. His face betrayed nothing and when his fingers were licked clean he withdrew them and inspected them as though scrutinising a manicure. He made no comment so she must have performed satisfactorily. Her breasts were hanging loose and pendulous, her nipples sticking out like bolts. Trapping the cane under an armpit he slipped his hands inside the neckline of her dress, slid them downward and after lingeringly stroking his open palms over their iron textured tips, tested their full weight in both cupped hands. In order to do this he had necessarily moved much closer to her, so close that through the fabric of his trousers the bulge of his rekindled erection brushed against her mouth. This was another test, she knew it. The pressure increased as the bulge travelled back and forth along the length of her desperate lips. She couldn't help herself, delirium seized her and out of control her mouth clamped itself over his constrained penis. The taste of cloth attacked her senses. This was not what she wanted, she didn't want her mouth filled with a mixture of wool and man made fibre, she wanted it stuffed with cock. His cock.

Instantly he backed away, tugging his hands free of her breasts and roughly pulling them out from inside her bodice. One hand went straight to the cane and wrenched it from his armpit.

"That, my girl," he said icily, "was gross misconduct. Inexcusable, deliberate disobedience."

She had displayed a total lack of deference to her master's wishes and completely ignored his instructions. The resumption of her education would cease temporarily whilst he considered exactly what punishment befitted her crime. He was angry, really angry this time. Not raging, but coldly infuriated and for the first time she felt real fear. And now that her dread was one hundred per cent genuine any wants, desires and thrills she'd felt before were as nothing. Her lust increased a hundredfold, her sex lips rippled, muscles contracted and she burst into an instantaneous sweat which flooded from her ankles, her legs, and her armpits, to trickle down across her breasts and even her hair flashed into flood. She was dripping from every part of her body.

She had been bound to the stool now for a considerable period and she was aching for relief, both sexual and physical. She'd expected an immediate thrashing but it didn't come. After some deliberation he approached her once more and she was surprised to see that despite his anger he was still displaying an impressive erection. He positioned himself before her and with the cane held firmly in his right hand he laid it on the back of her shoulder. There was hardly any sensation of weight but she knew better than to succumb to the idea that perhaps next time it wouldn't sting quite so much. With his flies directly in front of her open mouth his left hand moved to his zip.

"Now, absolutely no reaction," he instructed. "You must do nothing unless I so order."

The zip slipped slowly down its track and when it was fully disengaged he slipped his hand inside and uncaged his penis. It sprang skywards and laying his palm over its upper surface he pushed it downwards until it lay rigid but horizontal. It pointed straight at her hungry mouth. So, she thought, he was going to continue with the mental assault, knowing full well by now that she found that even more unbearable than physical torment. Correction by psychology, it was inhuman and she wanted to scream at him to whip her instead, but she took a grip on herself and held her tongue.

He pushed his glans closer. Her emotions were rising

dangerously and she gripped the legs of the stool tightly and her back pushed against the constraints of the strap as she fidgeted, trying to bring them to order. The cane whipped away from her shoulder and a cutting lash ripped across the top of one of her buttocks. She couldn't help herself, she screamed as the singeing pain bit into her.

"That's two misdemeanours in one go," he said, "not good enough."

She heard the swish of the cane once more as it cut through the air on its flight to her tortured bottom. She managed to stifle the scream that had rushed to her lips as the impact seared another weal into her delicate flesh. She couldn't see these fresh stripes but she knew they'd be in perfect symmetry, leaving enough space to accommodate the four which must now surely follow. She froze her muscles and remained immobile as he waited for any reaction. When none came he returned his attention to his member. His palm still lay across the top holding it down and she saw the blob of fluid which now trickled from its eye. It wasn't the real thing, she knew that, just some sort of lubrication or something but she was mad for the taste of it. Her tongue refused to obey her brain and rolled out in eager anticipation and at the exact instant she realised her transgression her senses were stunned by the impact of the third lash.

"Get a grip girl, control yourself," he barked. "Or are you just being wilfully disobedient?"

"I can't help it sir. It's too much to bear," she squeezed out through clenched lips.

"Well then, you'll just have to learn to bear it, won't you?" he said. "We will now resume the lesson. And take care, I will not continue to be so lenient if your flagrant insubordination continues." He pressed his bulbous glans up against her closed mouth. With the greatest effort of will she checked herself and managed to keep it clenched shut as he wiped his bell from side to side along the join where her lips met. He brought it to rest in the centre of the cupid's bow that shaped her mouth and prodded her lips as if trying to prize them apart. Sidelining the frenzy that was building in her crotch she did not respond.

"Very good," he congratulated. "You're not such a backward pupil after all. I think it's in order to proceed a little further." He told her to open her mouth, wide, but to make no contribution to what he might do.

He pushed his glans through the portals of her lips and laid it to rest on the salivating surface of her tongue. Only his bell had entered and he left it lying there, its girth stretching her lower jaw to its limit. He remained perfectly still, just a slight throbbing on her tongue indicating his heartbeat. He had a pulse in his cock, she never knew about that, but he had said she'd got a lot to learn so perhaps it was normal. Normal or not, the power of those pulses seemed to strengthen and they directed waves of stimulation coursing all the way down to the centre of her frustration. It was all too much. She couldn't keep still and her mouth leapt to devour his wondrous cock.

He was out in an instant. Her mouth gaped and her tongue lolled out, rolling around shamelessly seeking his shaft. She wriggled her backside, struggled against her bonds and cursed the impotence of her actions.

He was livid.

"A giant step backwards, after we'd come so far," he said. "You've received three strokes already during this session, perhaps another three will help you remember."

She said nothing.

"Well, will it girl?" he barked.

He was right, they had come a long way but she was beginning to despair. And yet she had to keep on trying.

"Yes Sir," she answered.

"You are a tart, a whore and a brazen hussy," he hissed as he commenced to circle around her, the cane continually slapping into his open palm. In passing he flicked one of her steel hard nipples with the tip of the cane.

Lolli stopped for a second, discontinuing her story and addressed herself directly to me.

"Compared to a good thrashing that may not sound much," she said, "but the pain is exquisite. And you've got to be a woman to really appreciate how agonising a blow to an inflamed nipple can be."

I glanced down, and saw that she herself, very clearly appreciated it. Her nipples were pushing the satin of her dress into hard little mounds, just at the memory. She caught my glance and smiled up at me. She really was an enchanting girl, that smile alone catapulting my pulse rate into the danger zone. She didn't miss the signals, laying a cool, smooth palm on my thigh to heighten my tension as she resumed the tale.

He completed several circuits, prodding here and there, never landing a full-blown lash but tormenting the nerve ends of her bottom, her thighs, her breasts and even her sex with cutting flicks of the cane.

"Discipline must be maintained," he said, as much to himself as to her, "and I will not tolerate your rebellious, ungrateful behaviour. You madam, are a trollop and I find myself in two minds as to the wisdom of continuing your training. In fact, to put it bluntly I feel you are something of a lost cause."

The atmosphere was tense, taut with his indecision. All her sexual passion flashed out of existence as iced water replaced the blood in her veins. Her clitoris subsided and retreated within its hood, the walls of her vagina relaxed and the previously warm musky flood bathing her intimate parts cooled into an uncomfortable stickiness that dripped coldly from the strands of her pubes. Her vagina might have frozen but her pulse raced, her heart thumped and she could hardly draw a breath. How long he stood deliberating she had no idea but in her tangled senses it seemed an eternity. At that moment she came as close to total emotional breakdown as she ever had, before or after. She couldn't lose him now; it would mean the end of her world, and the shattering of all her dreams. She determined that if he did cast her aside she'd end it all, if she was not to be his slave then she'd rather be dead than be a slave to an empty life without him as her master.

Eventually he addressed her and in detached icy tones asked if she had anything to say which might influence his judgement. A torrent of grovelling apology poured from her lips; she cried and she pleaded. She said she was sorry that she was just a foolish fallible girl, she'd never be disobedient again and she begged for one more chance to prove herself. He silenced her with a tap of the cane, and as he deliberated, for one agonising moment she thought she'd failed in her arguments. But then the verdict was announced and the sentence delivered.

"Very well, young lady," he said, "I'm prepared to make one final attempt to continue with your tuition but the slightest lack of adherence to my orders and you will find yourself dismissed from my presence, immediately and forever."

The relief was orgasmic in its scale. Muscles relaxed, her pulse slowed, and she managed to get her breathing back under control. She flopped into an ungainly heap over the stool, she was in heaven, and as long as he continued to test her, that was where she would stay.

His first recognisable pronouncement was that before they could proceed any further she must receive the outstanding three lashes due from her last indiscretion. She indicated neither acquiescence nor rebuttal, wisely opting for silence. She really didn't care what retribution he chose to extract; she just thanked every deity in the universe for her salvation. He circled her, very slowly one last time, firstly allowing the cane to slide along the groove of her vagina, then introducing it into her, finally flicking mercilessly at her swollen labial lips. That stung like the very devil. She didn't scream, or even utter a sound, but her involuntary wriggling betrayed her. Taking good aim he laid several swift, stinging strokes right across her sex and stood, awaiting her reaction. She squealed inwardly but with an effort of self-control she didn't know she possessed, she held it in check, no sound passing her lips. He seemed satisfied, turning his attention to her breasts. Using the tip of the cane, he molested her protesting nuggets, flicking up, down and from side to side in small, swift swishes. It was agony. Her nipples burned and her vulva pulsed in injured protestation. Then the blunt end of the cane probed the secrets of her anus.

Both sphincter muscles clamped shut in shocked surprise at the first ever penetration of her rear. But it was an erotic sensation and here was something she'd never before considered. Could something as slender as the end of a cane be the harbinger of future delights? Replace the cane with his throbbing cock and she'd be practically ripped apart. She thrilled at the prospect and the first stirrings of re-arousal rang alarm bells the length and breadth of her body. Calm down, stay cool, think of anything but sex she told herself. But that was far easier said than done, her anus welcoming the pushing, prodding willow, and heightening her already savagely intensifying emotions. This was another danger point and when his intimate exploration ceased and he pulled the cane from her bottom with an audible plop, she uttered a silent prayer of thanks.

\*\*\*

He stood contemplating her bottom. She had three more strokes coming and added to the nine he'd already delivered that would complete the design he intended to sear into her backside. He gave no warning, uttered no conciliatory words and laid the cane across the remaining unmarked area at the top of her buttocks with such vehemence that her protesting nervous system shocked her eyes into blackness. As her vision gradually returned via waves of undulating glimpses of reality, he lanced the second lash close beside the first. The agony was indescribable and then as the third and final lash burnt itself into her consciousness she again felt the rising tide of her desire flash into flood.

She fought to gain control of her senses as they threatened to run wild yet again. He said nothing, but looking in the mirror she was certain she'd caught a glimmer of satisfaction running over his stern features. She was going to come through this time, she knew it. Although the stinging in her rear and the growing tension in her erogenous zones were dangerously close to pushing her into betraying herself, she maintained her composure.

Caressing the cane as though he regarded it as an object of desire in itself he threw her a scrap of encouragement.

"A definite improvement," he complimented, "I see no reason now why we cannot proceed with your training."

His comment was a welcome balm to her ears, helping considerably to ease the pains which racked her whole body. She watched as carefully, almost ritually, he laid the cane back on the bed and despite the discomfort from her rectum she felt a pang of disappointment. But she consoled herself with thoughts of what he might next have planned for her instruction.

Then came the bombshell.

"But not today," he added.

She wasn't prepared for that. Complete and utter wretchedness extinguished the tiny spark of exultation which she had allowed herself. She fought an overwhelming urge to plead and beg, and moments later rejoiced at her fortitude as he stunned her with his following comment.

"You've done very well," he said, "the improvement is worthy of reward and I think a little encouragement would now prove more beneficial than further chastisement."

He once again put his hands between her legs and pushed them wide, very wide, apart. He ordered her to look in the mirror and then before her amazed eyes slowly and deliberately eased down his zip and freed his sex once more.

He left it on display momentarily in order to allow her time to see what he intended. Then he stepped between her legs and smacked the hard shaft down across the scarlet stripes glaring from one of her buttocks. Her backside bucked, the weals were still painful and it felt as if he'd struck her with a sand filled stocking.

She gasped and in an instant her vagina was dripping again. Clasping both hands around the girth of his penis and gripping it close up to his bell he ran its tip upwards from her clitoris, just delving into the crease between her labia. He did it again and the last vestige of self control remaining within her evaporated. Her body convulsed and every nerve ending sang with a kind of electricity as her lips drooled, her nipples hardened, and her clitoris seemed to double its length and spring erect.

"Try to hold back Lolli," he told her, "savour the experience."

And she did try. He opened her up with his fingers to make his entrance easier and with a struggle introduced his dome into her quivering vagina. That was as far as he got, just over the ridge. She bucked, squealed and writhed in manic frenzy as a mind-boggling orgasm tripped every fuse in the sensory circuit of emotions. He waited patiently as her convulsions gradually subsided, watching her boiling vagina try and grasp itself around his barely penetrating glans until he was sure her passion was spent.

"A very satisfactory but somewhat over eager reaction," he said calmly as he withdrew his glistening member from a hostess whose lips waved a reluctant adieu. He added that it was obvious she required intensive tuition but the next full lesson could wait until the following day. However her orgasm had been so swift that he felt she had not really taken the time to achieve any real depth of satisfaction. And so saying he returned to the seaman's chest and delved into its interior.

Did that mean he was going to give her another one? She

prayed that it did and uttered silent thanks as he once again stood before her, still with a giant hard on, running the three prongs of a short handled leather strap through his fingers. He told her he was going to ensure that she received the full reward to which he had judged she was entitled and that, although he didn't intend to thrash her again, she would certainly feel the tawse if she didn't make more of an effort to enjoy his benevolence to the full.

"You've never been taken from the rear, have you?" he questioned.

She didn't dare tell him she'd never been taken from any angle at all, the reason her maidenhead was no longer intact being the result of an over enthusiastic schoolgirl experiment with a candle, so she mumbled a muted response in confirmation.

"I thought not by your response to the cane," he said, "but it was obvious you found the experience intriguing and pleasurable."

That's where they would start, he said, but first there was something he must attend to. He leant over her jutting bottom and slipping his free hand inside the neckband of her dress, in one powerful tug he tore the garment apart from top to bottom. That one action totally eclipsed any thrill she'd yet encountered, barring the orgasm. She didn't know why but having the dress torn from her body was an extra, extra sensual experience. Carefully separating the two halves he let the ragged edges of the silk fall downwards from either side of her body, fully exposing her naked back and shoulders.

Now he was ready to proceed. He pushed up close to her yearning but apprehensive anus, his weapon clutched in one hand and the tawse in the other.

"We're really going to try this time, aren't we?" he asked.

On the far side of the stool her head bobbed up and down in agreement, but the image of his sex that stared at her from the mirror, so close to her forbidden zone, inflamed her passions to such an extent she doubted her ability to hold her emotions in check. She could already feel new lakes of love juice welling up inside her tortured vagina, just waiting for the stimulus that would burst the dam and set rivers of passion flowing once more.

He slid a hand between the firmness of her buttocks and pushed a finger straight into her anus. She yelped in surprise and her backside shot upwards. It was an extremely unpleasant experience and she felt as if he'd rammed a tree trunk up her backside. If that was only his finger how on earth would she cope with the girth of his penis? The prongs of the tawse flashed down on to her shoulder. There was no swish of sound, no whistling through the air as with a cane and its lash caught her by surprise. It still stung like the very devil but it was a different pain, more of a flattened blow than the narrow cut of the cane. At the exact instant the strap struck home he rammed his finger further up her back passage causing her backside and her shoulders to rear up together. That was very odd too, her stomach pushed down on to the stool bending her body into a bow shape, and her anus jerked backwards pushing itself over his finger until it was buried up to the knuckles.

The tawse fell again and a dull flush of pain radiated across her back from the spot between her shoulder blades where the leather prongs had struck home.

"You really must try to get a grip on yourself," he said, and there was a sort of sucking sound as he pulled his finger from her grasping anus.

He instructed her to compose herself and try to keep calm. He was now ready to introduce her bottom to the real thing, but her entire body was wound up like a giant spring and if she didn't relax her tensed muscles there was no way he'd be able to squeeze his engorged member past her crushing sphincters. But once he'd overcome that barrier, entered the tunnel beyond and she was opened up there'd be room enough to spare he assured her.

He put down the tawse so that it lay from side to side across the small of her back, just above the foothills of her rising buttocks. Feeling the heaviness of the plaited leather handle and the lighter, wide spaced touch of the three separated prongs, she fantasised over the delicious agony he would inflict upon her if he thrashed her with the pommelled end of the strap. Those thoughts vanished as with one hand he pushed her bottom higher in order to facilitate his entrance, grasped the other around his shaft and guided it to her anus. He struggled to gain an entrance and she grunted in discomfort unable to find any way to help. He clutched the fronts of both her thighs and attempted to pull her backwards over his swollen glans and the battle was on, rectum versus penis, and for the moment it seemed her rectum was going to stand fast and repel boarders.

He retreated, pulling out from the limited inroad he'd been able to accomplish and she could have shrieked in disappointment.

"I think we're going to need a little help here," he told her and disappeared into the bathroom. He reappeared seconds later with a plastic bottle. "Baby oil," he said, and unscrewing the top lathered his cock from base to bell with the oil. He stuck his now well-greased glans back into the cavity he had managed to open up and pushed hard. This time he burst through her contracted sphincters and slid straight in, half his length vanishing immediately and the rest immersing itself fully in response to a second brutal thrust. The pain really was exquisite as her anus widened to accommodate him. This was joy. At long last she was stuffed full of throbbing manhood but she was totally unprepared for the reaction of her body when he slowly began to slide up and down her rectum. She'd never read about this in any of the pornos she'd smuggled into the dorm.

Lolli stopped, feeling she needed to expand on this, offering me an explanation of her comment.

"In the books it's all ecstasy and pleasure," she told me, " but what they don't say is that when you've got something as big as that up your backside it makes your stomach want to move. At first it's weird but then you settle down and the vaginal walls get squeezed. There really is nothing like being buggered."

She said that it was a unique experience and one not to be missed, bringing a tingle of satisfaction to my face by adding that, of course, although there were also men who enjoyed that particular thrill, she had no doubts about me on that score. Once again those darts of burning sexuality flying from her eyes found their target and sank straight into the bull's eye. She turned me on as easily as I flick a dark room into light, except that I guarantee my bulb burned brighter. God, I thought, what wouldn't I give to own a woman like that? She had to coax my wandering thoughts back to the story, starting again twice before my mind was back on track.

Once he'd got into a satisfying rhythm he lifted the tawse from her back, reversed it and inserting it handle first between his own open legs he pushed the pommel between the gushing lips of her sex. With every thrust of his penis into her backside he pushed the tawse further into her welcoming vagina and working together like a coupled pair of pistons, prick and tawse drove her into a paroxysm of frenzied rapture. She exploded into another hurricane of an orgasm and this time he didn't hold back either. She could actually feel the buckets of sperm surging up through his urethra before they spurted from his jerking, thrusting manhood and flooded her with an ocean of steaming seed.

She was incapable of movement and lay helplessly inert over the stool as he withdrew both instruments of love from deep inside her. He let her lie, panting and gasping as he went back into the bathroom once again. He was gone longer this time and when he returned his newly washed penis was buried in the folds of a pristine white towel. He finished drying it, threw the towel down on to the bed and stepping around the stool stood perusing her.

He waited in silence. He didn't berate her, order her to pull herself together or lay a finger on her. Her breathing eased, some semblance of strength returned to her limp body and she gathered her senses together as best she could. When she could open her eyes again, he again grasped a fistful of hair and raised her head. He asked her if she now was beginning to understand the pleasures that were offered by restraint, and although she wanted to scream her affirmation from the rooftops all she could manage was a whispered, "Yes." He said that her reaction was most satisfactory and that her performance had been a vast improvement on her previously scandalous behaviour.

Proudly she looked up and was greeted by the sight of his wonderful, suckable cock waving imperiously a few inches from her nose. The adrenalin rush wasn't quite as immediate this time, but even so it was only seconds before her nervous system flushed itself clear and re-vitalised her. She was still soaking in juices from the orgasm but a fresh tumult in her belly relit the cauldron in her crotch. He said she was now displaying distinct promise and he was prepared to grant her further temporary dispensation from punishment if she could pass one more test. At that moment she could have passed her A-levels blindfold and eagerly accepted the challenge.

He told her that although he deplored the insolence she had displayed the first time he had entered her mouth, he did understand the temptation a member like his presented to any woman. However, he would train her to overcome that temptation and if she found herself running out of control this time, he would be as lenient as possible but in further lessons total control would be required.

This was more than her body and soul could survive. He was her master now, authoritarian and totally dominant, but not needlessly cruel and any slave would commit herself to an eternity in Hades for the chance to savour the reward he'd handed her. He'd fucked her into oblivion and she determined that as his obedient and willing vassal it was now her joy and duty to worship him utterly with her lips and mouth.

He dipped quickly behind her for an instant and reappeared gripping the tawse.

"Just in case," he told her.

Her mouth opened to its fullest extent.

Slowly and with almost theatrical deliberation he pressed his penis downwards and pushed it between her full, sensuous lips. She saw the tawse flex in his hand as he searched for any signs of failing restraint. She held herself in check and with a growing confidence and resolution awaited his next move. His glans pushed between her teeth and found her tongue. She didn't react, controlling herself with a new found steel. Her last orgasm had at last quenched many of her immediate desires and left her more able to manage her passion. Not that she wasn't once again incandescent with ardour, but now she was also fully aware of the consequences of any transgression. If she had allowed her feelings free rein she'd have sucked, and blown, and swallowed as much of his pulsing length as she possibly could.

And of course, that's exactly what she did. As he slid himself further through her straining jaws and along the surface of her tongue, her saliva jetted out, filling the tiny unoccupied pockets of her mouth and making her cheeks bulge. She sucked with every ounce of strength in her body and as his cock hit the back of her throat the leather of the tawse struck her bottom, provoking the already raised weals into a delirium of exquisite pain. She didn't care any more; let him do to her what he would because this was what she craved. She gobbled shamelessly at his shaft, attacking it with an appetite that was insatiable until he was uncontrollably thrusting himself. The thrusts increased in intensity as with each one, the leather continued to thwack down onto her screaming, burning buttocks until once again, but this time on her tongue, she felt the sperm racing up the thick tube on the underside of his rod. He convulsed, shattering spurts of seed whacked her throat and the wild jerking of his shaft pitched her head around as though it belonged to a doll.

But he didn't let her have it all.

"Watch, Lolli, watch!" he shouted, and wrenching himself free of her mouth, treated her to a spectacular display of male virility by shooting a giant fountain of semen feet into the air. It splattered down in showers, falling all over her hair, her back and her rectum. She was ecstatic.

At that point Lolli smiled at me. Then, with her eyes fixed to my own privates, she flashed a wicked grin.

"Of course, I did get a good mouthful," she said, "and as I swallowed it, I remembered my biology classes. Semen contains fructose you know, it's something to do with activating the sperm. So I couldn't help wondering, even in the midst of all the action, why it tasted salty and not sweet. But now of course I'm a connoisseur and it's a bit like tasting wine. I can tell quite a lot about a man just from the bouquet of his cock and the taste of his sperm."

Suddenly, under the direct gaze of her dark eyes, I felt the room was becoming uncomfortably hot. She took pity on me that time, disengaging her hypnotic gaze and continuing straightaway with her story. Breathing a sigh of relief I was able to return my attention to my notepad.

He recovered quickly and became his usual brisk self. Tuition would continue the following day, he told her, and he was encouraged by her improved behaviour. There was still a long distance to travel, but with hard work and strict supervision he was of the opinion that she might pull through.

He removed the leather shackles securing her wrists, unbuckled the broad belt from around her middle and pulled the wooden blocks from beneath her feet. Now freed from her restraints he motioned her to arise. Her heels dropped to the floor, her back straightened and she swayed a little with dizziness as she finally stood upright. The remnants of her dress hung from the stool and she stood naked, apart from her stockings and stilettos. The flushed, striped moons of her buttocks jutted defiantly above the stocking tops and she thrilled as he smoothed his palms around their contours. He took hold of her shoulders and stood her beside him to face the mirrors. The luxuriant bushy vee of her pubes stared back from its surface, her milky thighs and lacy stocking tops completing a devastating picture of newly awakened womanhood.

"An interesting pattern," he said, and turning her around, stood her with her back to the mirrors. He pushed her head sideways so that the field of her vision could just take in the reflection of her back.

"Here, look for yourself," he commanded.

She did as she was ordered and was thrilled at the sight of the twelve livid stripes radiating zebra fashion from the crease of her backside. Three evenly spaced parallel weals ran diagonally across the fleshy flank of each buttock so that they formed an open topped inverted V, stopping short of her coccyx, which if the stripes had continued would have been their natural apex. Three more lay horizontally across their tops on each side, only being prevented from joining into solid, unbroken lines by the valley dividing her bottom. They presented a silhouette somewhat akin to a trestle table viewed from the side.

That of course, is most definitely not what they represented, as I was to discover when Oliver Carlisle himself told me the story of Marie-Helene, he described the design as being somewhat similar to the mathematical symbol Pi. And although he warned me not to delve too deeply myself, it does seem that Lolli was much closer to the truth than she thought when she commented that it resembled a pattern she'd seen carved into several of the huge megaliths at Avebury, ones she'd seen on a school visit.

There were more wheals at the tops of her thighs and flares of redness from the tawse. But he told her to ignore them and look only at the pattern of the cane on her buttocks.

"Take good note of that design," he instructed, "maybe you'll see it again. If you do, in that exact configuration, you are in the presence of a Member of The Brotherhood and must obey his every command as if he were me."

It wasn't until her training was well progressed that she understood exactly what he'd meant by that, but she couldn't help noticing that he had a small birthmark which exactly replicated that design on his left upper arm.

He'd continued with her instruction throughout the whole summer, and after she'd left for Oxford, during the vacations when she'd return to the school. She was completely enslaved by him, but at the same time she graduated and came down from university he was appointed Head of the school. Now, no trace of impropriety or incorrect behaviour could be allowed to besmirch his name and he deemed it far too risky for her to visit him in his rooms. She had absolutely no desire to branch out into the world of everyday drudgery, although her first in Economics had prompted a generous offer of employment from a merchant bank. In any event he was of the opinion that her future lay in an entirely different direction.

And so he had brought her to The Lodge, where Madame Stalevsky had extended her training and she had found her vocation, now being one of the most keenly sought after of the girls. He did however, impose one condition, which due to her striking talent The Lodge was only too ready to agree to. And that condition was that whenever he was in residence she was to be his alone and must be in perfect shape, which means that Madame has to take her out of circulation a few days before he arrives. An irksome situation at times, but well understood and accepted by the members who have the greatest respect for him and the greatest desire for her. She's twenty five now and happy in her life, but happier still in that he says she's still the Lolita in his life.

So that's Lolli's story, although there is one telling little snippet to add. When that first night of tuition came to its end and it was time for her to return to the dormitory, he produced an all enveloping overcoat and placed it around her shoulders. As he led her to the door, she stopped and summoning up every last vestige of her courage, she posed a question.

"Please Sir," she said, "before you make me leave, will you please cane me one more time?"

# ROSA

*by Sean O'Kane*

"The problem I had was where to get a steady supply of girls Sean."

John Carpenter leaned back and blew out a cloud of cigar smoke. We were seated in the lounge of The Lodge. I was a little nervous; my first interviewee was none other than the founder of the club.

I had driven down from London and been royally entertained over lunch by John himself. It had been hard to concentrate on the food however; the Housegirls who served us were themselves so delectable. They all wore uniforms of long and full satin dresses with short, puffed sleeves and very low cut, tight bodices. In fact the necklines were so low that only a tiny piece of gauze hid the areolae and nipples of their creamy smooth breasts which swayed and moved as they bent to serve us. Alan had described the girls to me but the reality was breathtaking. As if that were not enough, several of the girls bore the marks of fresh beatings across their shoulders and breasts. Again I knew that The Lodge was an SM club but even so the calmly and openly displayed evidence was very distracting, and I couldn't help staring at the cleavages and noting how the red stripes would curve down the inner side of one breast and then up the swell of the other. I could sense that knowing smiles were being exchanged between the girls and John but I was spellbound at the sight. In the end John had informed me that, hidden in the copious folds of the skirts, was a slit at the back. And he demonstrated how a hand could be slipped up it to fondle any girl a member chose to. Never having taken such liberties with a completely strange girl before I was rather diffident but had at last fumbled with the dress of a pretty brunette, found the slit, and while she was clearing away my plates ran my hand up the soft warmth of her thighs. She immediately stopped what she was doing and stood still so that I could explore to my heart's content. My pulse raced at her calm obedience and the feel of the soft skin under my fingers. Emboldened I ran my hand over her buttocks and found to my surprise that there were discernible ridges running across them. She looked down and smiled at me when she felt my explorations stop.

"The cane, last night," she said. "A good hard fifteen."

John laughed at my confusion, dismissed the smiling girl and led me to the lounge where we now sat. Like most of the rooms at The Lodge, as I was to find out, it was oak panelled to the ceiling and furnished in quiet good taste. All the sofas and chairs were set around tables so that small groups of residents could sit and talk while the girls served coffee.

John now waved at one particular girl.

"Yes, I had everything set up to go. Madame, Yuri and Ivan were all here, the backers had been found, the house was nearly ready. But what I hadn't dared tell anyone was that I was still struggling to find a reliable source of girls for Madame to train."

The girl whom John had waved at now approached and I couldn't help noticing that she wore her uniform especially well. She had full breasts which were pushed up and together by the bodice so that they were displayed very provocatively, her thick, brown hair was tied back with a scarlet ribbon and her dark green dress set off her clear skin to perfection. As she bent over to pour our coffee I saw John's hand go into the slit at the back of her dress. But the only response she made was to shift her feet a little further apart so he could feel her more easily. And when she straightened up I could see that her breasts were rising and falling noticeably, and a faint flush suffused them. When John's hand released her she made to go but he stopped her.

"This is Rosa; the girl I want to tell you about. She belongs to Madame."

Alan had told me about Madame Stalevsky who trained and supervised the girls helped by the silent twins, Yuri and Ivan. She was worshipped by all the girls and held in awe by most of the members.

"I'm afraid that's why I take especial pleasure in breaking her rule about not interfering with the girls while they're on domestic duties," John continued, his grin becoming more mischievous. "She made the rule—but I designed those handy little slits in the dresses." I had heard about the close but tempestuous relationship between John and Madame.

John clicked his fingers casually and Rosa's hands flew to the zip at the back of her dress. But then she froze in horror.

"Master! If Madame sees, she will be furious!"

He patted her backside. "Then let her be. I'm sure Mr O'Kane will be delighted to watch you receive your due punishment. Now do as you're told."

The unfortunate Rosa bit her bottom lip—she was caught between the two most powerful people at The Lodge and really had no choice. Slowly she slid the bodice of the dress to her hips and then bent to clear it from her feet. I had a wonderful view of her heavy breasts swinging as she did so but then she stood up, dressed only in high heeled court shoes and sheer black hold-up stockings, which looked striking indeed against the pallor of her skin. She was an impressive sight as she stood naked before us, making no attempt to try and cover herself but holding herself proudly erect, only sideways glances at the door betrayed her nervousness. Her breasts were large but still stood high and prominent with large areolae. The stomach was pleasingly flat and in the dark hollow of the navel a jewel on a gold piercing glittered. At the join of her strong and smoothly skinned thighs a thick bush of pubic hair sprouted but it was what hung there which really caught the eye. A heavy steel ring pierced the left sex lip and from it, cushioned on the front of the closed thighs, hung a chain some four or five inches long, and on the end of it was a disc.

"Show it to the gentleman Rosa." John told her and she came to stand directly in front of me so that I could take the disc in my hand and read Madame's initials engraved on it.

"You should see her in a mini skirt Sean; very arousing. Now turn around Rosa."

Again she obeyed immediately and I was able to admire the view from the rear. She had broad shoulders and a strong back which narrowed to a nicely trim waist from which swelled good wide hips and from these curved out towards me two delightfully prominent buttocks, smooth, firm and unmarked. But on the back of each shoulder she bore striking tattoos. On each side of the spine, sloping diagonally up and out, was the carefully drawn image of a scourge in sombre black. The thongs of each whip spread out across the shoulders. Testament, I assumed, to her mistress's fondness for using such implements on her.

John leaned back in his seat and grinned again, but his eyes were suddenly hard; challenging.

"Give me your assessment Sean."

I stood up, my thoughts racing. I was being given a test and for all I knew if I failed that might be the end of the whole project. Here and now.

I had spanked plenty of girls and taken my belt to quite a few in the past, but then who hasn't? Professionally I had come into contact with the SM scene and found it exciting, but The Lodge with its calm and open acceptance of complete slavery—by both masters and slaves—had taken me by surprise. Somehow I had to adopt the mindset of a resident here, ignore the flesh and blood reality of the naked girl before me and assess the body purely on its merits as a slave. Maybe it was the bottle of excellent wine over lunch and the brandy afterwards which helped me, but for whatever reason I found I was able to approach the girl's body with the same casualness that she offered it. I ran my hands down the warm back, feeling the firm muscle tone before hefting the buttocks appreciatively. Their prominence and roundness invited the whip or cane but they were so youthfully smooth and muscular with not a mark on them. And yet how many beatings had they received, I found myself wondering. Her thighs were the same, smooth and unflinching under my hands, even when I reached round and brushed her pubes which set her chain swinging. I could have delved further and explored her sex, she would only have opened her legs and let me. But I could see that she was still watching the door nervously. So I moved on up across the stomach until I could weigh and finger the breasts. She was incredibly responsive, at the first touch her nipples hardened, and then went on hardening until they attained an unusual length while I teased and stroked them. I couldn't resist it; my hands went back down to her delta and before I got there she had opened her legs to let me in. It was the first pierced vulva I had come across and the cold steel contrasted excitingly with the soft folds of labial flesh which parted easily to allow me to find that the clitoris was thrusting up from its hood eagerly. I reached round a little further and pushed a finger into her vagina, which again allowed me access quite readily. She was indeed responsive to this open fondling and examination of her intimacies, as I withdrew my finger from her there was a soft sigh of regret.

As I stood back I became aware of a pounding erection pressing against my trousers. But I had to keep my mind on the business in hand. John was still watching me carefully and waiting for my report.

"Good stuff John," I replied as casually as I could. "Very responsive, strong. Good skin and muscle tone." Here I slapped a buttock and made a show of watching how it rippled under the blow.

John nodded carefully. "How about endurance under the whip or in one of our dungeons?"

"I reckon she'd be good for however much you wanted

to give her. Provided you took your time. She looks tough."

John relaxed, and so did I. "Pretty good Sean," he said smiling again. "And she had to be tough for the first few weeks believe me. I think that's why Madame bought her from the club. You see Rosa was our first girl…"

"Please Master…?" Rosa interrupted in a terrified whisper.

"What? Oh yes, get dressed."

Gratefully Rosa bent for her dress and I got a perfect view of her wide hips and bottom with the sex lips pouting invitingly at me. But it was too late. As she straightened up we saw that Yuri was approaching us having seen Rosa naked in the lounge, something which was strictly against the rules. But the big man's anger faded as he saw it was John who was in charge of her

"Ah Yuri. You've caught Rosa with her pants well and truly down. Make sure she tells Madame that, and that Mr O'Kane and I will look forward to seeing her soundly punished."

The man smiled briefly and then left while Rosa scrambled into her dress and followed him, bobbing us a little curtsy as she went. I was astounded at the cruelty of making Rosa take a punishment for obeying an order she was powerless to refuse and it must have showed in my face.

"Sean," John said, "you've made a good start but you must understand that it is what they expect. What is the point of being submissive to masters who don't take every opportunity to demonstrate their mastery? You could see she hadn't been beaten for some time, Madame keeps her for herself for weeks at a time and she loves being allowed out into the club to be used by the members. Anyway, you'll see later. Now as I was saying…"

Hastily I reached for my recorder and notepad.

Eastern Europe had always been John's speciality as a venture capital consultant, and his bonuses had provided the lynch pin around which The Lodge project had grown. And it had grown quickly; men of wealth and influence were queuing up to join, quite apart from those who were willing to invest. The house and grounds were nearly ready but the only girls he had were his own wife, Caroline, who was a submissive and some other girls whose masters had agreed to lend them until a proper supply could be established. And it was that problem he was pondering when, in a slightly scruffy end of London, he suddenly heard two men conversing in a Balkan dialect he recognised. But it was what they were discussing which really drew his attention. One man was offering the other the use of a girl. However he wasn't interested and when he moved off, John moved in. At first the pimp was deeply suspicious of the obviously affluent man who spoke his own language so fluently and wanted his girl, but the production of ready money soothed him enough to lead John to a back alley, halfway along which was a grimy door which he opened for John. Inside and up some stairs he was shown into a small living room and curled up on the sofa was the girl he would come to know as Rosa. She was dressed in a short, cheap cotton shift and was obviously in need of a good bath, but even so John could see her potential. She looked up in wide-eyed fear as the pimp entered. As she did so, John could see fresh red marks on her face where she had been recently knocked about, presumably by the pimp.

At a command she stood up and let John get a good look at her. She was strongly built but shapely enough, and pretty, under the grime.

"She's a good girl," the man said. "You do anything you like with her. Straight fuck is the cheapest but if you want more…?"

"Oh I want a lot more," John told him, taking in the girl's strong thighs, prominent buttocks and high breasts.

"You! Go and do schoolgirl!" the man shouted at her. She had been standing hunch shouldered and eyes downcast, but at his command she shot a look of pleading at him. He raised a hand threateningly and she went into what John assumed was a bedroom. Once she had gone the man crossed to a small table and poured two glasses of cheap brandy.

"I'll cane her when she comes back." John said once the fiery liquor had gone down.

"Of course," the man agreed. "But I watch. She's good merchandise and I don't want her too marked up, yes?"

"No. Two hundred pounds," and John counted them out of his wallet, "says you'll go and leave me alone with her." The man's eyes followed John's wallet greedily as he replaced it in his jacket and then he turned his attention to counting the money.

John let him for a moment and then with no warning kicked him hard in the crotch. No sooner had he folded retching onto the floor than he grabbed him by his greasy hair, hauled him up and slammed him against a wall.

"I know what you're thinking you bastard. I do the girl and you arrange to have me turned over as soon as I step out of here! Okay you'll make a few quid if you do that, but I can offer you more money than you've ever dreamed of if this bitch is any good. I need a steady supply and I'll pay well for it. So leave me with her and hope she performs!"

John threw him out still gasping, and turned to find that Rosa had reappeared. She was dressed in a short grey pinafore dress and filthy white blouse. If she possessed stockings she wasn't wearing them, just high heeled shoes; even so she looked good. But at the moment she was staring at the door through which she had just seen the man who had ruled her life flung out. And now she faced John.

"Yes," John told her, "I'm the one you've got to worry about now. But just do what you're told and I'll look after you. I expect the clients beat you when you're got up like that, so get me the cane please."

For a moment she hesitated but then reached down behind

the sofa and brought out a fairly presentable cane, which she handed to him. Her eyes were large and soft as she looked at him.

"Please…" she stammered in heavily accented English. "Not too hard. I know I've been naughty but I fuck better if I'm not too hurt."

John laughed. "Oh I bet the clients just melt under those big eyes. No, you just bend over and take whatever I want to give you."

Trembling she turned and leaned over to grasp the arms of a chair. The short dress rode up to reveal the lower half of her inviting buttocks.

"No, no! Out here on the floor, spread your legs and touch your toes!"

Slowly she did as she was told, encouraged by little flicks of the cane. When he was satisfied John lifted the dress clear of her bottom and ran his hands over the buttocks. They were good deep pillows of flesh, firm under his gripping fingers but pleasantly soft. Her sex lips were very full and attractive even though they weren't yet tumescent or open. Her thighs were broad but firm skinned. Altogether she was a durable package he thought. He noticed her watching him upside down, her hair trailing on the floor. To his amusement he realised that her gaze was fixed on the very obvious bulge in his trousers.

Regretfully he realised that the need for haste, if she was any good, required that he keep the beating to six strokes. To his way of thinking anything less than a dozen was poor repayment for a girl's obedience in bending over for a caning. It was the very least that Caroline would expect. But there might well be other opportunities; he had a feeling about this girl. Stepping back he began to cane her. At the first lash she gave a strange little cry—half gasp and half scream—John found it an exciting noise, and laid on the second. A guttural grunt was the response to that Crack! of the whippy shaft across the shuddering expanse of the globes. He waited for a moment while the lines filled and darkened, picking his spot for the third stroke. When he was ready he swung into it a little harder and her head jerked up while a sobbing yell escaped her.

"Please!..." she shrieked. "He doesn't let them do it this hard!"

"But 'he' isn't here. I am. And if you give me any trouble I'll double the beating, understand?"

She groaned but settled herself again. The fourth stroke was harder still, just to teach her, and a strange nasal sort of scream greeted it. And this time while he waited and chose his next target her sobbing continued so that at the fifth stroke, her shriek was merely a peak amidst her continuous noise. After the sixth had cracked home across the shivering buttocks and made them ripple again most delightfully, he watched her stand up, wiping her tears and sniffing. He put the cane down and reached out for her. Obediently, she came and leaned against him while his hand went down her front, lifted the little dress and began to explore her sex. She held quite still as he did so, just running his index finger along the groove of her lips. As he had thought, they were slick and with a deliciously moist parting they opened for him and Rosa gave a soft whimper as first one and then two fingers felt their way up into her lubricating channel. And when the heel of his hand rubbed hard against her clitoris she reached up for him urgently and drew him down to kiss him passionately, her tongue darting teasingly into his mouth, her lips as soft and compliant as her labia.

"We fuck now!" she whispered and pulled him into the shabby little bedroom. In a kind of frenzy she flung off her clothes and John looked at her. She was perfect, sturdy and well rounded. And naturally turned on by a good beating. The bed with its rumpled, dirty sheets didn't appeal and so he simply had her bend over onto it and went in from the rear. But before he did he took the opportunity to survey the well-striped expanse of buttock and in the midst of her thick fleece of pubes, the coral pink of her vulva beckoned eagerly to him. Penetration was effortless. Rosa cried out as she felt him spear up into her and ground her hips against him to extract every ounce of pleasure from the encounter. She arched her back to push back the better and he grabbed her hair to brace himself while he pumped into her. And as he thrust and withdrew he listened to her cries of joy; no faking there. And inside her he could feel her vaginal muscles contracting around his shaft. However long she had been a whore, she certainly wasn't shagged out. He relaxed and allowed himself to enjoy her, driving her to repeated climaxes before she was begging him to come inside her. He pulled harder on her hair and managed to get one hand down between their bodies so that he could rake at her wheals with his fingers. She squealed in anguished delight and then shouted in triumph as he finally spurted into her, finishing with powerful pelvic thrusts which slapped into her as the jets of sperm erupted.

When he stepped back she lay without moving, utterly spent. He wiped himself clean in her buttock cleft and she murmured happily as she felt his wet helm rub against her.

"Get up," he told her. "You're coming with me."

She propped herself up and looked at him, disbelief and delight on her face.

"Come on!" he repeated, and smacked her bottom hard. She gave a gasp of shocked pleasure at the stinging blow and then scrambled upright. He watched as she pulled the cheap dress over her head, slipped on her shoes, ran her fingers through her hair and finally grabbed a corner of grubby sheet and wiped between her legs where his sperm was seeping out of her. John found the vulnerable eagerness of her preparations to start a new life both touching and exciting.

As he had thought, the pimp was waiting for them at the foot of the stairs. But there was respect in his manner now. And all it took was a visit to a cash dispenser before he produced Rosa's passport and she was his. John gave him a contact number to use when his next girl or girls came in and then he took Rosa to The Lodge.

He had seen her eyes widen in hope when her passport had changed hands, but it was only when he took her to his car and she stepped into the leather upholstered luxury of its interior that he saw her begin to blossom into the truly pretty girl she would become. She sat quietly while the car smoothly eased its way out of London and onto the M4, accelerating silently to a speed which made her smile with excited disbelief.

"What's your name?" John asked at last.

She told him.

"Well then Rosa. Rosa with the passport to prove it." He tossed the little booklet over to her and she clutched it to her breast. "Open your legs and play with yourself for me."

"I can't...No I won't...not here!" she protested.

John made no answer but drove onto a slip road and from there found a quiet side road some distance along which was a lay-by. It was nearly dark now and when the car's lights were turned off the interior was softly lit by only a map reading light. Rosa watched him anxiously.

"You have your passport. You can either take it and go or stay and do whatever I ask. It's your choice, and you are free to make it. Nothing will be forced on you."

He knew it was a cruel choice to give a penniless girl in a strange country. But he was certain that it wasn't the choice itself which frightened her. He continued. "Either come with me and discover a new life of luxury and pleasure you have never dreamed of, or go ...You're free."

As he had thought, it was the freedom which frightened her.

"No," she said. "I do what you want. You are a strong man I think and all my life I have been beaten by strong men; Grandfather, Father, uncles. But that pig back there...he was weak he didn't know how to beat a woman.

It should be slow, like you did it, hard but careful I think and you like me while you beat me, yes?"

"Yes I enjoyed the way you took it."

"And I enjoyed it. It was how a strong man should beat." She handed him her passport, "I'll come with you and do what you say."

"Good. But you did disobey me. So now I don't want you to play with yourself, I want you to take me in your mouth."

Giving him a brilliant smile, she unbuckled her seat belt and knelt up on the seat so that she could reach over the console and free his sex from the confines of his clothing. John lifted his hips to help her and soon the semi-tumescent length of his shaft was encircled by her hand and hardening rapidly. Rosa bent lower to lick at it and John ran his hand up and down the length of her back.

"Did your pimp only use the cane?"

"No, riding whip too," she said lifting her head away from giving him long licks up the ridge of his urethra. "But too fast, always too fast. He was not in control like you are."

"Well then Rosa. If you make me come in your mouth too soon, I'll use the crop on you too." John was sure that he had struck pure gold, but this last test would show him for sure.

"Mmmm..." she purred and gave his gleaming helm a soft kiss before replying, "all down my back. Slow and hard."

Then she lowered her face once more, sucking and lapping urgently, nodding her head up and down to caress his length with her mouth and throat, impatient to taste the eruption of his seed on her tongue and in so doing earn herself the promised beating. John pressed his hands hard down into her thick hair when he felt the powerful spasms begin to run through him, and bucked up into the exquisitely soft little chamber of her mouth. Her tongue worked feverishly as he spurted, encouraging every last drop out of him. When she was sure that he was properly clean and that she had swallowed every last morsel of his spend, she sat up, flushed and happy.

John tucked his flaccid member back into his clothes and smiled at her. Madame's first real pupil was going to be a star; he was certain.

"Now you can play with yourself Rosa," he told her as he pulled back onto the motorway.

"Yes Sir," she replied eagerly. And for the rest of the journey John was treated to the sight of her widespread legs with all the fingers of one hand buried deep in the slit between them, spreading the labia wide apart. Her little dress was wrenched up above her hips so that her other hand could reach up under it to squeeze and caress her breasts. She moaned and yelled time after time, arching her back up off the seat as climax after climax ripped through her. It was the most enthusiastic performance he had ever witnessed. But as Rosa told him after she couldn't go on anymore, the clients never lasted long enough to please her and if the pimp caught her masturbating she starved for a week.

John just couldn't believe his luck, a pretty young submissive, sexually experienced but also pleasure starved. Madame would love her.

\*\*\*

"And Madame did," John concluded. "I gave Rosa the crop right here, and then she was whisked away for a bath. Poor kid you should have seen her face when she saw this place and found out she was going to live here. I had her strip, kneel down and stretch out over this very coffee table while Madame looked on.

"I don't remember how many strokes I gave her, but it was a pretty good thrashing, slow and hard, just as she likes it. We could see immediately that she was made of tough stuff, just like you said Sean. It took three or four full-blooded lashes before we even got a whimper out of her, and then maybe ten more after that before she was wriggling and crying out loud. Her back's a good one and there was plenty of room so I carried on until she was screaming and just about to come. Then Madame stepped in behind her and gave her a real fisting; four fingers in the front and her thumb up the back. Christ! The girl nearly took off. She was howling and yelling out for more, writhing and bucking up and down, and Madame just kept on pumping her hand in and out. You could hear her cunt squelching from feet away but Madame kept her at it till she nearly fainted."

John smiled fondly at the memory. "Of course we knew from that moment on that The Lodge was well and truly in business. There would be more where Rosa had come from."

He waved another girl over to refill our glasses and cups and settled back to continue.

***

It took only a fortnight before he got the phone call he was waiting for, and on a dark night in February he pulled into a desolate car park behind a run-down development in East Anglia. In his headlights he saw the pimp waving him into a dilapidated warehouse. Once he had driven in, the door was pulled across behind him and in the dim light John saw a container truck, a van, a table and some chairs and a line of girls against one wall guarded by several men. As he got out of his car he saw that the girls were chained with their hands above their heads. Like Rosa had been they were all skimpily and cheaply dressed, shivering in the cold. They were dull-eyed with tiredness and hunger but even so John could see that they were pretty enough, as the pimp eagerly pointed out. He had four men with him and at his order they went along the line, ripping open dresses, blouses and skirts, and slicing off bras and knickers with knives so that nothing should prevent John from making a detailed examination of the goods. The warehouse rang with shrieks of female fear and protest but in a few minutes John was presented with ten reluctantly displayed nude bodies. Some of the girls tried to twist at the ends of their chains and hide themselves by facing the wall, but one of the men went along the line again and cut at them with a short, thick leather strap. Once again there were yelps and screams as it slapped meatily across thighs and buttocks until at last all ten girls hung motionless in their chains and John could get a look at them. For a moment he allowed himself to admire the sheer quantity of woman flesh on display, the way the breasts ranged in size from pert to heavy, some small with uptilted nipples, some with full curves; some hips slender, some wide with sturdy hams and thighs. But as all of them had their hands raised high the curves and swells of their bodies were emphasised excitingly. He had to remind himself sternly that it was up to him to choose the first batch of girls for Madame to train. She wanted a maximum of four; but how was he to select the best for her purposes?

There seemed only one way to start.

He returned to the car and retrieved a packet of surgical gloves he had had the foresight to bring with him. He felt the only way he could really start to assess them was to examine their reactions to the most outrageously intimate examination he could concoct while they were frightened, cold, tired and hungry.

One by one the girls the men brought the girls over to the table and flung them roughly down onto it. John spent a happy hour or so forcing his fingers deep into vaginas and anuses. He tested them for tightness and elasticity, watching the girls' reactions and immediately rejecting those who had obviously been used too long as prostitutes. But he noted those who were still tight and there were even one or two who responded straightaway. Eventually he had a shortlist of six and had them presented again. This time he tested them further, he had them penetrated anally and vaginally by the men and himself delivered a few strokes with the strap to their backs and buttocks. Again he watched for their reactions and was rewarded by four of the bodies helplessly responding to their treatment. He chose these, paid over half the agreed fee, the balance to be paid on delivery, and drove away.

He spared a thought as he left for those he had rejected. The Lodge would not be staffed by demoralised, worn out whores. The girls he had chosen would have their passports returned and even be helped to return home if that was what they wanted. But he had every confidence that Madame's commanding presence would mean that very few would. And once they had chosen to stay, they would be well paid and looked after. John only wanted proud and willing submissives for his customers, as he considered that only they could provide the ultimate erotic experience.

Two days later John and Madame greeted the van as it pulled up outside The Lodge. To John's surprise it wasn't the pimp driving it but one of the men who had been helping him. He unloaded the pathetic cargo who stood shivering and naked, chained together by the ankles and wrists; they were in a filthy state by then. John was sure they had been kept in the van since he had selected them; they certainly looked and smelled as if they had.

The man approached John and handed over the dog-eared little booklets, which were all the girls had. But then he produced an ID card and for a moment the bottom dropped out of John's world.

"Immigration Mr Carpenter," he said, and smiled as John and Madame paled.

"But some of us get better assignments than others. And I understand you have better trained merchandise than this."

John's mind raced. Caroline was abroad, the girls who were to be loaned hadn't arrived yet and that left only Rosa—who had been in training for only a fortnight.

He told Madame to fetch her, and could see a flicker of uncertainty even in her impassive face as she went.

"You didn't let me sample the wares fully the other night, and they're a bit high now," the man continued. "But if everything meets with my approval today there shouldn't be a problem."

John took the man inside and ordered Yuri and Ivan to take the new girls to a cell and chain them until further notice. In strained silence he and the immigration officer drank a Scotch and waited for Rosa to appear. John poured himself a large measure. He was well aware of his predicament. All that stood between him and almost certain prison was Rosa…and Madame's training.

After what seemed like an eternity Rosa appeared. John hadn't seen her since he had turned her over to Madame and he was astonished. Gone was the grimy but willing backstreet whore; in her place stood a proud woman in a scarlet satin dress which exhibited the mature curves of her body to perfection. John had seen and approved the drawings of the uniforms—in fact he had delivered them to the tailors after making his little alteration—but it was the first time he had seen it worn. And he could see the immigration officer drinking in the sight of the twin swells of smooth breast flesh, displayed by the stoutly boned construction of the bodice which also constricted the waist to show off the curve of the hips, before the full folds of the dress swept to the floor in a cascade of shining satin.

After a second he ordered her to turn around and both men admired the way the wide and low cut back of the dress revealed the graceful lines of the shoulders and back of the woman herself.

"Very impressive Mr Carpenter, but does she perform as well as she looks?" the man said after a longer pause.

To John's surprise, Rosa answered for him.

Turning again she said, "I am a Housegirl at The Lodge, Sir. And where a guest of The Lodge is concerned, I welcome any use of my body. I will try to please you in any way I can."

"Very well," the man replied. "Let's get started."

Rosa herself conducted them down to one of the training cellars and after stripping began a very long afternoon's work.

John didn't know whether to admire the man's or Rosa's stamina more.

He started by chaining her wrists above her and leaving her just balancing on tiptoes, then whipping her back and buttocks with a dog whip. As soon as he began John relaxed a little. The man was good with a whip and delivered the beating slowly and carefully. Rosa responded with a slow building orgasm, gasping and moaning as she jerked under the heavy, braided lash. And it was only when her sweat gleaming body was laced with pink and red wheals from shoulders to thighs did her head go back and long shuddering spasms run through her, while her cries echoed round the cellar. She was taken down and John helped the man to strap her down spread-eagled on her back on a wooden table. Immediately she began to groan in excitement as the rasp of the wood against her wheals began to excite her. The man undid his trousers and climbed onto her, sliding effortlessly into her open and eager sex, driving her to a multiple climax before finishing himself with a throaty cry of relief. But there was no let-up. In only a few moments the man was ready to go again. Leaving Rosa where she was he took a short-lashed scourge to her breasts, stomach and pubic mound. She arched and yelled under the slapping lashes, the sweat pouring off her and making her flesh stick to the wood as she bucked up to meet the whip. Again she came, but the only time she had to get her breath back was while she was released and turned to lie with her breasts squashed down on the table while she was taken in the rear. The man's erection had no trouble penetrating and John watched as the long pole of hard sex slowly sank into her depths, making her shiver and whimper hoarsely. And as he reamed out her narrow channel, John watched her fingers scrabble at the wood while animal grunts and moans greeted each new thrust, but at last there were the unmistakable cries of piercing pleasure as she came yet again. And this time when he withdrew and released her, she slumped dazedly to her knees and then fell forward onto her elbows, leaving the men with an unashamed view of her wide open sex, still oozing semen, and her contracting anus between her striped buttocks.

But to John's dismay the man was still erect, panting from his exertions but still eager for more. So far he knew that Rosa had performed magnificently, but he had to buy her some time. He persuaded the man that a refreshing drink for both of them would give the girl time to recover and respond better to whatever else he wanted to do. They left Rosa hog-tied on the table and went to enjoy another Scotch before going back to finish off. As his finale the man shackled Rosa's ankles, spread wide apart, to a beam which hung from chains in the ceiling. He hauled her up, leaving her arms dangling, until her face was about three feet off the floor. He selected a crop and reaching up went to work on her thighs, while Rosa squirmed and spun, finally achieving a tumultuous orgasm, howling like someone demented as the overload of suspension and flogging drove her to realms beyond mere pain or pleasure. And then at last he stopped. Rosa hung nearly inert now but John could see that even in that state she knew how she was to serve, one last time. Her mouth hung open as she gasped for breath and the man's throbbing shaft made straight for it. She was helpless to control how deep he thrust in. He merely grabbed her head and moved it on his shaft to suit his own pleasure. John watched in amazement as somehow Rosa held on and even at his most brutal thrusts at the moment of emission managed to swallow everything, even reaching round him to grasp his buttocks and pull him towards her.

Quite calmly the man tucked his softening sex away and surveyed the wrecked girl.

"Good, Mr Carpenter," he said. "Very good. I should like to come and stay here... say three weeks a year? And if that's agreeable to you, there will be no problems."

***

John looked thoughtful for a moment.

"It was a close thing Sean. And it was only Rosa and Madame's training which got us through. But he's stayed for three weeks a year ever since then. The girls reckon he's got one of the strongest whip arms of all, and you should see how they queue up to go with him!"

At this point Yuri returned and handed John a note. Both he and his equally big twin, Ivan, were mutes which only added to their menacing presence and no-one got out of order while they were around, as I was to discover.

"Ah! Madame requests the pleasure of our company downstairs Sean," John said, reading the note. "Shall we go? She's put Rosa on the Beam and would like us to join her for the punishment. It should be a good show. Those two know each other inside out by now."

At John's suggestion I left my notepad and recorder behind, he promised that I wouldn't have any trouble remembering what I was about to witness, and we followed Yuri along a richly carpeted corridor, through a small door and down some stone steps. The corridor we then found ourselves in was low and dark, lit only by small bulbs, spaced well apart and lined on the left hand side with wooden doors. Each door had a small barred grill set in it and as we passed I could see that the rooms beyond were really just stone cells.

"This is where a lot of the training goes on," John's voice echoed off the walls and ceiling. "The members can bring girls down here as well if they want more than the common room or bedrooms can offer."

Yuri stopped outside a door and ushered us in. As I entered after John and looked around, I felt a strange, stomach lurching excitement grip me. This was a proper dungeon, fully equipped to deliver as much torment as a body could handle. I gazed around at the chains and ropes which hung from the walls and ceiling, and at the equipment, the stocks, the rack and the strangely shaped furniture on which I couldn't begin to guess how a human body could fit. But I began to get an inkling of just how a body could be contorted when I saw Rosa. She was completely naked apart from a leather hood which covered her from the nose up, leaving only her mouth free. And she was tied to the Beam.

The Beam was a simple baulk of timber; it was mounted on one wall at head height and then sloped downwards out into the room at about forty-five degrees until it met the floor. It was about six inches wide, and Rosa was mounted on it. Her arms had been shackled by wrist restraints to rings in the wall. They were pulled wide apart and back so that her shoulders had to arch against the Beam under her, pushing her breasts out and up. Her thighs were parted each side of the wood and her ankles shackled to the floor, at just the right distance apart to make her have to strain up on tiptoes to try and relieve the pressure on her shoulders. I could see how the sinews in her legs were corded with the effort, and as my gaze travelled up those legs I saw how the finishing touch had been applied. At her crotch her ring and chain had been tucked to one side, down the inside of one thigh. This left her vulva pink and open provocatively. But another chain had been attached. It was a fine one with a small clamp at one end which had been fixed to her clitoris. The chain had then been pulled taut and wound round the head of a screw some five inches below her straining body. Apart from the obvious discomfort, and Rosa was already sweating and heaving, I couldn't see the full significance of this clitoral chain at first. I was so involved with examining the erotic spectacle which Rosa made that for a minute I didn't see Madame standing beside her slave. But when I did I had to admit that she too presented a spectacle of complete sexuality: completely dominant sexuality.

Her torso was encased in a deep crimson basque with black lace trimming which just hid the tips of her breasts, surprisingly large ones on so tall a woman. The length of her legs was emphasised by the mid-thigh length boots with stiletto heels. She wore no stockings and her sex was uncovered, leaving a neatly trimmed bush of pubic hair fully visible. Gazing at her, I could see why she didn't bother with stockings; her skin was flawlessly smooth and clear despite her forty-odd years.

Her thick black hair which she had worn loose when I had been introduced to her earlier was now tied back, making her handsome face with its rather Roman nose seem even more stern than it had then. She ran a hand over Rosa's straining breasts and stomach, and immediately the hooded girl became still, recognising her mistress's touch.

Madame gave us a brief smile. "You have been playing with my poor Rosa, Mr Carpenter. And now she must be punished."

"I thought she could provide Mr O'Kane with some good material for his book, Madame."

"Ah yes, this book," Madame's smile faded and she regarded me coldly. I realised suddenly that not everyone at The Lodge was as keen on us being there as John was.

She looked down at her property where her hand was gently brushing between Rosa's open legs, the fingers tracing the contours of the clitoral hood and just touching the chain and clamp enough to make the girl squirm in her bondage.

"Rosa has never failed The Lodge. Has Mr Carpenter told you her story?" She looked back up at me and I assured her he had. She simply nodded and left Rosa who moaned when she felt her mistress's touch withdrawn. She walked over to a rack on the wall from which about twenty crops and whips hung by leather loops on their handles. I couldn't help watching how her hips and buttocks moved as she took long graceful steps. I had been told that she had once been a ballerina and now I could believe it.

She selected a two lashed whip, each lash being of braided leather, looped and knotted at its end. Her heels clicked on the stone as she walked back to stand beside the Beam. Rosa must have sensed something even from inside her hood. We saw her tense and her head move blindly trying to seek out where her mistress was and where the beating was going to come from.

Madame stood still for a moment while Rosa continued to try and sense where she was. She whimpered in suspense and then Madame struck.

Her arm came back, over and down so fast I hardly saw it, and the lash seemed to have every ounce of her strength behind it. The thongs snapped viciously across Rosa's breasts, the noise echoing around the dungeon. Blinded and deafened by the hood, Rosa had no warning at all and she screeched in shock at the blow. Her head went back and her body arched as much as it could, her legs shaking. John nudged me and pointed at the chain and clamp attached to her clitoris, her reaction to the whip had jerked it even more taut than before and it wrenched at the tender membrane. A long moan escaped Rosa and she let herself slide just fractionally down the Beam. A second lash cracked across her breasts, again she screamed and bucked, and again the clitoral chain was jerked tight.

"You see Mr O'Kane, the whip should always be applied hard…" Madame said and then broke off to deliver another lash which made me wince slightly as it bit across the smooth plain of the bound girl's stomach, making her twist as far as she could, and still pull at that devilish chain between her legs.

"Anything less is an insult to a girl…" Another lash across the stomach and four criss-crossing weals to show for it. "A girl…" she resumed, without taking her eyes off her target, "who is proud to call herself a Housegirl at The Lodge."

The next lash was laid across the pubic mound and was followed swiftly by another which allowed the thongs to bite into the tender flesh at the tops of the open thighs. Rosa was crying out and writhing constantly by now. Madame waited for a few moments until she was craning her head up again and obviously trying to work out where the next lash was coming from and where it would land. Then she cracked in two more in quick succession, both of them across the shuddering mounds of Rosa's breasts, the nipples by now dark red, hardened columns of extraordinary length.

Rosa went into a kind of frenzied overdrive even as she screamed. Briefly her head went back but then she craned it up again as if looking down her body to where the clitoral chain and clamp were tormenting her. Her moaning and crying stopped, all her reactions now were centred in her body. I could see her lips were pursed in fierce effort as she began to buck her hips with all her strength, yanking on the chain between her legs. She set up a frantic rhythm, making her stomach and breasts ripple while her legs trembled with the strain. Her buttocks beat out a tattoo on the wood beneath them, faster and faster. Then she began a throaty kind of growl as she beat against the chain and clamp. It was the most explosive onset of orgasm I had ever witnessed. Suddenly she began yelling "God! Yes! Yes!" over and over as her hip movements slowed but became even more fierce and desperate. I couldn't believe how much movement she managed to get in that bondage, but the tugs on her clamped clitoris were now so violent that I could see the stretched flesh protruding from its hood as Rosa deliberately tormented herself to climax.

Madame watched the writhing body in its demented struggles until the hip thrusts and Rosa's cries had reached an incredible intensity. And then she swung in two more lashes. One more to the already striped breasts and one more to the straining thighs. At last Rosa broke. I could see her sex lips flutter as shuddering spasms ripped through her, still she bucked and pulled at the clamp but the frantic rhythm became a series of violent jerks as she let out an ear-splitting yell of delight, froze rigid at her peak and then collapsed back onto the Beam, gasping and moaning. John had been quite right, slave and mistress knew each other perfectly, the timing of the final lashes had been exquisite, the pain and pleasure of the slave had encouraged the cruelty that both of them enjoyed.

As Madame replaced the whip I found that my throat was dry, so absorbed in the display had I been. I suddenly became aware that I had a pounding erection straining against my trousers, and I also realised that the sight of the whip striped, sweating and exhausted body before me, her sex open and obviously lubricating, was the most erotic I had ever seen.

Madame returned carrying a smooth, black and featureless dildo attached to a harness. She smiled knowingly at me and quite openly parted her legs to feed a strap through her crotch and then gather it behind her buttocks before attaching it to two other straps which encircled her hips.

"If you gentlemen will excuse us…?" and she pointed to the black rod which now speared up from her loins.

"Of course Madame." John answered, and we headed for the door.

I couldn't help one last look before we left. Madame had straddled the Beam and unclamped Rosa's clitoris, who now groaned as the circulation was restored to the engorged tissue. She moved up the sloping wood and as the door closed I heard Rosa's throaty cry of contentment as her mistress penetrated her.

Outside I took a deep breath, my mind whirling with excitement, arousal and questions. Lots of questions.

"John," I began, "how on Earth does she get them like that? What does she do? I mean I've seen some subs but…"

"All in good time Sean," he interrupted. "But first of all I think we could both do with some relief."

Again I became aware of my erection. But as we emerged back into The Lodge proper I realised that it was early evening and I had a date in London. Reluctantly I decided that I would have to leave that pleasure for another time. I was meeting a girl for dinner, a girl who I had been asking out for some time and who had finally agreed. Before that day I had been looking forward to it, and what might follow. But now all I could do was wonder how she would respond to domination. The memory of Rosa's frantic orgasm under bondage and the whip was overwhelming.

I knew I would be back at The Lodge soon; I still had a lot of work to do. But I was quite certain that what had started out as just another job had turned into a life-changing experience.

John saw me to my car, and before I pulled away he told me that Madame did not trust easily and it had been against her wishes that Falconer and myself had been allowed into The Lodge.

"But don't worry. We'll work on her and see if she'll talk to you once she's got used to the two of you being around...but you must understand that even I don't really know how she does it," he said finally. And I drove off quite determined that somehow I would get an interview with Madame Stalevsky.

# MELINDA

*by Falconer Bridges*

ONE.

It was a warm, sunny day, and so what better place to conduct my interview with Melinda, than in one of the splendid themed gardens dotted around The Lodge. The rolling grounds surrounding the fine old building are a horticulturist's dream and she led me to one of her favourite spots overlooking the lake. We settled ourselves on an ornamental bench and after some initial inconsequential chitchat, got down to the business in hand. What follows is Melinda's story, in her own words.

The day had dawned wonderfully.

Not only was it my birthday, I was nineteen, but it was also to be my first day as a fully qualified Housegirl. What an honour! I'd arrived at The Lodge not exactly a virgin, but not exactly experienced either. I knew that I'd given Madame Stalevsky more problems than she'd wished for during my training but now she had decreed that my tuition was complete and released me from the direct supervision of either herself or her two assistants, Yuri and Ivan. They still kept a watchful eye on me of course, but basically I was free to take up my duties with the Gentlemen of The Lodge. This was to be my initiation and my excitement was unbounded. Looking back now, I think I saw it as a sort of parallel to a pilot taking her first solo flight, a truly momentous occasion.

I entered the common room that evening, nervous but full of eager anticipation, and fantasising wildly as to the possible outcome of my first unaccompanied foray into the heady world of domination and subservience inhabited by these few select, accomplished and powerful men. You'll understand that having lived for this moment throughout the rigorous, and at times seemingly tortuous training, it was with a thudding heart that I glanced discreetly around the room. One of Madame Stalevsky's basic instructions being that there must be never be any trace of wanton or flirtatious behaviour on my part, I took great care not to meet any of the members' gazes directly. An advance was strictly the prerogative of a member and must come directly from him. But all the same I was desperate to see which of them were in attendance.

Uncontrollable, shimmering shivers of desire and expectation ran through my body as I saw John Carpenter and Alan Masterson lounging in opposing armchairs, enjoying a cigar and an after dinner cognac. These were two of the most powerful men ever to be found together in one place. Apart from his importance in the commercial world, Master Carpenter was also the controlling influence in the operation of The Lodge, and here he was, accompanied by an equally important colleague. And one of them occupied an almost continual presence in my thoughts. What if he should be the first to reserve me by tagging me with his room disc? My legs instantly turned to jelly at the thought, and when, having noticed me, John Carpenter directed his companion's attention to me, my cheeks coloured into a spectacular shade of scarlet. My composure flew out of the window in the blink of an eye and if Madame Stalevsky had witnessed my crimson hued embarrassment, I'm sure the consequences would have been dire. Luckily for me, she did not and the two men seemed to be more amused than indignant.

John Carpenter concentrated his gaze upon me for what seemed an eternity. I shrank into myself, wishing I was anywhere else on Earth. If ever there was any man to whom I'd give my soul, it was him. My whole being was in turmoil. All through my training, I'd watched him from afar. He entranced me. I worshipped him. I don't know why. All I know is that I longed for him to command me, to control me, to take me and use me in any way he desired. I was crazed with lust, wantonness and desire. The heat between my legs turned itself up to volcanic proportions, and if I'd been wearing knickers they'd have been drenched by the involuntary torrent of lubrication from my vagina. As it was, the juice just trickled down my inner thighs as I fought to control the fingers that desperately longed to caress, fondle and satisfy the raging need that now gripped my sex.

Oh God, please, please let him be the first.

I repeated that phrase again and again in my mind as he turned to his companion and entered into a languid conversation, punctuated by lazy but obvious glances in my direction. They were appraising me. I stood, maintaining my composure to the best of my ability, until at last, much to my dismay, Alan Masterson looked me straight in the eye and beckoned me over. Oh no. That wasn't what I wanted. I wanted Master Carpenter. I couldn't be sure whether or not I showed any outward sign of disappointment, I prayed that I had not as that would have been an unforgivable sin, but mentally I drooped. Of course I would follow my training and submit myself to any of the Masters who wished to use me, but my heart was bursting with longing for the discipline, and hopefully, the sexual gratification that I was certain he would provide in a superior manner to any of the others. Why did I have such intense feelings for that one man? There could only one answer: it was love.

That was it. The reality I'd fought to hide burst through the barriers of suppression, flooding my senses with a sudden flash; I was in love with Master Carpenter. That was far worse than anything I'd envisaged and I startled myself with the shameful admission as Madame Stalevsky's words stabbed themselves into my consciousness. All the Masters were Lord to me; I must obey each and every one without question or favour. I was their slave, to be used, abused and treated in whatever way they desired. No one

Master must take precedence over another in my thoughts or attention. I was nothing, whilst they, collectively were God. And yet, here I was on my graduation outing, inwardly breaking every rule. How could I help myself? Master Carpenter had a presence, a majesty that eclipsed all around him and I was hopelessly gripped in the vice like jaws of the spell he wove so effortlessly.

I'd had no experience of true love, but once I'd admitted the undoubted truth, I wondered why it had taken so long for the light to dawn. From the moment that he'd put the proposition to me in Prague I'd been in thrall to him. The Lodge was to be my own personal Valhalla and on our journey to England I'd spent every moment conjuring up visions of him taking me, punishing me and using my body. Of course he explained to me that I would be common property, available for use by any and every denizen of my illustrious destination, but that did nothing to stop Technicolor images of his undoubtedly magnificent phallus penetrating my mouth, my sex and my anus, drawing themselves in my mind. I dreamt of the whip and the cane. I saw chains. And straps. And all manner of wicked bondage devices. And he was using them all to deliver pain, humiliation, discipline and joy to my undeserving self. But most of all I dreamt of orgasms. Giant body wracking ferments of pleasure, that transported me from the commonplace into the realms of unimaginable ecstasy. But he'd never so much as laid a finger on me. He'd remained at all times a perfect gentleman, I'd remained exquisitely frustrated and as with all his recruits, Madame Stalevsky welcomed a student ripe for tuition.

Alan Masterson's angry voice ripped through my reverie.

"Come here girl! Good God, what's wrong you?"

Gathering my emotions together as best I could I walked over to where the men were sitting and set myself, in the prescribed position with legs apart, in front of Alan Masterson.

"Pull yourself together," he admonished, "you're not here to stand around dreaming. Now, step closer."

I obeyed immediately and without question. Alan Masterson seemed to find that gratifying.

"That's better," he grunted, "now let's have a good look at you."

His eyes swept over my body, appreciatively taking in the curves of my young, taut breasts with their jutting nipples, and the easy swell of my hips. He reached out, running his palm over my bottom and caressed my buttocks through the silky smoothness of my gown. Despite myself I felt the heat returning to my sex and when he slipped his hand inside the split skirt of my dress and ran it slowly up the inside of my thigh I trembled in anticipation. His hand found my crotch, cupping my mound sensuously before rippling his fingers along the length of my slit. Arousal was not to be denied, I shamelessly pressed myself against the strength of his touch and as I grew ever wetter his index finger slid easily inside my vulva, finding the bud of my clitoris. I couldn't stifle the moan that escaped my lips and as if to heighten my discomfort he gently stroked my stiffening bud for several long seconds before removing his finger.

"My, you are a naughty little girl, aren't you?" he said icily, as he took his hand from beneath my dress. "Am I to gather that Madame Stalevsky taught you nothing? Did I give you permission to allow yourself to be aroused?"

I'd failed. Again.

He questioned me with his eyes as he wiped his glistening finger on a tissue. He expected an answer but his frosty attitude and my own inability to follow my training had numbed my mind and frozen my tongue. I remained mute.

"God damn it, answer me," he exploded.

"Yes Master... er, I mean no Master," I stammered

"If you're unable to give a sensible reply, you'd better keep quiet altogether," he said.

I was thrown into confusion and stood in awkward embarrassment as he sat tapping his fingers on the buttoned, stuffed leather arms of his chair. Under his unwavering gaze the heat in my sex swiftly subsided, leaving my labials and the tops of my thighs uncomfortably sticky with my cooling secretions. He surveyed me intently for what seemed like hours and then, lightening his demeanour he spoke gently, ordering me to bend closer.

"After careful consideration, it comes to my mind that you would benefit greatly from a little personal tuition from myself," he said and producing his room disc, he slipped the chain over my lowered head.

"You are now mine for the night," he continued. "I have a little business to settle before I can allow you to immerse yourself in what no doubt will be for you, a rewarding and unique experience. Now, re-fill our glasses and then take yourself off and wait for my call."

"Not so fast," a voice interjected. It was John Carpenter. "I can't let you to get away with that. You know full well that in this room a girl is communal property, or were you just hoping that I'd let it go and leave you to claim this delightful young creature without protest?"

"Oh well, it was worth a try. I suppose we'd better discuss the matter. But not in front of the stock." Then, addressing me directly, he ordered me to go and stand in the corner of the room whilst they resolved the matter.

I was exhilarated, John Carpenter had now shown a real interest in me. Me! Maybe my dream would come true after all. As I made my way across the room I was gratified to notice heads turning as I passed occupied armchairs, although I found one particular braying comment somewhat disconcerting.

"Pretty damn fine filly, eh what?" it said. "I wouldn't say no to a few hours in the saddle with that myself." The voice had a grating, Hooray Henry, kind of intonation and I once again found myself at odds with my training as I crossed my fingers and secretly hoped this coarse person would never get his unwelcome bit between my teeth.

I reached the designated corner and stood facing the wall as I knew was expected of me. With legs apart, my hands clasped together behind my back, my breasts thrust proudly upward and my head held erect I adopted the classic position of a subservient chattel, whilst I waited in increasingly nervous suspense as my Masters deliberated over my fate. It seemed as if some kind of hush had come over the room, of course it could have been my fevered imagination working overtime, but I could almost physically feel the searing heat of massed lechery burning into my back. It took every ounce of self-control to stop myself turning to glance rearwards, but I didn't really need visual confirmation, the atmosphere in the room had changed. And the cause was me.

I was the new girl. Fresh territory, ripe for exploration and the fading British pioneering spirit seemed to suddenly re-awaken deep in the loins of all present. Everyone was looking at me, mentally peeling away my dress, fondling my breasts, my buttocks and my sex and in their minds' eyes selecting the cane, the crop, the whip or whatever item of correction and pain they considered the most suitable with which to discipline me. I knew it. And they knew that I knew. And that knowledge was seemingly stimulating previously resting libidos into red-blooded awareness. Every single one of them now felt the call to enter into the race to be the first to conquer my previously uncharted regions.

Yes, I was young. And yes again, I was relatively inexperienced. To find fulfilment I had thrown aside my independence and was now owned, body and soul, by my Masters. Without their patronage I was nothing and must never allow myself to fall into the trap of attributing to myself false values of worth or desirability. Vanity and pride had no place in my life now that I had abandoned myself to a future of ordered discipline and outside control. That much had been made very clear to me during my training and therefore those basic principles were instilled into my subconscious. But subjugation of my will did not equate with relinquishment of thought. My brain was still free to roam unchecked in spheres not directly involved with matters of domination and subservience. Apart from total obedience, the Masters also expected a girl to display a reasonable level of intelligence. We had, after all, to spend a great deal of time in their presence, not all of which was dedicated to sexual or physical domination. They had other requirements which begged fulfilment, a reasoned conversation and enlightened attitude in their playthings being two of them, which is why the Housegirls of The Lodge were in themselves treasured highly. We were special. What's more, I had overheard a supposedly private conversation between Madame Stalevsky and an unseen Master during which she described me as a valuable asset, an appreciating piece of property that with the right handling would eventually figure highly on the Lodge's balance sheet. It's little wonder therefore that I didn't check the wild thoughts and fantasies that flew around my spinning head. The Masters wanted me. And I loved it.

However, I did not love the animal roughness of the hand that from nowhere suddenly clamped itself hard around one of my breasts. Its twin attacked my other unsuspecting mammary, a powerful erection pushed the satin of my gown into the crease between my buttocks and a heavy jaw, complete with overwhelming whisky breath, laid itself on my shoulder.

"Now then, my beauty," brayed the same tones I'd heard earlier, "let's see how you run over eight furlongs."

Both paws finally retreated, but not before a pair of forefingers and thumbs cruelly mistreated the sensitive, hardened nipples that during my fantasies had strained against my dress. With a final double squeeze that left me gasping, the hands leapt from my cleavage, clasped the hem of my skirt and in one mighty heave, pulled it up over the roundness of my bottom. In an instant a horny finger savagely thrust itself past the barrier of my labials and sank into my unsuspecting vagina, only to be accompanied almost immediately by a fat, truncheon like, thumb jabbing painfully at the entrance to my virgin anus. The thumb would brook no denial, thrusting and prodding, until with a breakthrough that brought tears to my eyes and a scream to my lips, it finally parted my sphincters and became the first adventurer to penetrate previously unsullied territory.

Although I couldn't see him, I knew who it was and I hated him with the same intensity that I loved Master Carpenter. And yet, as the thumb and finger worked together compressing and titillating my two most intimate regions that same, uncontrollable fire burnt into my senses and I felt the stirrings of arousal once more. Lascivious comments of encouragement, along with murmured speculations as to the future course of the encounter exploded into my consciousness. Startled, I suddenly realised that my assailant and myself were surrounded by an eager, expectant crowd. All the Masters had risen from their seats, abandoning their previous diversions in order to observe, and perhaps participate, in the initiation of the New Girl.

Without warning the digits were pulled with distinctly resounding plops from my increasingly appreciative orifices. The same two animal-like, hands clamped themselves around the front of my thighs and I was pulled roughly backwards for a pace or two.

"Legs wide apart and touch your toes," came the command.

A flat palm smacked stingingly several times across my buttocks, the unexpected pain causing me to bite so hard on my lip in order to deny the threatened protest, that I tasted blood. Further gut wrenching blows landed on my back before a heavy hand pushed urgently between my shoulders to hasten my obedience, causing my head to scrape the panelling on its urgent, forced descent. He was in a hurry. Not a good example for a Master to set. I remember that thought flashing through my mind. Self control was one of the most important attributes that not only a Housegirl, but also a Master, was expected to possess. This arrogant, horsey, buffoon was not in the same league as John Carpenter, he didn't belong on the same planet. The backs of impatient fists pressed into both my inner thighs, and after forcing my legs even further apart, resolved themselves into palms, which after delivering a barrage of crippling slaps to my most tender flesh, cupped my buttocks, lifting them higher and setting my pudenda at an angle far more suited to both observance and penetration.

What was this man doing in an establishment such as the Lodge? He was nothing but a beast and I decided that the only possible reason he was admitted must be due to immense wealth or power. My opinion of his animality was confirmed as my sex lips were torn unceremoniously apart and a rock of a bell end hammered at my vagina. All was lost, or so it seemed. I gave myself up to my fate; the crock of gold at the end of the rainbow was not to be mine after all. Master Carpenter was not to be my initiator. My golden dream faded to black.

And then.

"*Hold*, gentlemen."

It was him.

My knight in shining armour.

Master Carpenter.

\*\*\*

Montague D'Arcy DuPont was a boorish lout at the best of times it seemed, and later, in a rare moment of social intimacy, Madame Stalevsky told me that. She said his vanity was unbounded, he was the only man she'd ever known who carried a mirror in his pocket. He was also a bigot, a fanatical know-all full of his own self-importance, and as such he had forged no close bonds with any other member. And that's why Master Carpenter got away with his totally unprecedented action.

Stunned silence had greeted the initial interjection. It was heresy, totally unheard of and absolutely against the rules. The very rules which he himself had help to draft. DuPont paused in his onslaught although his bulbous helmet had already drilled a limited entry into my surprisingly slippy and responsive tunnel. I didn't want him, but the reaction of my vagina to his assault signalled anything but rejection. His piston had stoked the flickering embers of my lust into something akin to a forest fire and pre programmed conditioning had eased my legs open wider and lubricated my sheath in readiness to accept the entire length of his cannoning cock. I sensed him straighten up and knew that he had turned his head to face the interloper. His twitching weapon however remained firmly wedged a couple of inches or so over the threshold of my sex.

Electric tension crackled through the air as with bated breath and pleading genitals I waited for Master Carpenter to continue.

"Gentlemen, gentlemen, this is no way for us to behave. We have rules and set procedures to follow," he said, contradicting his own outburst of a few moments before. "We must maintain the dignity of our positions here and not allow ourselves to indulge in behaviour unsuited to our status as Masters of all we survey."

I was only a servitor, a mere item on the inventory of the Lodge, he went on, but correct and proper treatment of the lower orders was paramount to maintaining both the authority of their betters and the unquestioning respect and servitude of those same inferior creatures.

"To descend upon this initiate like a pack of hounds harassing a cornered fox is most inappropriate," he added.

They were in danger of becoming a rabble, and if I really

was the undeniable temptress they seemed to think, then perhaps I should be brought out into the centre of the room where they could each share in, and enjoy my undoubted attributes. The inference was obvious. He meant that they could all fuck me. Or beat me. Or anything else their inventive minds could envisage, but I let that wash over me like drizzle in the breeze, because if they accepted his proposal then I was sure he would be obliged to participate. And if that's what it took to have his wonderful shaft firmly plumbing the depths of my uterus, then so be it.

In the meantime my increasingly demanding vagina had not remained inactive. I cursed myself for my inability to dampen my excitement, as totally of their own volition my labials spread wider, my juices flowed with a musky, arousing aroma that even drifted to my own nostrils, and my sex lips rippled in a frantic attempt to pull the bulbous pleasure dome blocking my hole further into my sheath. I wanted the whole of that pulsing weapon thrust inside me right up to the hilt. I needed to feel it stretching me to the limit. I lusted for its engorged girth to block my channel and plug me up as tight as the cork in a bottle of champagne, even though it belonged to the hideous DuPont. He obviously felt the tug on his manhood and landed a further barrage of painful, heavy blows on my straining back, knocking the breath from my lungs and leaving me gasping.

"Keep still, you damned foreign whore, I'll fuck your arse off when I'm good and ready," he yelped. "Just keep that sluttish twat of yours in check whilst I decide the best way to sort out Carpenter." His monstrous outburst provoked a universal sense of outrage amongst the Masters, breaking the impasse that had developed in the moments of indecision following Master Carpenter's intervention. Straining to peer backwards between my ankles, beyond the closeness of DuPont's calves I saw the Masters turn away, disperse and return to their seats. He had succeeded in demonstrating once more his absolute caddishness to them all. So, I wasn't

English, and maybe I wasn't as pure as the driven snow, but I was a Housegirl at The Lodge and that stood for something. And his insolence in addressing John Carpenter in such a derogatory manner had left them stunned.

But for the moment, he was still a member of The Lodge and entitled to all the services and privileges that entailed, including the right to do with me as he pleased. He stood glaring at Master Carpenter who I could see holding his position and countering DuPont's leering triumphant stare with an expression of absolute contempt. In a sudden act of petulance DuPont slapped both palms stingingly down on my backside and heaved me off his penis with such violence my head crashed into the panelling with a mighty thud that sent my senses reeling. My knees buckled and I fell to the floor in a daze, but he immediately grabbed a bunch of my hair, hauling me to my feet, and with his free hand on my shoulder, spun me around to face him.

"Alright, he wins for now," he said, "but not until that whore's mouth of yours sucks me drier than the sands of the Sahara." And with that, he laid both heavy paws on my shoulders and pushed me unceremoniously down on to my knees in front of him.

"You can leave it to me now Carpenter," he bellowed defiantly, "I'll return her to you and your cronies when I've filled her gullet with spunk." I could foresee that there'd be trouble over that remark later, Master Carpenter being a strong man in every sense of the word, but for the time being he could do no more than reluctantly return to his seat and exchange frustrated glances with Alan Masterson, who himself appeared to be deeply offended by the whole incident.

"Suck, you crossbred bitch," DuPont menaced, "you darkies are supposed be good at this, so let's see you prove it."

There was nearly a mass uprising there and then, and I saw Master Carpenter's face turn crimson with rage. Fascist racism would not be tolerated by him and had no place in The Lodge. He knew full well that my mother had been of mixed race, being a product of what the French termed 'La collaboration horizontale' after her own mother had formed a relationship with a black American officer during the closing stages of World War Two. After one further dilution, the ebony of my grandfather's skin had turned to a creamy coffee in me, and upon our introduction Master Carpenter had told me that he found the combination of what he termed my enticingly sensual colour and my eastern European accent a beguiling mixture. A view later wholeheartedly endorsed by Madame Stalevsky.

Totally oblivious to the furore he was causing, Dupont allowed his thickly veined penis to rear up in front of my face before pushing it down to a level position with one hand. He then clamped his other hand around the back of my head, and roughly pulling it closer, plunged his purple hued glans straight into my mouth. I wasn't ready to take him and the violence of his entry dragged both my lips inwards, pressing them hard against my teeth. I gagged as his vile instrument scraped over my tongue and banged up against the solid wall of my tonsils. With absolutely no expertise or finesse he fucked my mouth just as if it were any other orifice, lunging in and out whilst pulling my head backwards and forwards to meet his frantic thrusts. I was choking, fighting for breath and when, on my tongue, I finally felt his urethra expand as the swelling river of his sperm rushed to ejaculation, I was overcome with relief. Soon my ordeal would be over.

I licked, sucked, and rasped his jerking member in order to accelerate his climax. The sooner the better, I thought. And yet, as the fountains of seed spurted into my already overfilled mouth, I thrilled as its salty taste washed over my expectant taste buds. The first delicious flood of come gushing down my throat almost drove me into a seizure. I didn't care whose sperm it was, I was crazy for it and half choking I hungrily swallowed geyser after geyser. As the storm of his ejaculation abated, his penis slackened and with a palm pressing firmly on my forehead he started to pull the still throbbing shaft from my battered mouth. But I couldn't help myself and totally losing control I frantically licked and slurped in an attempt to feed on every last drop of magical ambrosia. Inwardly, I cursed myself for being so weak, but there was nothing I could do. Sperm to me is like a narcotic, I can never get enough, but unlike heroin there are no harmful effects. There is no such thing as a fatal overdose of semen, and for that I can only thank God.

But DuPont hadn't quite finished with me yet. Stepping forward he harvested a fistful of the hair falling over each side of my face and buried his penis in the thick strands, wiping away the final traces of seminal fluid that I had been unable to capture for my own delight. As he turned disdainfully away, I noticed for the first time, Madame Stalevsky, accompanied by Yuri and Ivan, standing surveying him with arctic frostiness. He saw them at the same moment, displaying evident surprise. He was even more surprised a moment later when, without ceremony and not even allowing him the opportunity to return his penis to its lair inside his trousers, Yuri and Ivan both took one of his arms and steered him firmly, but with as little disruption as possible, from the room. John Carpenter and Alan Masterson both rose from their chairs, but Master Carpenter waved his colleague back into his seat and then hurried to follow in their wake.

Madame Stalevsky approached me displaying a tenderness and concern which I could never have previously imagined. Smoothing back my tangled locks, she helped me to my feet.

"My child," she said, "such a disgraceful episode. It has not happened before in all my time here. Never."

Looking me straight in the eye, she asked me in a voice so full of compassion that I could hardly relate it to the authoritarian tones she'd used during my training, if I wished to return to the special experience of my 'coming out', or if I wished to be excused until I was more composed. I was overwhelmed, my previously strictly disciplinarian Mistress had a heart. There was obviously much more to The Lodge than I had realised. We girls were treasure. Here I was valued and protected. I had worth. The Lodge truly was Valhalla.

Although I was distressed, and not a little shaken by my experience, I assured her that it had not been too unendurable, and confirmed that I had not made any protest, or sought at any time to prevent DuPont from carrying out any of his actions. Privately, to myself, I added that I'd found the quality and flavour of his sperm most satisfying. I had to be truthful with myself and also admit that I'd found his rough and demeaning treatment strangely exciting.

But my ultimate fantasy was dashed. Master Carpenter had not been the first, and now there seemed no possibility that he would use me that night. And that hurt. I was cut to the bone and as Madame Stalevsky took my hand to lead me away, real tears of disappointment welled up into my eyes. But, crossing the floor, I was blessed with one, last wonderful vision. Through the windows of the room, I saw Montague DuPont, clutching one hand to an obviously injured jaw, running from the building.

Moments later Master Carpenter pushed through the door, blowing on his knuckles, and heading, as I thought, straight in my direction. I lost all sense of reason, waves of joy swept through my being. At last my dream was coming true. He had returned. For me! All my self-control vanished in an instant, as totally unable to contain myself; I pulled from Madame Stalevsky's grasp and rushed towards him. Flinging my arms around his shoulders, I clung to him in rapture, my head laid upon his chest.

The silence of death fell upon the room.

Everyone stared in horror. Utter disbelief radiated from glacial features as he disengaged my arms and pushed me away. Oh God, what had I done? The hot surge of blood turned to ice in my veins, as the full realisation of the gravity of my actions dawned on me. I'd made a travesty of my training, and a mockery of Madame Stalevsky, which would reflect badly on her. He said nothing, just surveyed me through eyes of steel. And that look delivered an admonishment more blistering than any vocal reprimand. I stood trembling and afraid, awaiting my fate.

Finally, he turned to Madame, addressing her in a cold, intimidating but perfectly controlled tone.

"You assured me, did you not, that this trollop was thoroughly housetrained?"

She was allowed no opportunity to reply.

"However, I now see that I was misinformed. Take her away, clean her up and bring her to my rooms in precisely one hour. During that time, I will appoint a committee to judge precisely her suitability and worth to this establishment."

We were dismissed with the wave of a hand, the depth of Madame Stalevsky's fury transmitting itself to me through the intensity of her grip on my arm as she escorted me from the room.

Without further ado, I was marched to my room and ushered inside. I stood immobile as she laid her hands at the base of my neck and slipped the short sleeves of my dress over my shoulders. The dress fell to the floor, but there was no sexual innuendo present, and now naked apart from my stockings and stilettos I allowed myself to be led to the shower. Shedding the hosiery and footwear I stepped into the soothing jets, directing the steaming water on to my hair, my face and then my breasts. Unhooking the showerhead I shamelessly sprayed between my thighs, sweeping the forceful jets along the length of my labials. My fingers strayed to my sex and I lazily explored my dripping vagina, massaging my emerging clitoris with easy strokes. My legs widened involuntarily as my thumb concentrated on my nub and two fingers lost themselves inside the accommodating well of my vagina.

A forceful cough from Madame Stalevsky returned me to consciousness. Turning off the spray she pulled me from the shower, and after helping me to dry myself, pushed me down on to the seat in front of my dressing table. Attending to my make up with professional expertise, she skilfully applied shades and colours I'd never previously worn. Colours that I would never have had the courage to choose for myself. Opalescent, almost white eye shadow and lipstick complemented delicately blushed coffee coloured cheeks, and stroke after stroke of the brush transformed my long tresses into a sheen of satin ebony. A matching shade of pearly polish was applied to my finger and toe nails, and after painting my broad areolae to emphasise their already impressive size, she removed the small rings from my pierced nipples, replacing them with much larger, heavier circles of gold.

I had been allowed to keep my luxuriant thatch of pubic hair and she now attended to this, brushing and combing it with detailed attention until she was satisfied by its appearance. Finally she had me lie on the bed, knees bent and legs wide apart as she coloured my labials and inner sex lips, in what shade I couldn't tell, but I knew well enough that at her hands, the effect would be perfect.

But would it be perfect enough for him? It was obvious that Master Carpenter was a man apart. But he was the man of my dreams. And I'd placed my dream in jeopardy. My ultimate fulfilment was without any doubt to submit and subjugate my entire being to his will. Submission is joy, and it had been just around the corner. So close and yet now, so far away. But Madame was not about to give up on me.

When she was satisfied with my appearance, I stood and looked at myself in the mirrors. No, that's a lie. What I really did, was allow myself the unforgivable satisfaction of appreciating the splendour that the reflected image of my body presented to me. Madame Stalevsky had excelled herself. I could have fallen to the ground and kissed her feet. I clenched my nails into my palms as I slowly pirouetted before the silvered glass.

A leopard.

That's what she'd made of me.

A jungle goddess.

My milk chocolate skin was oiled, shiny and glowing. My hair was swept tightly back from my face, accentuating my high, blushed cheekbones. Huge golden skulls dangled from either earlobe and my neck was circled with a diamond-studded collar, also of gold. She'd returned me to my roots. Now there was no doubting my African origin. A giant sapphire glistened above my pierced navel, gold bangles circled my wrists and upper arms, and anklets of that same precious metal hung above my feet. This was grandeur in the extreme. I fancied the jewels were treasure, plundered by pirates from the harem of some Arabian potentate. What would he have made of the thick golden circles threaded through my jutting nipples? Did his women dance before him with jewel-encrusted chains cascading over their pudenda, suspended from similarly sparkling belts clasped around their waists? Were their labia decorated with descending ladders of golden rings threaded through the pierced outer lips of their sex as mine were? How could I know? I couldn't. I could only wonder as I studied myself. Luxuriant ebony pubes. A glistening oiled body. Jutting breasts and smooth thighs. Exultant nipples, walnut brown and stiff as pokers. I looked, and that's what I saw.

And that's what he'd see.

I could only guess what sort of visual stimuli he might find pleasing, but I thrilled, unable to control myself. Surely he wouldn't reject me. Not now. Not presenting an image such as Madame Stalevsky had now endowed me with, I began to hope. I tingled. I allowed my lust to run wild. My debt to her was incalculable and I resolved from that moment on, I'd be the best, most obedient girl in her charge.

As she fussed over the final finishing touches to my appearance, the tension was mounting in my loins, making me increasingly impatient and restless. I fidgeted uncontrollably and was rewarded with a series of smarting slaps as I was ordered to keep still. I couldn't help myself. I just wanted him to fuck me. Whip me. Beat me. Put it any way you want, I couldn't live for much longer without the lashing sting of his cane pulsing across my flesh.

And I now possessed the ultimate image to bring my dream to reality. He would do it. I knew he would. Madame Stalevsky knew it as well. She was triumphal, almost haughty, in her attitude as she clipped a thick plaited leather lead to the ring on my collar and tugged me towards the door.

TWO

There was silence.

Madame Stalevsky had allowed me to walk upright along the darkened passages leading to Master Carpenter's apartments. But now, adopting the stance of a jungle predator, I balanced on outstretched fingertips and toes as I waited with bated breath outside his door. After what seemed an interminable period of time, the door opened in response to her summons. He looked out. On all fours I lay below his gaze and so his eyes greeted my Mistress with a questioning look. Her own eyes dropped downwards. His eyes followed. They settled on me, drinking in my sensuality.

Have you ever known Heaven?

I did at that moment.

Sensing his approval, Madame Stalevsky took her leave in an instant, disappearing back into the dimness as he scooped the lead from her hands and tugged me into his presence. I entered Master Carpenter's rooms not really knowing what to expect. I'd hoped for the best, but prepared for the worst. After all, I'd failed drastically at my first real test, and my performance now had not only to guarantee my own future, but also that of Madame Stalevsky. Master Carpenter surveyed me for several long minutes. To me it seemed an eternity. Eventually he reached a conclusion, and leaving the room, he fastened the lead attached to my collar to a hook on the wall, firmly instructing me to remain as I was. I heard the beeps of an electronic telephone. Seconds later, long before the call could have been connected, the phone was slammed back onto its base and very shortly afterwards he strode back into the hall, carrying a bowl of water. A dog's bowl. He laid it in front of me in the manner of an owner trying to calm an expectant pet.

"Drink," he said, "your future is about to be decided."

Moments later I heard him dial once again.

I remained splayed out on all fours for what seemed like hours. I'd drunk from the bowl as I heard him re-dial and now still balanced on my now protesting digits, I contemplated my future. He looked in on me once or twice, checking that I hadn't relaxed my position. That was something I dared not attempt to do.

"You," he'd told me, "are no more than a dumb animal. Animals are trained to obey their masters instinctively and immediately, no matter what the circumstances. Very shortly, my colleagues and I will endeavour to ascertain once and for all, whether or not your training has been successful."

So, he intended to share me. To farm me out. To allow me to be beaten, abused and degraded by all and sundry. Well, all right, if that's what he wanted then I wasn't about to argue. I'd learnt my lesson. His very words alone ignited the unstoppable heat in my loins that accompanies any mention of chastisement or correction. I was dripping in no seconds flat. Surely he must have known by then that my greatest wish was to surrender myself totally to his control. And not only that. Love, or lust if you prefer it, such as mine was insatiable. There was absolutely no command he could issue that I wouldn't obey. And if that included fucking his associates, being sodomised by them, sucking them dry, or simply submitting to a whipping or beating, then I'd carry out that task utilising every last ounce of my ability.

Is there any greater love than that?

Of course, all those acts of submission and sex would be part of my normal duties at the Lodge in any event, but I revelled in the fantasy that I was there only for his use and pleasure. I was still oozing juices freely from the stimulation of my lascivious reverie when the first knock came upon the door. And I was ready. I'd been parked beside a mirror, so that not only would anyone entering the rooms be welcomed by my thrusting bottom, but they could also soak in all my other delights by glancing in the glass.

Master Carpenter strode past me, dimming the lights on the way, and pulled the door open. In the half light I looked in the mirror. I was oiled and gleaming. I had the well-hung breasts of a Page Three model and the buttocks of an African angel. Looking up, I recognised the visitor. It was Oliver Carlisle. Stepping through the door he welcomed the sight of my expectant sex with a series of stinging open palmed slaps, laid squarely across my well-fleshed rump. I crumpled mentally, fighting to make no outward sign, but inwardly I screamed for more.

There was no more.

And that was torture in itself I thought as I was ordered by Master Carpenter to return my gaze to the floor. Oliver Carlisle was followed very swiftly by two others, both of whom, to my delight, dealt me a blow from a crop, or a whip, or something similar as they paused on their entrance into the apartments. I was unable to see who they were; so unidentified fingers explored my sex and my anus. Rough palms delved under my chest, pulling and squeezing my breasts and nipples. My legs widened involuntarily, hungry for further exploitation.

"Good solid haunches."

That was the initial comment. From Master Carlisle, I was certain of it.

"Looks like perfect breeding material, if you don't mind my saying so old man," quickly followed. "The right hips, and juicy where it matters."

I had to be very much mistaken if that wasn't Dandy McIntyre.

"God knows how you find these broads." There was only one accent in the Lodge that owed its origins to a deep study of old American movies: Joseph Wright.

Following their initial assessment of my attributes, I heard them all move on into the main room. Then, a spicy, subtle aftershave approached. It was Armani, my favourite. A lingering caress rolled over my backside and edged its way shiveringly upwards along my spine, before sweeping languorously down to roll my nipples into a stiffening awakening. The fingers pinched hard, raising an instant protest from my surprised nubs before they succumbed to the numbing pleasure of pain, and started those same old shivers rolling unchecked through my body. Whoever he was, he'd felt my reaction and dealt me an immediate flurry of stinging slaps across my haunches.

"Don't be in such a hurry, my horny little petal," said a voice from the ether. A rich, cultured voice whose tone thrilled me almost as much as its owner's strong fingers. Instantly, even before the event, I forgave that magic voice for any and every indignity or punishment it might inflict upon me. That voice alone ignited the kindling in my loins, sending surges of expectation rushing through my veins. Smooth palms rolled over my hips, fondling my buttocks on their journey to my most intimate parts.

"Open wide," said the Voice in the manner of a dental surgeon, and even though I was feeling the first twinges of arousal, I had to fight to suppress a giggle.

He was playing with me. He was playing with me in a

much more serious fashion seconds later when, after widening my stance in obedience to his command, he laid a trail of vicious pinches up my inner thighs to my vulva.

"Ouch!" I screamed. I couldn't help myself; the nips had been so violently and unexpectedly inflicted.

"Oh dear, John was right," came the comment, "you really are an undisciplined wench, aren't you?

With a final slap on my rump he moved on to join the others.

"I must compliment you on your judgement of livestock," he said as he entered the room. "Smooth. And well muscled. Not pure bred of course, but none the worse for that. She'd make a first class addition to my own stable."

I was intrigued. Who was he?

Bidden to remain in my animal subordination, I strained against my lead in an effort both to ascertain who it was that possessed such a sensitive touch and to overhear the conversation being carried on in the adding room.

"Beautiful merchandise," I heard from the unidentifiable voice. "Beautiful.".

Eloquent and suave, it remained a mystery.

"So, how did you rate my performance?" it questioned.

"One hundred per cent," came the reply, "quite unlike the girl," this time in the totally undisguisable tones of Master Carpenter. "Your association with The Lodge and your trust in me personally is valued in the extreme." And then, obviously addressing everyone present, "Now, let us concern ourselves with the business in hand. My lead was unhooked from the wall and unable to see anything but the five pairs of legs surrounding me, I was hastened through the door and out into the darkened corridor.

THREE

Torches flickered. Five gleaming bodies swung by their wrists, glistening in the faltering, uneven light. A circular overhead conveyer chain was fixed into the arched ceiling of a bare walled training cellar; a quintet of suspended carcasses hanging from hooks spread equidistantly around its circumference. The five Masters who had escorted me from John Carpenter's chambers stood behind them, one Master to each naked body.

My own nude frame was first in line, Master Carpenter intently absorbed in the task of selecting a weapon of correction, stood close to my rear. My eyes traversed the circle. Identifying three of the other Masters offered no problems, until partly obscured by the others and seemingly in much dimmer light the last member of the squad defied recognition. He had to be The Voice. Suddenly, for the first time, I caught sight of the full training team, Madame Stalevsky, Yuri and Ivan. They stood together, steely eyed and observant.

Fright.

Surrounded by flames, imprisoned in an airless cellar and with a platoon of dinner-jacketed warriors pressing in on me, my initial reaction was of terror. I was strung up, as were all the other girls, completely helpless and subject to the whim of the Masters. But it wasn't them who terrified me. I could take any amount of punishment, I was certain of that. No. What cut me to the bone was the possibility that once again I wouldn't have the fortitude to live up to her expectations. Unexpectedly she caught my eye, and whether it was self-delusion or not, I swear she gave me a gesture of encouragement.

That was enough.

"Gentlemen," I heard Master Carpenter say, "let us begin."

I promptly lost interest in anything other than my own immediate situation, as without warning the cutting slash of a cane lanced across the fronts of both my thighs. I gasped in surprised hurt. This was what I'd been yearning for, but caught unawares I had not been able to ready myself and so what should have been delicious torment presented itself as searing agony. With a mighty whoosh, the cane struck again further up my thighs. And then again. Six times in all, each one a little higher and excruciatingly more painful. I screamed. I couldn't help myself. He certainly wasn't holding back, I'd never endured a flogging such as this before. He knew what I wanted and he was ensuring that I got it.

He stepped back, his eyes alert and questioning. Given a moment's respite my senses re-orientated themselves, a tide of worshipful rapture flooding my entire being. Enlightenment at last. I was being sacrificed on the altar of love, and it was nirvana.

"Please Master, more," I begged.

"Remember your training," he cautioned, "for the other girls, this is a rite of passage. Important enough on its own, but for you, it is also a test."

Madame Stalevsky had prepared me for the rituals that took place from time to time amongst the hierarchy of The Lodge, and it appeared that my evaluation was to be conducted in tandem with this particular one. I was not aware of what event or occasion it celebrated and Master Carpenter made no effort to inform me. But, what did I care?

"Beat me, please Master! Thrash me! Fuck me!"

I heard myself yelling all these demands.

John Carpenter remained aloof. I suppose, looking back on it now, I was acting just like a common whore. But, at that time, such treatment of my body by the man of my dreams was enough to propel me into paroxysms of ecstasy.

And the ritual had barely started.

The golden ornaments: the earrings, the bangles, the loops piercing my sex, the hoops threaded through my nipples, flashed and glistened in the strobe like beams of light generated by the smouldering torches.

"You love it here, don't you?" he asked.

Was he insane? I didn't just love it; I'd die without it. What was he asking me?

"Yes Master," I whispered.

"Very praiseworthy," was the reply. "Now, look around."

I did. Four girls hung from their chains, totally unattended now. He swept his arm towards the place I'd seen Madame Stalevsky.

I really did have a lot to learn. Completely unconcerned, she was conversing with the other Masters, who having cruised through stage one of the ritual were now taking refreshments, attended by Yuri and Ivan.

"You have more to prove than the others," he said, as with a wave of his arm he beckoned a figure from the shadows.

"The other Masters and myself are having a brief respite," Master Carpenter said, "but as this gentleman was, in fact, the first to claim you earlier this evening, during our first intermission you will attend to his every need. Is that clear?"

With that, he strode over to the other men. I looked over to the other girls. They were all swinging free, and with the Masters now well supplied with champagne, Yuri and Ivan were attending to each girl in turn, sponging and cleaning them as they slowly turned beneath their hooks. They all bore the marks of punishment and they'd all obviously been penetrated in one or more orifices. I burned with envy. I desperately wanted to get fucked as well.

And fucked I was. Unceremoniously. Swiftly. And with great vigour.

Alan Masterson had suffered the equivalent to my ardour all evening. He'd wanted me in the common room. He'd quietly gone berserk when DuPont abused me, and after being claimed by Master Carpenter, he'd confided his lust to Madame Stalevsky. This was the outcome. During the intermission, with Master Carpenter's permission, whilst the other girls were allowed a respite, I was to be used in any fashion by Masterson. But there was no time for any prolonged joys of punishment. The other Masters were only taking a short refreshment break, so it had to be quick. And it was.

Circling me, he flicked at my straining breasts and my ringed labia with a mean looking fly tailed whip. Suddenly, with machine gun delivery he lashed me stingingly half a dozen times across my breasts and stomach. There was no doubting the surge of pleasure that accompanied each strike, but I wasn't allowed the time to luxuriate in that pleasure. Lifting my legs, he wrapped them around his back, for which I was thankful, as resting my calves upon his hips allowed me to take some of the weight from my arms and shoulders. He possessed a true King of a penis. Big. Bulbous. And breathtaking, as it thrust unceremoniously through the portals of my sex. I'd been ready in any case, expecting Master Carpenter, so barely able to control my ardour, I welcomed this very capable substitute. His pleasuring caresses, plucking and tweaking my nipples, as he thrust deeply into my welcoming canal brought me to orgasm in an unbelievably short space of time. But that was acceptable. He wasn't part of the test. I hadn't failed. In fact, he'd done me an unrepayable favour. Now that my first orgasm was out of the way, my lust was somewhat sated, giving me more fortitude to fight whatever trials followed. He pulled out very reluctantly. In fact, more than once he actually thrust his retreating member back into my still welcoming orifice. Hot sperm gathered into a huge globule before running from my sex as Master Carpenter approached to reclaim me.

"Alan, you've left something behind," he called.

"Indeed I have," came the response.

What he'd left trickled slowly down the insides of my thighs.

With hot water and a soft sponge Madame herself cleansed me in readiness for my next encounter.

Then.

"Gentlemen, resume your places," came the command from Master Carpenter.

I wasn't quite ready for what followed.

A switch was thrown and the overhead belt jerked into movement. Along with the other girls, I swung precariously as I was tugged along the conveyor. It couldn't have been far, just a few feet, but it was unnerving. Hands reached out to halt my uncontrolled swayings as the belt came to a halt. Firm, strong hands grasped my thighs, halting my gyrations. I was confused. I'd expected Master Carpenter to continue with my education following the intermission, but after a little thought, all became clear. Five Masters, five girls, five thrashings and five couplings. And the continuous overhead chain transported us from one Master to another as the proceedings were repeated. Ingenious. I was just sorry that in my case I couldn't be beaten and molested five times by the same person.

I looked to my left. Master Carpenter was already positioning himself behind my replacement. It was Lolli, my roommate. He struck her, moments before another line of fire erupted across my unprotected buttocks. They liked my backside, the Masters. Several times during their evaluation of me I'd heard mention of how only females of African descent possessed just that jutting roundness of the rump. Another blistering stripe burnt itself close to the first. I couldn't see what implement of punishment was being used on me, but from the numbing fullness of the blows, I thought it most likely to be a riding crop. I did know who it was however. Oliver Carlisle was next in line. I liked him, he seemed a reasonable man, but I didn't lust after him as I did Master Carpenter. And Master Carpenter, although he'd beaten me, had relinquished his right to fuck me, to another. He didn't care! I was just another girl after all. My disappointment was so great that although Oliver beat, thrashed and ravaged me in a manner guaranteed to bring any normal slave to a slavering climax, I remained detached to such an extent that my orgasm, when it came, can only be described as adequate.

And so it continued.

A beating. An orgasm of sorts. A break, during which the Masters refreshed themselves and we were cleansed, and then passed on to the next in line.

That is, until the Voice became the next in line. I still had no idea who he was. Somehow he was always shaded, half hidden amongst the flickering light. It was infuriating. Dandy had done me proud, but all through his undeniably exciting and stimulating treatment of my compliant body, I twisted and turned in a useless attempt to determine the identity of the unknown personage. I'd now been thoroughly beaten by four different Masters, five if you include Alan Masterson, experienced four more or less satisfactory orgasms and was striped, bruised and aching all over. But Master Carpenter was still seemingly indifferent, having shown no further interest in me. Perhaps that was part of the test too. I'd done well so far, I thought, having remained true to my training and only climaxing when given permission.

So. 'The Voice' was next. At last I'd solve the mystery of his identity.

But then, before the overhead chain moved us on, whispering calming encouragement in my ear, Madame Stalevsky covered my eyes with a blindfold of totally impenetrable material, tying it tightly behind my head. I was doing very well, she told me, bidding me to ensure that I maintained my resilience throughout this one last trial.

"But, the blindfold?" I asked.

The reply was firm. This was what 'the Voice' ordered. I was not to be allowed full sight of him. Involuntarily, I started to protest, checking myself just in time. I'd wanted so much to find out who he was, that approaching the final hurdle I'd nearly fallen. A cold shiver ran through my body. I'd averted failure by a hair's breadth. Finally, I swung suspended in front of him. That same Armani essence I'd encountered in Master Carpenter's entrance hall approached and steadied my pendulating frame. The hands were strong.

But sensitive. The touch was magic.

"Now then my pretty," murmured the velvet tones, "shall we find out just what you're made of?"

That voice alone brought about total meltdown.

Smooth palms ran sensuously down my thighs, flowing over my calves before terminating in a delicate stroke over the tops of my feet. One leg was bent backwards behind me. A toe, the biggest, was taken into a mouth that knew every nuance of stimulation as an unrelated finger lent itself to the exploration of my already overused sex. Only now, under this completely new investigation, I tingled inexplicably. My muscles tightened. Excitement replaced complacency. I thrilled. My body renewed its resources. This was going to be something remarkable. All the lusts and desires I'd relegated to a futile dream now once again became possible. Again I asked myself, who was he?

I didn't know. And within minutes I didn't care. Heaven had sent him to satisfy my every prayer. The lips released my digit, and now, with both hands clasping my trembling legs, an open mouth traced a trail upwards along the back of my calves, onwards over the increasingly sensitive skin of my inner thighs and lingered tantalisingly on the very portals of my sex. I tensed in expectancy. The next step had to be his tongue penetrating my welcoming vagina. I felt so feminine it hurt. The delicacy and tenderness of his approach generated a desire that, unfulfilled, was more painful than a thousand lashes. Orgasm was imminent.

Then it stopped.

"Not yet," he said, "that would be too easy. Name your favourite instrument of correction"

I was taken aback. Prised from my indolence.

Once more I'd almost allowed the rising tide of my expectant senses to override my training. He'd saved me. I realised that immediately.

"Take your time," he added, very quietly, in a confidential whisper that could not be overheard.

If my hands had been free, I would have crossed myself at that point. He really was helping me through the final phases of my ordeal.

"Anything the Master desires," finally came my reply.

It was a whip, firstly. Six lashes. Followed by the tawse. Six more welts. Every one exquisite in its pain. Then, a velvet touch explored the trails left by the strikes, following their path towards my erogenous areas. Impossibly long forefingers threaded themselves through the huge golden rings piercing my nipples, leaving behind broad palms that massaged and caressed my thrusting breasts. One hand remained, clasped around a fleshy teat as the other withdrew, tracing a one-fingered descent towards my vulva. The finger slipped downwards, delving between the upper valley of my labials, sinking deeper as it progressed, until finding my vagina, it crooked, investigating its well-lubricated entrance.

The other hand slipped from its breast to join its partner in the hollow between my legs. Gentle palms eased my thighs apart and sweet lips replaced fingers as guardians of my breasts, taking in the golden rings as well as their rock solid hosts. Training is all well and good, but this was too much.

How could I deal with so much pleasure? And it got worse. Or better, according to how you judge it. He was unrelenting. He actually kissed me!! On the lips I mean, at the same moment as I felt his pulsing penis stroke itself along the length of my sex. One hand clamped itself around my bottom, pulling me closer to him, as the other opened me up before returning to guide his throbbing member into my welcoming hole. Pleasure such as that wasn't meant for mere mortals like me. If this was what awaited on the other side then I for one, wouldn't be sorry to hear the last trump.

My arms were useless, still stretched above my head, but now, light as butterfly wings my legs needed no help to loop themselves around his waist. Using all the strength of my calves I pulled him closer, jamming his wonderful weapon further into my sheath. He filled every inch of me, sliding unhurriedly in and out, each new thrust taking him deeper until it seemed that he must be about to penetrate my womb itself. All the while pleasing fingers danced over my body, tweaking a nipple, teasing my anus or joining his phallus to stimulate my bullet of a clitoris. The fight not to climax too soon became a head on battle between my lustful sex and my restraining brain. It was Hell. And it was Heaven. Oh, what a man! Nothing could have prepared me for torment such as that. I felt his penis throb and swell as the power and intensity of his thrusts increased. He was approaching ejaculation and I prayed for permission to come myself.

Suddenly he stopped.

I was bewildered, and only by valiant effort of will did I stop my legs from attempting to pull him closer and so propel his stationary sex into motion. With surprising gentleness he disentangled my limbs from around his waist and withdrew. Nothing happened. I was in a panic. Surely he wasn't going to let it go at that. No, he wasn't, for without warning the tension on my arms decreased as I was lowered sufficiently for my feet to plant themselves on the floor and support my weight.

"Now I'm going to let you down further," he whispered, "until you can kneel."

And he did just that, so that I was on my knees in front of him, but he kept the chain tight so that my arms were still stretched above me.

"You've done well," he said, "and this is no more than you deserve."

With that I felt the tip of a bulbous glans press against my lips. I rolled out my tongue, running it over the eye and the whole head of his pleasure dome. His seminal fluid and my own juices intermingled into a salty nectar, and a wonderful combination of musky manhood and designer fragrance drifted into my nostrils. I cursed the blindfold and the chains. I could taste and I could smell, but I couldn't see and I couldn't touch.

He cupped one hand around the back of my head to hold it steady, whilst with the other he threaded his pulsing penis into my mouth. He was big. My lips, my tongue and my cheeks worked together to aid his entry. Right down into my throat. He moved gently back and forward as I salivated, sucking and rolling my tongue continually. His thrusts became increasingly more powerful, and I sucked furiously in response, until I felt the rising surge of semen race up from his testes to pour from his ejaculation in a gushing torrent. It was like swallowing Niagara Falls. There was so much I could have drowned. But I didn't care; I feasted on every last drop.

He left his member resting on my tongue as it slackened. And it still filled my mouth. Hauling it from my lips with slow deliberation, he allowed me the honour of licking it completely clear of all the last traces of his magical emission. I felt hands fumbling around my wrists and moments later they were free. My arms dropped to my side in blessed relief. But not for long.

"Adopt the position," came the command.

I hesitated, unsure.

"The jungle cat," he said, "on all fours, rump up."

I fell forward on to my fingertips, spread my legs as wide as was possible and once more balanced on my extremities. I thrust my bottom shamelessly upwards. All of my sex, the ladder of rings and the pucker of my anus must have presented themselves to his gaze. I felt, more than heard him circling me. A whiplash cut across my shoulder blades, then my back and a third curled under my ribs to sear my breasts. More delicious pain.

"How do you find the whip," he asked.

I found it wonderfully exhilarating and gasped out an answer to that effect.

"That pleases me greatly," he said, "for there is no honour in beating a woman who does not wish to be so treated."

Three more lashes fell in quick succession, stoking the furnace heat in my loins to boiling point. My vagina and my anus were probed and then I heard the whip fall to the floor. Hands looped around my feet, he was standing between my wide-open legs.

"Support yourself," he ordered, lifting and straightening my legs until my rump was on a level with his crotch, much the same position that children adopt when playing wheelbarrow'. He shuffled forwards, transferring his grip to the fronts of my thighs, my legs now resting on his hips. His penis, once again rigid, large and glorious, slid into my grasping vagina like a pellet cartridge into a shotgun. Muscles contracted of their own volition, gripping and tugging in an endeavour to pull him all the way in.

"No, not yet my pet," he said, "your vagina was not my target, it's difficult to score a bull without a guiding hand."

With dread I realised that he intended to penetrate my anus. It was an experience I'd longed for, but the one and only previous entry into that region had been earlier that very day when DuPont had so brutally savaged me. And he had only assaulted me with his thumb. And that thumb had hurt. How could my bottom possibly accommodate an organ of such proportions as that possessed by the Voice?

I soon found out.

Easily.

It was just a matter of technique, although the granite hardness of his penis, together with the film of lubricating vaginal fluids that had clung to it when he withdrew from my sex, was paramount in the storming of my sphincters. Together, they assisted his mighty phallus on its initial journey into my interior. His grip on my thighs was numbing as he supported my weight, sometimes actually lifting my hands from the floor, whilst sliding tightly in and out of my most private area. He filled me to bursting, squeezing my vaginal walls in the process and giving me the strangest sensations in both holes. This was definitely a thrill out of the ordinary and as he approached ejaculation, I tried to increase his satisfaction by thrusting my bottom rearwards to meet his thrusts. It was impossible. My physical situation, the manner in which I was positioned, was such that I could really only wriggle unsatisfactorily. A smart slap stung my haunches. We staggered uncertainly for a moment as he grabbed to retrieve the thigh he'd dropped in order to deliver the reprimand.

"No," he said, "keep still, I have to do this on my own."

And he did, until jerking wildly, he propelled what felt like oceans of semen into my bottom. What a waste. I'd wanted that creamy ambrosia washing once more over my taste buds. However he wasn't altogether unfeeling, in that after I felt him pull his still tightly clamped organ from my rectum, he dropped my legs and allowed me to kneel before him, once again to devour the sperm that remained swimming over his semi flaccid penis. Even after every drop had vanished I continued to lap until with a gentle hand on my forehead he pushed me away.

"Your performance has proved most satisfactory".

Heady words from an unknown someone who was rapidly replacing Master Carpenter as the man of my dreams.

"And now you deserve a little heaven of your own. This time you may climax at will."

Those words drained me.

Elation so great that it left me weak, gripped me as a tremor rippled through my whole being. Already rock hard nipples hardened into steel. My clitoris stripped back its protecting hood even further, seemingly attempting to push itself clear of my labia. There was a churning in my stomach. Juices drenched my sex as I abandoned myself solely to the pursuit of my own release. That was permissible, authorisation had been given.

"Bend over and touch the floor. Legs wide."

It seemed I'd heard that command before. What did I care? I leapt to obey. In an instant his iron helmet was nuzzling my dripping vulva. Only the slightest push and he was in. I was ready. I was desperate and his whole length was rippled in by my flexing tube. His legs pressed against my rump, a hand reaching over to allow those sensitive fingers to stroke my clitoris whilst the other reached for my breasts, massaging and tweaking.

"Please Master." I hesitated... and then, "now, Master, NOW," I screamed.

He didn't torture me any further. He brought me to fulfilment in an instant. Just a few solid, well-controlled piston strokes and I was there. Again and again the multiple surging waves of a prolonged, earth moving orgasm shook my body. No one could experience such a stoking and remain with their feet still planted on this world. But somehow I did even as again, and then for a third time, he detonated further controlled explosions in my sex. I was jelly, weak with rapture, as he continued towards his own climax. When he finally withdrew I remained as I was, unable to move, my fingers limply scraping the floor, with great tears of joy falling from my eyes.

What length of time passed I had no idea, I was lost in my own private paradise. Then, gentle palms eased me to an upright position, fingers fumbled for a moment or two, and the blindfold was untied. I blinked. The light, although subdued, hurt my eyes.

Now I would see.

But I didn't.

The cellar was empty.

Apart from Madame Stalevsky and myself that is.

He was gone. And so was everyone else. He had departed, in true Masterly fashion, without acknowledging my existence. And with him he took my heart and soul.

Hot water, sponges and delicately scented soaps worked their magic on my ravaged, despoiled body. In seemingly no time at all, Madame Stalevsky transformed me back into an eminently desirable creature.

"Your dream is coming true now," she said.

Except I'd stopped dreaming.

Master Carpenter was waiting outside his door as she walked me, animal fashion, on all fours, up to his apartments. She handed the lead over to him. He'd known of my lust, my cravings for him, and he'd saved himself until last. This was to be my Eden, my passport to the Promised Land. That same morning I would have given my life just to be in his presence. Now, I didn't care, I dreamt of a different destination. All through the night, although I responded to his demands as a true Housegirl should, when he was finally sated, I slept on the floor beside his bed dreaming of the 'the Voice'.

Collecting me the following morning, Madame Stalevsky's murmurs of sympathy were long and seemingly heartfelt. She inspected me thoroughly, from tip to toe. I was striped, bruised and marked all over, including distinct finger and thumb impressions on my thighs, where 'the Voice' had supported me during our frantic anal lovemaking. I had the feeling that she was somewhat impressed, not to say taken aback by my appearance, when she pronounced an unprecedented two weeks leave from anything but household duties.

So, that evening I began serving at tables.

After dinner, John Carpenter, although alone, ordered two cognacs and two Havanas, to be served to him in the common room. I assumed that he must be expecting someone, and entering the room, I saw him conversing in an animated fashion, but with whom I couldn't tell, as his companion was seated with the back of his armchair facing me.

Then I heard it.

The Voice.

At last, the mystery was about to be solved. Piercing

needles of anticipation peppered my senses as I approached them. But I wasn't prepared for the lightning bolt that struck me when I saw who it was. In shocked surprise I dropped the tray, the drinks and cigars crashing to the floor, an action for which I was soundly punished later by both 'the Voice' and John Carpenter.

Melinda then lost herself for a few moments in a private reverie. The memories were obviously joyously precious. Recovering her composure, she went on to tell me that she stood, frozen in disbelief and wonderment, until a sharp reprimand brought her back to awareness. The Masters owed her no explanations, but Madame Stalevsky told her later that the events in the common room at her initiation were a test, part of her final assessment. The members were all in the know, and 'the Voice' had played his part perfectly. Melinda determined that never again would she judge anyone at first sight, now realising just how much her vision had been clouded by false impressions.

Her feelings for 'the Voice' had only grown stronger and much to her delight, he used her services with frequent regularity. In fact, she added, fingering the room disc hanging around her neck, he had reserved her for that very night. I took that as an indication that I should take my leave of her and was about to do so when I heard footsteps crunching on the gravel. They stopped beside us and I looked up at a rugged, distinguished face.

Melinda and I rose together.

"Mister Bridges," she said, "please allow me to introduce Montague D'Arcy DuPont."

# CAROLINE

*By Sean O'Kane*

About a month after I had interviewed John Carpenter, been told Rosa's story and witnessed her punishment by Madame, I got my next communication from The Lodge.

Rosa's story had been written up and the editor was as pleased as editors ever get, that is he wasn't complaining or asking for re-writes. But I wasn't happy.

After that first day at The Lodge I had come back to London and made my dinner date with a truly beautiful girl, her name was Kathy. It had been a pleasant evening but I had struggled to get the day's events out of my mind. Despite that we had a great evening and finally ended up in bed at my place, but even as I was making love to her I knew that it was no longer enough. I wanted more from sex, I wanted sex the way it was enjoyed at The Lodge.

Some weeks later we had a second date, and again ended up at my place. After a couple of bottles of wine in the lounge I had tipped her over my knee, face down and hiked up her skirt. She was wearing stockings, suspenders and just a little thong, the back of which ran tightly up her buttock cleft and left the globes themselves enticingly naked. She gave a little shriek when I first pulled her over onto my knee and giggled when she felt her skirt being pulled up her thighs, but didn't make any more than a token struggle. When I laid the palm of my hand on her left buttock she looked up at me and pouted.

"You chauvinist brute! Spanking a helpless girl like me."

And all at once I was utterly out of patience with playing games. I wanted a real woman, a woman who had passed through pain to find pleasure, a woman who had been taken to the limits of her sensuality and who could provide both herself and her man with the ultimate in physical pleasure. I gazed down at the bared bottom and wished I had a much more severe implement than my hand to use on it.

"Are you going to admire it all night? Or has your manly courage failed you?" Kathy asked with an irritating grin.

My only answer was a ringing smack on her soft flesh, swiftly followed by another to her right cheek. It was a classic backside, rounded and smooth which shuddered and rippled under the assault of my hand. She wriggled and squealed.

"Ow! Sean that stings! Ow! Ooh, God you do it hard!" She struggled for a bit and then as the heat in her bottom grew began to giggle tipsily. "I won't be able to sit down tomorrow! Ow! Ow! The neighbours'll hear! Ow!"

I realised that I had given her ten good hard smacks and her cheeks were glowing. I let her up and she stood in front of me trying to adjust her clothing and regain her dignity, but when I stood up too and took her in my arms she came to me passionately, pressing against me and purring when her stomach felt the bulge of my erection. But even as her lips parted softly, offering the promise of an equally eager reaction down below, I wondered if she might be worth experimenting with. Lots of girls enjoy spanking as foreplay, but could this one be taken farther? And it was those thoughts which haunted me as we thrashed about in the bed. She was an active and responsive partner with a warm and eager body; I wanted to possess it and the act of penetration took on a whole new meaning for me.

She left at about ten the next morning after some more sleepy sex and a hasty breakfast. She was no sooner out of the door, having been pleasingly keen on another date, when the phone rang.

I suppose I was expecting John to ring but it was my editor. He told me that my presence was requested at The Lodge the next morning.

"Does that mean they're happy so far?"

"I suppose it must do or they wouldn't want you back. Apparently you're going to be interviewing Mrs Carpenter this time. Make sure you're down there for eleven o'clock."

When I put the phone down I was a bit disappointed at first. I knew that John was a powerful man in financial circles and I had enjoyed talking to him, but Falconer seemed to be getting the real celebrities. There again, I knew that Caroline Carpenter was a submissive woman who had been trained by Madame, so by talking with her maybe I could edge closer to an interview with Madame herself. And after my day at The Lodge and the previous night with Kathy, that suddenly seemed the most important part of the project for me.

\*\*\*

Once again I was a little ashamed of my rather elderly car when I parked at The Lodge. It seemed out of place amongst the gleaming Mercs, Rolls Royces, BMW's and Ferraris which were already there. And as I walked up the steps to the imposing double doors with the neo Gothic tower to their right I was tempted to go and look for the tradesman's entrance, but John had told me last time I came to use these doors and so I rang and waited for an answer. To my surprise it was Madame herself who opened the doors for me. She gave me her rather wintry smile and got straight down to business.

"Now," she said, "I have been told that you are to speak to Mrs Carpenter. Mr Carpenter is busy today. So I will take you to her. Come." And she swept away while I hurried after her.

My pulse raced with excitement when I realised that I was being taken towards the back of the house and then down another stone flagged staircase. Once again I was being taken to the cells.

This time I found myself in a completely different corridor. It was still like a stone tunnel with heavy wooden doors every now and then, but they were on both sides this time. Madame stopped at one and opened it for me. This time I was a little more prepared for the sight which met me, but even so the reality was still pretty astounding. All the equipment I remembered from Rosa's dungeon was there, but looking absurdly out of place there was an office desk and chair in one corner. In the centre of the room one of the Russian twins stood, patient and impassive. And over on our right was Caroline Carpenter.

She was slung from four chains hanging down from the ceiling and attaching to restraints on her ankles and wrists, which left her torso about four feet off the floor and parallel to it. The chains which held her wrists were quite close to the wall so that her head was propped against it and she was able to look along her body and between her wide-open legs. I found myself standing some distance from her but directly between those legs, staring at John's wife's wrenched open sex. She must have already been suspended for some time because she was moaning at the strain on her limbs and as I had seen with Rosa, this discomfort was beginning to arouse her. Her labia were full and open so that I could plainly see the entrance to her vagina and the way her clitoris was beginning to emerge from its hood of pink flesh.

"The girls call this Madame's hammock Mr O'Kane," Madame told me as she approached the suspended body and ran one hand up the length of a tanned thigh, making it quiver at her touch. "Apparently Caroline was a little reluctant to talk to you so Yuri here will loosen her tongue. After that you may do as you wish with her, when she is here she is just a Housegirl. So don't feel restrained in any way. I will leave it up to you to judge when she is ready to co-operate."

She clicked her fingers at Yuri and abruptly left. Once again I was left with questions seething in my mind but Yuri approached Caroline and stood close in front of her crotch. Her moans became more urgent and she attempted to twist in her chains when she saw the riding crop he held.

My heart pounded as I realised what he was going to do and how the crop he held had a particularly wide flap of leather at its end. I held my breath.

The Russian raised his forearm and delivered a wrist flick with his crop so that the flap of leather cracked down onto her clitoris. Immediately every tendon in her legs tightened and she shrieked and twisted frantically but could do nothing to shield herself against the second cruel flick, or the third. Utterly absorbed I watched Caroline buck and swing under the steady flicks. Her eyes were fixed on the Russian's arm as the wrist steadily delivered the blows. They were not hard but the shocks of pain must have been building remorselessly because all at once I realised that the leather was landing with less of a Crack! It was making more of a smacking noise and I could see a fine spray of moisture thrown up each time the crop descended, and suddenly Caroline's torso arched and shook. Even though the beating stopped her hips continued to heave and rotate for some seconds until, with a deep sigh she went limp and hung inertly in her chains. Yuri simply turned, replaced the crop in the rack from which he had selected it and then left as well.

I remained standing where I was, looking at the throbbing sex before me and noting how completely open it was now and how the nub of the clitoris was standing erect and obviously excited by its vulnerability. Farther up the body the nipples were also erect, tight little peaks on the heaving breasts. Caroline opened her eyes and stared at me. She had large hazel coloured eyes beneath thick dark brown hair which now hung partly over her face. I noticed that her expression was the same as one commonly finds in women experiencing the aftermath of a thunderous orgasm, calm and replete.

"I think we'll talk now," I told her.

She nodded and I set about releasing her ankles and then her wrists. For some time she leaned against the dungeon wall, her hands cupped between her legs, but eventually she straightened up, shook her hair back and adopted an open legged stance with her hands behind her back. At last I had a chance to fully appreciate her suntanned body. Her breasts were of a good size and stood out from her chest at a pleasing height, her stomach was flat and smooth and although her hips were narrow and girlish the waist was very slender. A neatly clipped bush of dark pubic hair covered her mons and drew the eye to the long thighs.

"Caroline," I said. "Please understand that I had no desire to have anyone forced into talking to me." I had found her beating very exciting indeed but felt that I should explain that I was not its cause.

She laughed at that, and immediately I realised that I had made a bad mistake.

"You don't understand do you? John thought you mightn't. You see, as Mrs Carpenter my husband wanted me to reveal very intimate details about myself to a complete stranger; not an easy thing for a woman to do. But here I am a slave, and when I have been humiliated in front of that stranger by being displayed and whipped to an orgasm, what choice do I have? A slave can have no modesty, she can only do what her master and mistress command."

Suddenly I appreciated the logic of her slavery. She was right, I hadn't understood. This way Caroline could hide behind the lack of choice her slavery left her with. I saw the amusement in her eyes as she saw understanding dawn— and I made a mental note to repay her for that condescension.

Anger allowed my arousal to subside and I got down to work. Curtly I ordered her over to the desk but I couldn't help noticing how enticingly her body moved as she walked, she was used to nudity and knew she looked good. She stood in front of the desk and awaited the next command. There was only one chair; I could order her to sit on the desk or kneel at my feet, but then a better idea occurred to me. Caroline's body was slender and graceful, I was determined that I was going to have my revenge on it, so why not enjoy it while she talked to me?

"Lie on your back along the desk. Put your hands up to hold the edge of it either side of your face." She did exactly as I had told her and the result was that her torso was stretched by her raised arms and the full breasts stood proudly up from the ribs. But it wasn't enough. She wanted slavery and I was going to show her that I understood that right enough.

"Raise you right leg and put the foot on the desktop. Move your left leg to the side and let it trail down the side of the desk." Again she obeyed without a murmur and I was able once again to look along her body and see her sex opened, exposed between the obediently spread, long and smooth thighs. She wriggled a little to get comfortable and then looked calmly up at me as I moved to stand by her shoulder.

"Can you see everything you want Sir?"

I could detect no sarcasm in her voice or in her face. But I noted the 'Sir' rather than 'Master'.

"That will do for the moment. Now tell me how you came to be a common Housegirl—a slave at an expensive SM brothel."

I had expected some spark of anger in her eyes as I delivered that last line, but what I got was a look of surprise and to my astonishment I saw her dark nipples start to harden and redden with excitement. She was a slave all right and needed to be treated as such. I barely had time to turn on my recorder before she began her story.

She had met her husband soon after graduating with a first in English Literature, she didn't really know what she wanted to do and John's utter certainty that he was going to be rich and successful had proved a powerful aphrodisiac. He simply swept her off her feet, and quite literally that first night they met at a mutual friend's party. He had taken her to his flat, put her over his knee and spanked her, hard. No-one had ever treated like that but he had followed it up with sex like she had never had before. They were married in only a couple of months and less than a year after that John was well on his way up the corporate ladder. Two years later they were wealthy and living in a luxurious house in Kent.

The first time she was caned was one evening when they were due to go out for dinner with one of John's associates.

Caroline had settled easily into the role of 'trophy wife', learning quickly that her full breasts, mounted on so willowy a form as hers could excite a lot of male attention at whatever function they were called on to attend, and ease the passage of whatever deal John was negotiating. Consequently she was in the habit of wearing low-necked and well-tailored dresses to show off not only her breasts but also the inviting swell of her buttocks above the long legs. She had also learned that after these evenings when she was on display, John's spankings would be especially hard and their beautifully furnished lounge would reverberate to the sound of his palm cracking down on her squirming bottom while she squealed and moaned in delight at the mingling of excitement and just enough pain. The heat in her buttocks would inexorably spread into her lower stomach, pressed down against John's powerful thigh, and then lodge firmly in the molten crease between her legs, which would open with shamelessly moist servility to his hand when he had reduced her buttocks to quivering, scarlet mounds of desire.

And then on their bed she would crouch on elbows and knees—well spread—so that his rampant sex could spear into her from behind. Usually he would spend himself first in her vagina, ramming his pelvis against her tenderised buttocks and driving her to a violent orgasm as she felt his hot seed erupt into her spasming channel. A few minutes' rest and then he would push her head down to lick at his flaccid sex, pungent and sticky with their mingled juices. She loved that taste and would suck hungrily at the soft member until she experienced the joy of feeling it throb erect once more, filling her mouth and forcing her jaws wide apart to contain it. Carefully she would allow her tongue to rub across the slit in the engorged helm until he pulled her away. Then once again she would crouch in front of him while he admired and stroked her buttocks before pressing his saliva-lubricated penis against the tight button of her anus. She always made a show of protesting at this perverse use of that entrance but couldn't disguise the shattering pleasure she took in feeling his length slide, inch by inch up the tight tunnel until he could thrust and withdraw easily. And when he was ramming himself home deep into her lower stomach she would yell with ecstasy as she felt his rod swell and pulse and finally discharge. Sometimes she took her weight on one arm and rubbed frantically at her own clitoris as he shot his second spend into her dark passage.

So on that evening, as she descended the stairs she was looking forward to a night of convulsing orgasms after dinner.

But she wasn't ready for the cane.

She was wearing a long silk dress, slashed to the left midthigh and cut in a sweeping curve at the front of the slit so that a tantalising amount of leg was revealed as she walked. John was in a dinner jacket and enjoying a drink in the dining room when she entered and saw the cane lying on the dining table.

"Ah Caroline! You look wonderful," he greeted her. "But we're meeting someone rather special tonight. And instead of spanking you when we get home, I'm afraid I'll have to cane you before we go."

For a moment she gaped helplessly at him. But then he spoke again, calm, self-assured and full of self-belief. All those things about him which had always made her stomach melt and her loins churn.

"You'll look even more beautiful afterwards. You always do after a beating, and our guest will appreciate it. So bend over the table and take six strokes."

She found her voice at last. "No! I won't! You can't…John please no," she trailed off feebly.

"Caroline you know you can't resist doing what I want you to do. And think how much you'll love it later when I take you in your delightful little arse, knowing how much I enjoyed striping it with the cane."

Her throat went dry. He was reading her innermost thoughts. He must have known all along how much she loved the subservience of the position he usually took her in, her buttocks seething and burning from a beating. And of course she had never protested too much when her sphincter had gradually opened for him and her own saliva would ease the penetration. How much greater would be the secret pleasure of feeling her bowels fill and empty as he thrust and withdrew, if she had been really punished first.

John would own her completely then. Silently she watched him reach out and take hold of the wickedly slender implement. She would undoubtedly scream and writhe under the beating which was surely coming her way—and for which she would just as surely bend over. But she would howl and cry out with utter fulfilment when he took her later on.

Without fully realising that she was doing it her right hand began to bunch the dress up in front of her crotch as she took a faltering step towards the table.

"Come on Caroline," John snapped. "We haven't got all night and you'll need to repair your make-up when I've finished."

The imperious tone connected with something so deep inside her that quite suddenly she found herself standing with the edge of the table pressing against her pubic mound. And only dimly aware that she was crossing some kind of gulf from which there would be no return, she leaned forward and spread her arms out to the sides, grasping the sides of the table and settling her breasts against the hard surface.

"In future Caroline, make sure your dress or skirt is raised or removed when you are required to receive a caning." John's voice came from directly behind her and she felt him bunch the skirt of the dress fully up in front of her thighs, and she even lifted her pelvis enough for him to tuck it under her, while the gossamer weight of the back of the dress was piled in the small of her back. Absurdly she found herself being thankful that the silk wouldn't crease. But then she felt John's hands reach round her hips to snap the thin straps of her knickers and pull them off. The feel of the strength of his hands and the contemptuous ease with which her last shred of protection was brushed aside served only to send the blood pounding through her body as her fingers gripped the table even harder.

"Not good enough Caroline! Relax your buttock cheeks; I want to see how the shock waves run through your flesh at each lash. It is the pleasure I require you to give me."

Somehow the sheer arrogance comforted her. However bizarre the scene; John was in control, and she was his to command. She let her tense muscles relax, settled her feet a little farther apart and prepared to give him whatever he wanted. She closed her eyes and waited.

He took his time

Six hard strokes let off bomb bursts of colour behind her eyelids and detonated explosions of incandescent pain as each stroke sliced in, preceded by an audible 'whoosh' as the cane descended. But each stroke was followed by an agonising pause which allowed the numbing pain to spread and take root in her sex while she thought of what a craven spectacle she must make. Her pale buttocks, framed by her suspender straps would be shuddering under each slash of the cane, her labia would be clearly visible between her opened legs and even as she shook and gasped in the wake of each stroke, she made no attempt to escape. Afterwards she was proud of the fact that it took until the fifth stroke before she screamed. It was a thin wail which burst from her clenched lips and she fidgeted and lifted her feet in turn to try and distract herself from the scalding mass of pure, bright pain which burned in her bottom. But even as the scream escaped her she was dimly aware of the fact that her feet were settling themselves wider apart still and at last the heat burned in from her flesh and ignited the fires deep in her loins. And she knew that in advance of the sixth stroke, John would be able to see the moist proof of her degradation seeping from her open vulva. He would know that she was far more aroused than she ever had been by a mere spanking.

She was right.

"Well done Caroline," she heard him say. "That's a pretty sight. Just one more now and you'll be done to a turn."

The final stroke made her head arch back and she shrieked as the pain hit a scarlet crescendo which blended with the heat in her vaginal channel to completely wipe out the boundaries of where pain stopped and pleasure began. And for the first time she glimpsed the landscapes of sensation that await the truly submissive when they cross the pain/pleasure border.

From a long way off she heard John order her to her feet. And as she blinked away the tears she saw him holding the cane across the fronts of his thighs and smiling at her. A wave of the most naked hunger she had ever felt for him swept over her.

"Thank you John," she murmured, aware only of an aching void between her legs. She was desperate to feel the man who had just caned her, thrust himself brutally into her body and grasp her scalding buttocks in his strong hands as he took possession of her utterly.

Again he knew her thoughts.

"I'd like nothing more than to have you on the table, here and now. But I'm afraid we do have to go… maybe later…"

A few minutes afterwards she came downstairs again, still dazed and still trying to come to terms with the throbbing in her backside and the strange way it seemed to hotwire her sex. To replace her knickers she had chosen her briefest G-string. She told herself it was to avoid having even the lightest of coverings rubbing on her buttocks, but she couldn't deny the thrills coursing up and down her vagina at the prospect of having only the silk of her dress between her caned bottom and the rest of the world.

They had a few minutes to wait at the restaurant before their table was available and before their guest arrived, and as Caroline settled herself carefully onto a chair she couldn't help giving John a long and openly flirtatious look as he grinned at her manoeuvrings.

"There'll be a lot more yet Caroline, believe me," he whispered.

When his associate arrived Caroline was impressed. He was a grey haired man, exquisitely dressed, suntanned and clearly very wealthy. He had piercing blue eyes and a ready smile. She warmed to his faultless courtesy, delivered with a slight South American accent, but gradually she became aware that his eyes were boring into her and they seemed very knowing somehow. Her buttocks seemed to burn anew at the thought that somehow he did know. She blushed deeply and looked down as his eyes swept over her. But business rescued her, the men's conversation turned to finance and they were summoned to their table.

The meal and the wine were as superb as she had come to expect and for a while she relaxed—even speculating about what might happen when John got her home again. He would do things to her, he would subjugate her again, and she felt herself lubricate at the thought that everything, anything, would be done to her and with her—she herself would do nothing except respond. For the first time she had a sexual fantasy about being completely passive in the face of a stern master and husband.

She was woken from a scene she had concocted, where John was using his hand to beat her on the marks the cane had left, by the stranger. Carlos, as John had introduced him, was talking to her.

"John told me that before we met this evening he would 'prepare' you."

At the careful emphasis on 'prepare' Caroline blushed furiously once again. The man did know! John had told him! She knew that she should be outraged—she should storm out—leave John before it was too late. But too late for what? And wasn't it already too late? She had been—was still being—treated appallingly and yet she knew her labia were tumescent and her vulva was seeping copious amounts of juice into the tiny gusset of her G string. She wanted whatever lay ahead for her and John. She found herself staring at Carlos' hands; they were slender and strong like John's. What could they inflict on her willing body? Did John plan to turn her over to him? She felt her blush begin to creep down across her chest and her nipples harden and jut out through the thin dress. She wanted whatever lay ahead, whatever was required of her.

"If...if you mean," she stammered softly, "that I've been...caned. Then yes, John has caned me."

She lifted her eyes to meet the men's.

"Bravely done Caroline," Carlos told her. "You have no idea how much more lovely even a beautiful lady looks when she carries the marks of her master on her body, especially when they are so lightly hidden. But I must ask, are you wearing any panties?"

She nodded. He calmly told her to remove them. "You should be naked under your outer clothes."

Caroline swallowed hard. The audacity of the command had set her pulses racing once again, and a fresh spurt of heat erupted in her lower stomach. It was a thrilling idea; to be completely naked under her clothes with only these two men amongst all the diners to share the secret.

Using the thick linen tablecloth and her serviette as cover, she ran her left hand up her stockinged thigh, up under the slit of the dress and hooked the thin strap off her hip. Then with a twist and a furtive lift of her bottom she pulled it as far down as it would go. A quick glance round told her that no-one was looking. She reached between her legs into the warmth between her thighs and grasped the wet gusset. The touch of her fingers on her labia sent shivers down her spine and she had to pause for a second. Then she opened her legs a little wider, lifted her backside again and wrenched. The heat of the room and her near-constant arousal had transformed her sex into a cauldron of mingled sweat and juice. The flimsy material of the G-string unglued itself with sticky reluctance, but still the thong at the back was buried deep in her buttock crease. Another quick glance, then another lift, her hand reaching down shamelessly till her fingers felt her anus then a last tug and the G string was round her thighs. From there it needed only a little wriggling to get it to her knees. And lastly a quick drumming of her heels on the deep pile carpet allowed her to step out of it. Breathless and ruffled she looked around. No-one was any the wiser.

The two men lifted their wine glasses.

"To the pleasures that lie in store for us... and for a lot of others as well."

Carlos proposed the toast and although Caroline didn't understand the last part, flushed, excited and proud she drank to it.

The men immediately returned to business leaving her to savour the breaths of cool air which caressed her overheated sex as she opened her legs under the table. She tried to follow the conversation and it seemed as though John was setting up some kind of club, and was courting Carlos as a backer for the venture. But in only a few minutes John waved away coffee and liqueurs and suggested they return to the house. As the waiter moved Caroline's chair back for her, she managed to lean forward quickly and retrieve her knickers from the floor before stuffing them into her bag. But as she walked out on John's arm she nearly laughed aloud at the thought of how the figure-hugging silk of the dress would press back against her body as she walked and show in clear relief the bush of her pubes. She did catch sight of one or two raised female eyebrows, but the subtlety was lost on the men whose eyes followed the sway and ripple of her breasts as she moved.

Back at home she served two glasses of John's best Armagnac and was about to take her seat beside him on the sofa when he ordered her to go and stand in front of the fireplace and take her dress off. Immediately the fires at her belly ignited in earnest and she felt her vagina clench in excitement. Here it was, the unknown into which she had been journeying all that evening. She wore only stockings and suspenders under the dress and she knew that there could only be one reason for asking her to strip; it was so that both men could admire the marks of the cane on her buttocks. Nothing was forcing her to obey except the insatiable hunger between her legs. She glanced at Carlos and saw the desire kindling in his eyes. She knew John was proud of her body and its effect on other men; and she was proud of it too. Suddenly it didn't matter to her that she was for the first time being asked to display herself nude. She wanted Carlos to desire her as much as John obviously wanted him to, and the caning had been part of the preparation.

Without needing to be told she stood facing away from the men and let the dress slip from her shoulders to glide soundlessly to her feet and she stepped away from it.

"Now lean forward, spread your arms out along the mantelpiece and open your legs wide." John's voice was calm as he delivered the orders which would display his wife to a complete stranger. Caroline did exactly as she was told and for a moment there was complete silence. But then she heard soft footsteps and Carlos spoke from just behind her.

"Very beautiful John. Everything you told me; and more. You can have my two slaves for a month until you get your supply lines set up. And if this Madame Stalevsky is as good as you say, then this lovely creature will make a perfect complement to the services we can offer for that first month."

Caroline couldn't make sense of it but in any case she was distracted by a cool hand stroking her shoulders and back while Carlos continued.

"A strong back; slender but strong. And see here—I like this—the extent to which the breasts swell out sideways. Unusual on so slender a frame." Caroline felt the hands stroke the sides of her breasts and with tantalising slowness make their way forwards to cup the hardened nipples. She risked a look down to see the sun-tanned fingers, dark against the pale flesh of her breasts themselves, roll and pull at them deepening their cherry red colour as they pounded and strained with arousal. She moaned softly when they were withdrawn, but inevitably they made their way down her back, out over her hips and then felt along the raised weals on her buttocks. She shivered at the touch.

"Ah!" Carlos chuckled, "as sensitive as she is beautiful. And what shall I find Caroline when I reach between those lovely, opened thighs?"

She could make no reply but only shivered again as the fingers trailed down her buttock cleft and at last—at long last—slid forward to feel along the soft crease of her sex and explore the plump ripeness of her labia, peeling open to allow him access to the moist pink flesh within. She cried out and trembled when she felt him press on her erect clitoris. Carlos paused only to rub at it briefly and then he plunged two fingers into the roiling depths of her vagina. Caroline closed her eyes and surrendered totally to the expert manipulation. The fingers twisted, opened and clenched within her until she could only groan with delight. And as if to underline her body's complete subjugation she felt the pad of his thumb press against her anus. With an ease born of many penetrations her sphincter relaxed and allowed it entry. With this double invasion Caroline's pleasure began to spiral towards its crisis. For some moments Carlos moved his fingers inside both her channels while her hips bucked and rotated, letting her writhe openly, her cries mounting towards a crescendo, and then with cruel suddenness he withdrew and left her only one resounding smack to a buttock to savour. She had to bite her lip to prevent herself from cravenly begging him to go on. The blood pounding in her ears made the men's voices seem to come from a long way off.

Carlos was requesting that he see her beaten while he was here. John was telling him that he could choose a whip or a crop and that he had made arrangements in his study so that she could be suitably restrained. She was so far gone now that the complete certainty in John's voice that she would do whatever she was told only made her simmering excitement threaten to boil over. Still spread-eagled before the men she waited patiently to be beaten until another glass of Armagnac had been enjoyed and then John allowed her to stand and precede them into the study. It was a room she was rarely allowed into. Apart from two leather armchairs and a low table the room contained only his computer station, the walls were lined with bookshelves almost to the ceiling.

Caroline was told to stand in front of the shelves just to the right of the computer. From beside the keyboard John took leather straps and she watched with a strange kind of remote curiosity as he wound them round her wrists and then tugged her arms up in front of her to wind the straps around hooks which he had embedded in the leading edge of a high shelf. When he had tied them off she was stretched up so that even in her high heels she was nearly on tiptoe, her nipples rubbed on the cool leather of some book spines. She craned her head around to watch what would happen next and saw that from the other side of the monitor screen John pulled a leather flail. It was the only word she could think of for it, it had many thin leather lashes and seeing her eyeing it, Carlos swooshed it in the air a couple of times. Hurriedly she turned her head away and faced the books in front of her, but even her momentary terror at her first sight of a whip couldn't entirely quench her excitement at the thought of how utterly vulnerable she was to whatever they wanted to do to her. Her nostrils inhaled the scent of leather from the books. Leather—just like the leather of the whip she had submitted herself to.

Her wandering thoughts were shattered when Carlos swung in the first lash. There was just the briefest of hisses in the air behind her and then a clubbing impact across her shoulders which rammed her against the shelves. A second and third followed swiftly, Caroline heard herself make strange grunts and moans as she was jerked about by the impacts. The pain was duller and wider than the intense sharpness of the cane. She felt a sullen sort of itchy heat that grew with each lash until her back was a sea of white-hot waves into which the whip seemed to crash endlessly. For the second time that night Caroline made the strange journey from pain and humiliation to the dazzling regions of ecstasy. Somewhere deep inside her she knew how invitingly her body was shaking and twisting under the lash, how well the marks of the flogging would suit her and she cried out in abandoned joy at each thudding caress of the leather thongs across her back and felt herself almost orgasming.

But before she could achieve her climax the beating stopped, strong hands gripped her thighs from behind and wrenched them so far apart that their soft inner skin pressed against the wood of the shelves. Those same hands supported her as her feet came off the floor and she hung by her wrists. But then she felt the pressure of a hugely engorged sex ignore her wide-open vagina and instead press against her anus. With slavish eagerness her body welcomed the intruder into her most private regions, she even hoped it wasn't John; she hoped he was watching; enjoying. She yelled in triumph as the shaft slid smoothly up into her whipped body, exciting the familiar, curious sensations in her bowels, and the delicious pressure on her vaginal walls.

She came in an animal frenzy of humping back and pumping hips, bouncing up and down on the hands under her thighs, grinding down against the root of the erection which impaled her. On and on the ecstasy went until at last she felt the hot jets of sperm gush up into her. She cried and moaned and shouted until at last it was over and she hung once more, her feet barely able to support her. Sweating, panting and completely spent, she felt the wet and flaccid sex which had reamed her, wiped clean in her buttock crease. The men ignored her again and left her to gasp her way back to a semblance of normality while semen seeped out of her anus and ran down her thighs.

She had just about recovered when John returned. He bent and kissed her neck, her shoulder and some of the still throbbing weals, and she was more peacefully content than she had ever been. He undressed and stood behind her, and when she craned her head around she saw he was holding the whip.

"Now it's my turn," he said. She smiled.

A strange fortnight or so followed for Caroline. But never for a moment was she allowed to let the events of that night recede in her memory to the point where she could pretend they were some sort of temporary madness or even a dream.

She was kept under a strict regime by a husband who never, during that time, touched her to mistreat her in any way. But she was forbidden any underwear except her basques, over which she could wear blouses or light pullovers with short skirts and high heels. Caroline at first thought she looked rather tarty and was embarrassed to appear in front of her home help who came in three days a week to clean. But the first time she caught the train up to town to meet John for lunch, at his express instructions, she saw why he was doing it to her. It was to underline the lesson she had learnt in the restaurant. Whenever she stood, walked, and especially when she sat, she was acutely aware of her thinly covered nudity, and the marks on her back and bottom. No amount of tugging at the mini skirt would hide her long thighs and she kept her legs pressed tightly together whenever she sat, terrified that someone would see her naked sex if they studied her for long enough. On several days he phoned her when he was starting for home and told her to go to the study and play the audio tape he had made of her whipping She was ordered to sit in one of the leather armchairs, open her legs wide, sling her thighs over the arms and masturbate while she listened to it. Never having played with herself before she was hesitant at first but for a woman who had willingly submitted to the cane and the whip, it was no big thing, she chided herself. And she was amazed at how passionately her body responded to her own fingers expertly playing with her hardening clitoris and how her vagina responded eagerly to those same fingers as they twisted and probed inside her. Soon she was able to get all four fingers up and rub her thumb hard on her throbbing nub. She found herself crying out in unison with her own voice on the tape as the steady swish and meaty smack of the whip on her own back drove her to orgasm all over again, and by the time she heard her moans of delight as she was sodomised after the beatings, her hips were right off the chair and both hands were working frantically at her crotch. She would obediently lick her fingers when she had finished and then phone John back, dishevelled and dazed, to report that she had done as he ordered. On those evenings she hated the self-control he exerted, which wouldn't allow him to beat her again.

But at long last the waiting came to an end, all her marks had faded and John told her she was ready. But for what?

The phone rang mid-morning and she was told to dress in Basque, stockings and court shoes, and to wait in the study. As soon as John returned he selected a short coat for her and with no explanations, ordered her into the car. In silence they drove for a long time, John refusing to answer her anxious questions. Eventually he stopped the car on a narrow country road. Caroline looked around her, the countryside was open and rolling, dotted with woodland. There were no houses visible apart from a small gatehouse right beside them. It stood just inside tall wrought iron gates which stood open to give access to a long drive, lined with lime trees and fenced off from the acres of parkland on either side. If it led to a house then Caroline couldn't see it.

"Take off your coat and get out now Caroline." John told her. She looked at him in horror.

"Go on, or I'll tie you over one of those fences and beat you here and now."

She knew he meant every word and hesitantly she began to shrug the coat off. The only comfort she received was when she leaned forward to slide it down her back. John reached over and ran his hand over the soft mounds of breast flesh she was offering to him over the half cups of the Basque. Immediately she felt herself melt and heat to his touch, she opened her legs for him but he only smiled and told her to walk up the drive.

"You're expected. Just obey anyone you meet as if they were me and I'll come and collect you in a month," he told her and then leaned across to open the door for her.

Helplessly she climbed out and immediately the car pulled away, leaving her standing on the road half naked. Gratefully she noticed that the gatehouse appeared to be unlived in. There was nothing for it. She folded her arms across her chest and started up the drive, horribly aware of the wide-open spaces around her, the way the basque left her buttocks naked and how the cool air moved between her legs as she walked. For what seemed like an eternity she walked, seeing no-one and hearing nothing except occasional bird song and the click and rasp of her shoes on the tarmac. But at long last the drive curved to the left and went through a gap in a high brick wall, and as Caroline approached a woman stepped out to greet her.

She was tall and slender, one of the most impressive women Caroline had ever seen. She had thick black hair piled high on her head and a sharp, authoritarian face. She was dressed in a swirling, calf-length dress and high-heeled boots which stretched up beyond the hem of the dress. In her right hand she carried a long, thin riding crop.

"Caroline, yes?" she said in thickly accented English. Caroline could only nod dumbly. The woman walked slowly around her until she stood in front of her again.

"Take you arms away from your breasts."

Caroline hesitated and in a blur the crop flashed out to her left and then her right, scoring bright stabs of white-hot pain across her hips. Instantly Caroline's hands flew to shield herself and she was left as the woman wanted her.

"Very nice. Good breasts indeed." The crop's tip ran down her cleavage and Caroline shivered.

"You will call me Madame and you will obey me and my assistants, Yuri and Ivan, without question no matter what we order you to do. It is what your master requires."

For a second Caroline thought about querying the use of the word 'master' to describe John, but then he had become much more than a mere husband in these last weeks. She looked up and met Madame's gaze.

"Yes Madame," she replied meekly.

"Good. Follow me."

The woman turned and strode away, forcing Caroline to break into a trot to keep up with her. Shortly the drive took a final turn to the right and Caroline saw the neo-gothic splendour of The Lodge for the first time.

***

Caroline fell silent at that point.

"And what happened then?" I asked sharply.

She stretched her body languidly on the desk and smiled up at me as I came to stand over her.

"Madame has forbidden me to talk of it. But John did come and collect me a month later."

"Caroline!" I said angrily, "your master, your husband directly ordered you to talk to me... to give my readers a story."

"I'm sorry Sir, but when I am here, I am under Madame's command."

That was true unfortunately. And for some reason Madame didn't want me finding out any more about her training methods, she didn't trust me or Falconer and was setting limits on our reporting. John might not be pleased but he would have to back her up if push came to shove. I had one more try nonetheless.

"John will not be pleased with you," I pointed out.

Caroline smiled up at me, licking her lips lasciviously. "A slavegirl's lot is often a hard one." She lifted her head and gazed down along her exposed body. "Of course, you could always try beating it out of me yourself." She gave me a long look, up from under her eyelashes. It seemed that everyone was testing me, John already had, Madame was doing it now...and so was Caroline.

I was tempted to get angry but managed to keep calm enough to think.

"Very well. If my readers aren't going to get their story, I might as well get some pleasure." I let her think that I had given in and was just going to give her an enjoyable thrashing and then leave. She would have kept faith with Madame, enjoyed being beaten to orgasm and could look forward to John giving her another session.

She was wrong.

And she only found out how wrong she was when I had

her ankle restraints clipped to ring bolts in the floor and her wrists clipped to chains from the ceiling. I cranked these up good and tight so that she was stretched taut and spread out in an X shape.

She was so smugly confident that I didn't understand her and would whip her to repeated orgasms while she happily refused to tell me what I wanted to know, that I had the greatest pleasure in selecting a thick, single thong whip and showing it to her. She moaned in anticipation of the braided leather biting into her unprotected back, breasts and thighs. But a few minutes later she was groaning a great deal more…because I wasn't using it on her. At least not the way she wanted.

Instead I stood in front of her and gently draped the lash over her shoulder, then drew it slowly up her back, letting the leather caress her skin, very lightly. She gasped and shuddered in pleasure at first, still quite certain that I would give it to her the way she wanted any minute now. But I moved to stand beside her and reached down to place the handle of the whip against her mons, at the same time I reached behind her and in my other hand grasped the lash. Then, very slowly and gently I sawed the leather through her legs, letting it slide along her crease, back and forth. Very gradually I increased the pressure and sure enough, after a few moments I could see the leather emerging from her shining with her juices.

"Are you good and moist now Caroline?" I asked. "Are your lips full and open so that the whip can slide along between them. Are you creaming yourself just imagining how much the thrashing is going to hurt?"

"Yes…oh yes!" she murmured, her eyes closed and her face soft with desire.

I moved behind her and let the lash trail down over one shoulder so that this time it hung down over her right breast and dangled between her spread legs. Once again I drew it gently up and watched her shudder as the leather softly crawled over her skin. I made sure that the tip of the lash stroked her nipple, already rock hard and deep cherry red.

"Oh please use it!" she whispered, "whip me! I need it!"

"Why should I Caroline? If I do then you get your pleasure but I don't get my story. No I think we'll just carry on like this."

I moved round in front again, never touching her with my hands, just teasing her with the whip, stroking her and sometimes flicking with just the last inch or so of the lash. She moaned and twisted with frustration, finally breaking when I flicked very softly at her sex, she tried to buck her hips towards the lash but couldn't and when I stopped doing it, she screamed.

"For God's sake, I'll tell you everything! Just do it properly, finish me please!"

But I had the power now—the real whip hand. And I was in no hurry.

"You'll tell me everything about how Madame trains the girls?" I brushed the lash against the insides of her thighs.

"Yes, yes! Everything, just whip me! I promise I'll tell you!"

Unfortunately, Madame chose that moment to enter the dungeon. She took in the sight of my teasing Caroline's crotch with the whip and her body trembling like a bowed violin string, then she strode up to the girl and yanked her head back by the hair so violently that she screamed.

"What have you done Caroline?" she whispered fiercely.

"Nothing Madame! I haven't told him anything except what you told me to say!"

Madame gave me a furious glance and I saw her free hand reach down Caroline's body. Immediately the already stretched torso writhed and she screamed again. I looked down and saw all four of Madame's fingers buried to the knuckles in her sex, pushing the labia wide apart. Caroline screamed again and I realised that Madame's thumb was probably rammed up into her backside and her hand was gripping the membranes inside her which separated the two entrances to her body.

I made a decision and stepped back from the girl.

"It's alright Madame. She hasn't told me anything...yet. She was about to but you caught her in time."

I wasn't going to get the whole of the story and in a perverse way I was ensuring that Caroline got the punishment she craved. But for the moment Madame increased the savage treatment she was dishing out to both ends of the chained body in front of her. Caroline's screams echoed off the stone walls as she frantically tried to wriggle and twist away from that awful grip inside her and the tension on her hair.

"Is this true?" Madame hissed.

"Yes, yes! I swear it!" Caroline shrieked and then gasped as the hand was withdrawn and her hair was released. Madame came to stand directly in front of me and stared hard at me. I returned the stare.

"You are a fast learner Mr O'Kane. You understand how slaves work, and I didn't think you would...so soon. But understand this. I will talk to you only when I trust you completely; not a moment before."

There was nothing for it. I had to take what I had got and be content for the time being. Madame watched me pack and leave. And as I closed the door and walked down the passage, then up the stairs and back through The Lodge proper, in my mind's eye I was seeing Caroline's superb body twisting and writhing under a savage thrashing.

By the time I had got behind the wheel of my car I had a pounding erection. I retrieved my mobile and phoned Kathy to fix up a date for that night. I was determined that her bottom was going to taste my belt. It was scant recompense for not having given Caroline the beating she had so wanted. But I was quite clear in my mind that if Kathy objected to the lashing I wanted—needed—to give her, then she could go. I knew what I wanted and I was going to get it.

# MARIE-HELENE

*By Falconer Bridges*

PROLOGUE

When the opportunity arose for me to meet Oliver Carlisle I grasped it with both hands. I knew all about him, or at least I thought I did, having a bad case of hero worship as far as he was concerned.

I admired him greatly because he was the only person I could think of who'd successfully bridged the credibility gap between culture and capitalism. He was a rock music legend whose band had stormed to prominence in the seventies, and although he'd stopped performing with them years ago in order to concentrate on his business empire, they still remain a major force on the world music scene. It takes a very special type of person to span two such diverse enterprises as rock music and high finance, and the fact that he enjoys the highest level of respect in both those spheres is a measure of his undeniable brilliance.

During our interview I learned he possessed other, more private, talents and left his presence a wiser, more enlightened man with a new direction of my own to follow and I fully intend to accept his invitation to visit one of his establishments in France. It's a very exclusive club, a counterpart of The Lodge set deep in a Breton forest, there is nothing to advertise its existence and membership is strictly by invitation only. It's very close to a spot where he enjoyed an early experience with Marie-Helene and a French policeman who is now a great friend of his. It's well hidden but if you try, you never know, you might find it.

ONE

It was lust at first sight.

She was without any doubt the most coolly sensuous creature I'd ever encountered. Sophisticated and self-assured she most certainly was, but nothing about her was overstated or ostentatious. I had no idea how old she was, I could only guess, but I thought thirty-five or maybe forty, and believe me, whatever her age, she was one very, very tasty lady. On the third finger of her left hand she wore a plain gold band and snuggling up against it was her only concession to grandeur, a ring set with a diamond that must have been one of the most spectacular rocks ever to be dug from the Kimberley mines. But for all its brilliance, she put it in the shade; she was dazzling.

I was young, just turned twenty, and spending the summer break from U.M.I.S.T. working as a waiter in Brittany; both for the money and to improve my French. I'd never for a minute believed that women like her actually existed in real life, I thought they were just images conjured up by writers and artists and you only found them in literature or art galleries. She was a revelation, a total one hundred per cent ball breaker and every inch of her was pure, raw sex appeal. Her hair was black as midnight; cascades of its anthracite locks framed her cheeks and folded over both shoulders. She had the intrigue of the Mona Lisa and a body that wouldn't have shamed the Venus de Milo, with glorious breasts that swelled above the neckline of her gown. I caught a glimpse of the upper circumference of a broad hazelnut areola and the tip of a darker chocolate brown thimble. My prick boggled, and to put it bluntly, it went berserk.

There was no way I could control it and as my state of arousal became increasingly obvious I felt a red tide surge upwards from my neck and cover my face in embarrassment. From across the table she studied my bulging trousers and her tongue emerged from between her lips and ran enticingly over their smooth, delicately painted surfaces. Her eyes lingered on my constrained, but only too visible manhood before sweeping upwards to hold my own in a sultry gaze. Instantaneous involuntary ejaculation became an imminent possibility. I was in an utter funk, incapable of lucid thought or action. I wanted to run, but I stood rooted to the spot, mesmerised by her beauty. What I wouldn't have given for the chance to plunge my throbbing penis into the ice bucket that stood at her elbow.

I tried to speak but no sound came out. My throat was arid, my tongue a useless floundering lump of flesh and my hard-on so granite solid that it hurt. In desperation I waved my order pad and pointed at the menu that lay in front of her.

"You'd better sit down," she said, "before the other customers begin to wonder just what it is that you're offering me for dinner."

Her voice was an aural aphrodisiac; husky, inviting and as liquid as virgin olive oil. She spoke in English but with a French accent so laden with sex it could get a twitch out of a corpse. It was hopeless. My cock jerked in an imitation of a jackhammer that semaphored my predicament to the entire room.

"Sit down," she whispered urgently.

"Madame, I'm sorry. I don't know what to say."

"Say nothing," she interrupted, "just sit down."

"I can't," I said, "staff aren't allowed to associate with the guests. I'll get the sack, the Maitre D will go crazy."

"If he sees that," she said pointedly, " he'll have a heart attack. And in any event there will be no problem, I'll deal with him. Now, *sit down*."

I slid down onto the chair opposite her and arranged the tablecloth over the Alpine proportions of my trousers in an effort to conceal the evidence. I'd had the king of all erections for so long my balls were screaming for release. The pain was incredible, as if both testicles were clamped in an ever tightening vice. I stole a glance in the direction of the kitchen and found that the Maitre D was standing transfixed, staring in my direction. I squirmed in my seat, waiting for the explosion. Moments passed. I looked again and saw him seething with rage but apparently unable or unwilling to take me to task. Abruptly he turned on his heels and stormed into the kitchen.

Once again she fixed me with those limpid black eyes.

"I find you, shall we say, interesting," she said, "I think perhaps you should dine with me and later we'll see if there isn't some way to resolve your little personal problem."

That was it. Any semblance of self-control evaporated in an instant. My bollocks found their relief. My cock writhed and jerking wildly, with no stimulation other than her words, spurted buckets of sperm into the straining confines of my pants. I'd been in embarrassing situations before, but this was terminal terror, humiliation beyond belief. I was drenched, gallons of sticky seed soaked my underpants and I was certain there'd be a damn great patch all over the front of my trousers, but there was no way I dared lift the cloth from my knees to take a look. My face changed species and turned into a beetroot. From the look on her own face I knew she must have guessed what had happened, and in a tone that was more amusement than admonishment, she said that I really must learn self control, adding that she'd better get me out of the place before I suffered any further untoward inconvenience.

"What is your name?" she asked abruptly.

I told her it was Oliver.

"Olivier," she repeated in that prick-twitching accent. "O-leev-e-ay," adding the extra vowel of the French version of my name. If she'd have leapt up, pulled my dick out of my pants and stuffed it down her throat she couldn't have provoked a more instant reaction than she did with that one utterance. If Action Man had been taking a quick nap, he was up again and straining at the leash in no seconds flat.

She couldn't help but see it and after a few moments deliberation she told me that I had the most desperate case of priapism she'd ever encountered and if I wished to enjoy her company further, I had to conduct myself in a more gentlemanly manner. I was desperate. There was nothing I could do, my penis had a will of its own and I hadn't got a clue what she was talking about. Here I was, a university student and she'd got a better English vocabulary than me, I had to look it up afterwards and she was spot on the mark.

Persistent erection of the penis, that's the dictionary definition and I've never forgotten it. But to get back to the point, there she was cool as a cucumber and as if I wasn't in enough bother as it was, she beckoned the Maitre D, who'd come back out of the kitchen. Now, he was a splenetic character at the best of times, so I was amazed when he scurried over to the table like a pet poodle.

"Oui Madame?" he fawned.

"Jean Paul," she said, "Olivier will be taking the rest of the evening off, we have a delicate matter to discuss, so I suggest you find someone else to take over his duties."

I was thunderstruck and I know my mouth gaped open. If dirty looks were bullets, I'd have been riddled, but choking back his rage he bowed very slightly to her and stalked off. She told me to clean myself up and meet her in the foyer in fifteen minutes. Trying to look inconspicuous I sidled out of the dining room, covering my wet patch with my waiter's napkin. I was in my cubbyhole of a room, taking a quick shower, when there was a knock on the door. Well, this is it then I thought, and opened the door, fully expecting a member of the management to be standing there with my cards in his hand. But it was a maid, she was English as well, and she was carrying a white tuxedo, a pair of black trousers, a wing collared shirt and a black tie.

"Jammy bastard," she said, thrusting the clothes into my arms. "With Madame's compliments."

I put the clothes on and they fitted almost perfectly. I didn't have a clue what was going on, I mean, how did she know my size for a start? I gave up wondering once I'd taken a gander in the mirror. I looked pretty good and it seemed as if she'd got something interesting in mind, so bracing myself I went down to meet her.

You don't need to know all that happened. It's enough to say that she had a Ferrari outside and she drove like a demon, to the Casino. We fed the slot machines, played the tables, bet on the wheel, drank Dom Perignon and generally lived it up. It was all new to me, I was amongst privileged society for the first time and I soaked up the atmosphere like a sponge. She made no deliberate effort to create an impression; she didn't need to, drawing admiring glances from every quarter and garnering constant attention from the management. Of course, at that time I had no idea of the extent of her fortune and influence, though I was staggered by the size of the stakes she was laying down, both for her and me. But, I was having a damned good time and I wasn't picking up the bill, so go with the flow I told myself, after all nobody was looking at me.

And then it was time to leave.

We didn't go back to the hotel. Instead she took me to one of those wonderful little Breton stone cottages, all white walls, black roof and masses of flowers in baskets. It was her little hideaway, she told me, and it stood high on a clifftop overlooking the Atlantic. The view was amazing but she didn't give me a chance to admire it, she had something else in mind. No sooner were we inside than she said, "I think you'd like to make love to me, no?"

No? Was she crazy? I wanted to fuck her all the way from there to England and back. I was speechless and couldn't do anything but nod in agreement. She took my hand and led me into the bedroom. I grabbed her and ran my hands over her jutting breasts, feeling the solid nuggets of her nipples pressing into my palms.

"No, no," she cried, pushing me away, "Calm yourself, do not be in so much of a hurry."

She said we had the whole night ahead of us, and if it would make me happy and I had the stamina, I could spend all of it making love to her. But there was something I had to do in return to make her happy.

"Anything, anything," I said, "just tell me what you want."

And she did. And I was even more staggered. It turned out she liked to be dominated by a lover, to be punished and feel pain. She told me that all her pleasure was in submission and obedience, and in order to ensure her fulfilment I had to dictate her actions and beat her soundly. I was out of my mind, I'd wanked myself sore time and again having fantasies about this sort of thing and now the most shaggable woman I'd ever seen was actually asking me to do it to her.

She pulled open the drawer at the bottom of a huge antique wooden wardrobe and took out a thin wooden cane. She pushed the drawer closed and stood bending the cane into a tight circle, demonstrating its flexibility.

"I think this will be perfect for your first experience," she said, "and do not forget, be masterful!"

She handed the cane to me and then turned towards the wall. There was a small ornate desk, another antique, pushed up against the wall and it was weird, I'd never seen anything in England like it. It was about three feet wide and about two and half feet high, with carved legs at each end, and it stood directly underneath an icon of Ste. Anne. She crossed herself, and with her back towards me, very slowly and deliberately started to bend forward. I was nearly out of mind with frustration and whipping the air, I slashed the cane down into my own open palm. Christ, did it sting, and it left a livid weal.

That did it. I yelled at her and ordered her to bend right over. She obeyed without question and I tugged her dress up over her thighs and threw it over up over her backside. It was like throwing open the gates to Heaven. Halted in my tracks, I stood mouth agape, soaking in the spectacle of her femininity. What a glorious bottom she'd got, full juicy buttocks that stretched her knickers to the limit, and mile long legs, encased in sheer nylon that reached to within six inches of her pleasure site. Rose embroidered suspenders held up the stockings and the milky flesh between them and her knickers was smooth and inviting. I wanted to touch it, to feel the smoothness for myself, to run my palms up the silky insides of her thighs and probe the mystery of her clearly outlined sex, but I knew full well that to do so would have been flirting with disaster. Marie-Helene had defined clearly enough the parameters of our relationship and I found myself fighting a bruising battle to rein in my raging emotions. I teetered uncertainly on the threshold until I'd pulled myself into some semblance of self-control, and then, taking a deep breath I stepped over into the Promised Land.

I laid the cane lightly on her rump positioning myself for the first stroke. A tremor ran through her body at its touch and despite my best efforts, my ardour rose to fever pitch. Still struggling to contain myself, I whacked her with more force than I'd intended, a shocked scream catapulting from her lips as a scarlet welt etched itself across the back of one of her thighs. I struck her again; lashing the tender rear of her other thigh and you should have heard her wail; her yelps and squeals sparking such a violent reaction in my cock that it threatened to blast its way out of my trousers. It was like a ten thousand volt electric shock surging through my manhood and numbing my senses. I lashed her again, and again, and again, I couldn't stop myself.

Suddenly, it hit me and I pulled myself up, the cane hanging loosely in my fist. What was I doing? I was saddled with a rock hard erection, a bucketful of guilt and I was ashamed that I'd let my emotions to run away with me. But I'll tell you this, underneath the remorse I was exhilarated and I'd got to do something about my dick, it was well in danger of spontaneous eruption all over again. She didn't move, she just stayed as she was, bent horizontal with her fingers still locked on to opposite edges of the desk with her bottom thrust towards me. She was trembling and breathing in short rapid gasps. She tried to say something but between the breaths her words were incoherent.

An edge of fright crept in then, I thought perhaps I'd really hurt her, but I couldn't tear my sight away from her savaged thighs. My eyes latched downward, leaping from weal to weal and each time they locked on to a fresh mark my cock throbbed with more intensity. It was so hard it hurt. I tried to mumble some kind of apology but she stayed as she was. It's still as clear in my mind as it was then, I can still see myself standing there, staring at her backside and playing with myself through my trousers.

Then, out of the blue, she spoke to me, loud and clear.

"It was wonderful," she said.

I couldn't believe my ears. And then she said it again.

"It was wonderful. You were wonderful. Strong. In charge; just as a man should be. I want you now. Do anything you want. Tell me to do anything you want. Please. Anything, anything at all."

I wrestled my shafter out of captivity in a second, and there was no way I could wait for anything at all. I couldn't take things slow and easy, I was desperate. I ripped her knickers from her bottom, clasped both hands around the milky heights above her stocking tops and thrust at her sex. I'm not ashamed to say I was totally inexperienced then and my organ floundered around the portals like a hooked salmon, sliding up, down and around but never succeeding in locating the gateway to heaven.

Then suddenly, my bell end hooked into a welcoming notch. It was tight as a pig's ear and I couldn't get in, but I shoved harder until she gasped and then, gripping her thighs even tighter I pulled her on to me and gained an entrance. It was gritty and dry and it sure as hell didn't want to let me in but I worked on it, pushing in, retreating and then pushing in further again. She moaned and I grunted, but I wasn't going to be beaten, and with an almighty thrust I pushed my entire allocation of throbbing gristle straight in up to the hilt. She loved it; she went crazy and shrieked in delight. I was in the Promised Land and in the blink of an eye both goolies had emptied their reservoirs, spurting bucket after bucket into her accommodating well.

"Thank you, thank you, thank you," she gasped and started to straighten up.

"No," I shouted, I didn't want her getting up.

There was no hesitation; she immediately took up her position again. I liked it, this was power and my word was law. I was young and I could go again straightaway, my weapon didn't slacken and anyway I was still practically stuck inside her. It was my first time and I didn't realise I'd gone in through the wrong door. Don't laugh, I'd got a lot to learn but I soon made up for lost time. It was a little easier the second time because there was some lubrication there now, my own sperm.

"Stop," she said, "Don't you want to do this one in my vagina?"

I thought that's where I was already but I wasn't about to let her know that. I had to think fast and I told her that I'd do it again where it was and then I'd take a ride up the Tunnel of Love. And so I did, and after that I caned her again for her insolence in questioning my intent.

At that moment I left my youth behind me. I became a man.

## TWO

Marie-Helene was forty-one and the reason the Maitre D had been so cringingly servile was that she owned him. Well, she owned the hotel, which in that business is the same thing. Needless to say, I never went back there, what few belongings I'd taken with me to France, including a guitar that never left my side, she had sent up to the cottage and we spent the next few days getting even more intimately acquainted. I was a quick learner and in no time at all, I was on top of the situation, in more ways than one. I lived up to her expectations more fully than only a few days before I would ever have thought possible. Our initial relationship was completely reversed, I was now her master and she was my slave, totally subservient and desperate to obey my every command. She asked me for just one favour, that being that I wouldn't humiliate her in the presence of her underlings or business associates. I granted her plea obviously, I wasn't about to undermine her authority in that sphere but apart from that, she was mine, body and soul.

A week flashed by in the blink of an eye; the weather was glorious and it didn't rain once, which had to be a record for Brittany. The cottage was set amongst tall pine trees, close to the edge of the pink granite cliffs, and had been built just an arm's length away from an absolutely enormous megalithic standing stone that was higher than the building itself and was covered in runic symbols. In the short periods of recuperation between our frenzied love making, I'd sit outside, leaning up against the megalith, playing my guitar and drinking red wine. It was as near to Heaven as you can get without actually keeling over and kicking up your heels.

By the end of the week I'd learned a lot more about Marie-Helene. Of French aristocratic stock herself, she was the widow of a Swiss businessman, whose financial interests had ranged from pharmaceuticals through banking to the leisure industry. He'd been a fair bit older than her and it was him that had nurtured and developed her need for discipline and domination in her private and sexual life. His legacy to her had been a mountain of cash, a majority shareholding in any number of blue chip companies and the hotel. But not only that hotel, a whole chain of hotels stretching across Europe. To a working class git like me, her wealth was incomprehensible, but I didn't give a monkey's anyway, I didn't want her money, I wanted her body.

On about the seventh or eighth day she told me that she'd had an inspection tour of some of her properties lined up for some time which she couldn't back out of and I could either stay at the cottage, or if I wanted, I could go along with her. Well, I didn't want to miss out on a single day's shagging and the chance to do it in some fancy surroundings sounded pretty good to me, so I signed up for the tour, ostensibly, for the benefit of her employees, as her personal assistant. She suggested rather tentatively that in order to play that part properly, it might be a good idea if I had some better clothes. In that area she was the boss and if she thought a designer label was going to help establish my credentials with the lower orders that was fine by me. She said that Rennes was the best place to find anything even half decent and so that's where we headed.

In her wardrobe I found a long blue denim skirt, tastefully patterned with small hummingbirds picked out in real silver thread. It buttoned all the way the down the front and looked as if it could be fun, so I ordered her to put it on, together with a thin satin blouse and stockings and suspenders. She did as she was told and then picked up the keys to the Ferrari.

"I'll drive," I told her, and she passed me the keys immediately.

I jumped into the car and roared off. It was bloody exhilarating, I can tell you. I'd only just passed my test, all I'd ever driven before was my father's old banger and here I was doing a Fittipaldi in one of the world's most exclusive sports cars, with an even more exclusive lady at my side. Fields of maize whizzed by in a blur, but the roads weren't too good, and after I almost piled us into a tree trying to take a bend too fast, the speed fever cooled and I calmed down a bit. Marie-Helene hadn't said a word but as my speed dropped, she gave a sigh of relief and I saw her hands unclench. Once I'd taken a look at her, my interest in the car immediately dropped into second place.

Her hair was blowing out in coal black streamers and the satin blouse was flattened to her breasts, her nipples almost punching holes through the thin material. I eased my foot back off the pedal and slowed to a speed where I could ogle her and still drive safely. Her hair fell back around her face and I thought again what a magnificent woman she was

"Unbutton your skirt up to your knickers," I instructed her.

Starting from the bottom upwards she obeyed my order. She did it very slowly, undoing each button with teasing exactness until she finally dispatched the one that sat over her crotch. The skirt still clung to her legs and I told her to pull it open and let the folds fall on either side of her thighs. One look and there it was again, instant hard on. I'm a hog for satin undies, white stockings and suspenders and I could have stopped the car there and then and rogered her over the bonnet, but I steeled myself to hang on in there, I had to if I was going to maintain our relationship. Self-control came top of the list in her table of priorities and now she was under my domination it was necessary that I proved myself equal to the task.

But I had to see more.

"Take them off," I said.

She didn't need me to spell it out and hooking her thumbs into the waistband of her knickers, with a not inconsiderable amount of shuffling and wriggling about in the tight confines of the bucket seat she tugged them down until they stuck fast on her backside, a luxuriant copse of curly black pubes sprouting over the waistband where it was halted just above her sex. She lifted her buttocks up from the seat and leaning forward she put a hand between her thighs and grasping the gusset of the knickers she pulled them from under her bottom. Once they were freed she slid them sensuously down her legs, wrestled them over her high heels and kicked them into the corner of the floor well.

"Now, open your legs wide," I ordered.

She did, and I took my right hand off the wheel and slid it over the top of her thigh and down between her legs. I edged the side of my hand up to her vagina and rubbed it up and down her moistening labials. Almost instantly she was wet through and my hand, from wrist to the tip of my little finger, was sucked into her welcoming lips. I carried on massaging her in that fashion, taking good care to excite her clitoris, but made no attempt to manoeuvre my fingers into a position where they could force an entrance into her orifice. I could feel the excitement rising within her as her juices flowed out and she pushed her soaking sex against my hand. She was getting really fired up and by now my own hose was making a determined attempt to unreel inside my jeans. I grabbed another quick glance at her and the flushed, eager expression on her face warned me to cool it, I didn't want her coming yet, I'd got other plans.

I pulled my hand free from her sucking vagina and her disappointment was almost painful. She slumped in her seat and I was sure she was going to beg me to carry on but she bit her lip and said nothing. I ran the side of my hand under my nostrils and snorted the warm musky scent of her sex and to this day I've never found anything you can put up your nose to equal the buzz I got from that. She still sat with her legs wide open and the magnificence of what was on display, combined with the headiness of her sexual aroma only served to stiffen my already rampant penis into a solid rod of iron. My need was now greater than hers and I was forced to amend my strategy. I was swept with all the authority that General Patton had commanded as he'd cleared those fields of France thirty years before. My orders were straight to the point.

"Get down and suck it!"

She didn't have to be told twice, she was fiddling with the buttons of my jeans before I'd completed the sentence and slipping her hand inside my flies, she delved into my underpants, hooked her palm under my straining serpent, and wrenching it free from its confines she pulled it out into the sunlight.

It was a rare, very hot day for that area of the country, but despite that her hand clasped around my shaft was cool and sensuous. I wanted to enjoy this to the full so I slowed to a crawl, dropped down a couple of gears, took my foot off the clutch, opened my own legs as wide as I could and with my right foot very gently caressing the accelerator, cruised down the lane at minimum speed. She shuffled round in her seat until her bottom was pressed up against the passenger door and her head was positioned directly over my throbbing shaft. I was leaking myself by now and her tongue flicked out and lapped up the salty pre come fluid that was flowing out over my bell. She looped her thumb and fingers very loosely around my weapon, stroking it upwards into her wide-open welcoming mouth.

I was lost in a wonderland of lust but I pulled myself together just in time to negotiate another potentially fatal bend in the road. Once around the curve I wished I'd let myself go and taken the trip to paradise, because I ran into one of those idiotic situations that couldn't possibly happen anywhere else but rural France. A Renault Four, or one of those other stupid little shoe boxes the Gendarmerie used was nose down in the ditch; the lane was littered with artichokes that had spilled from an overturned cart and a 2CV6, with a sack of potatoes in the passenger seat and a panic stricken pig in the back were completely blocking the road. The Agent de Police, the two labourers in charge of the cart, the farmer who'd been piloting the Citroen and several cauliflower pickers who just fancied an argument, were involved in a push and shove fracas in the middle of the road.

I rolled to a stop and turned off the ignition, it was obvious we could be in for a long wait. Marie-Helene, whose head was below dashboard level, had by now worked her mouth halfway down my shaft. The Gendarme couldn't see her and taking a quick look in my direction, dismissed me instantly and returned to his furious argument. Marie-Helene stopped slurping for a moment and raised her head with the intention of looking around her. I pushed her straight back over my vital equipment; I'd watch, she'd suck.

And suck she did. She tongued every straining inch of my manhood, her greedy lips sliding slowly up and down its quivering length, tasting and savouring it as if it came with three Michelin stars. I uttered silent thanks to the Swiss industrialist, he'd taught her well. Further and further down she went as she took more and more into her mouth and in order to get it all in, right down to my testicles, she was forced to shift her position and kneel on the passenger seat. The Ferrari was obviously an open topped sports job and her backside necessarily now jutted well above the passenger door as her head bobbed busily around under the steering wheel.

It didn't take long. One of the cauliflower pickers was the first to notice and immediately losing interest in the promised punch up, disengaged himself from the altercation and sauntered over. He stood, open mouthed, gaping at the action inside the car. One by one they followed, forming a silent semi-circle around the car, until only the gendarme and the farmer were left in the middle of the lane, poking each other violently in the chest. They were an appreciative audience and watched in jealous admiration as Marie-Helene, with her eyes closed and unaware of their presence, took even more of me into her mouth until my glans touched the back of her throat. Trousers were turning into tents all around me, when suddenly the two remaining adversaries realised that they were alone and they both hurried over to investigate what could possibly be more interesting than a fight.

One of the labourers made room for them and the gendarme stood directly behind her jutting backside.

"Mon Dieu," he gasped, alerting Marie-Helene.

She slid her lips halfway back up my shaft and with it still clamped tightly in her mouth looked up. She skipped the pink and scarlet, and colouring straight into a deep shade of purple loosened her jaws and pulled her head upwards, but once again I stopped her retreat from the penile zone by laying a restraining palm on the top of her crown and she was left with just my bulbous bell stuck between her lips. I surveyed the lascivious palpitating circle of peasantry and threw a questioning glance at the gendarme. Her raised buttocks were staring him directly in the eye and he was having great difficulty trying to conceal a burgeoning erection. Globules of sweat trickled down his temples and after a moment's indecision, he nodded and I pushed her saliva filled mouth back downwards.

"Entertain them well," I told her.

She proceeded to do just that. Her lips and tongue got straight back to work and very slowly and deliberately she began to pump them up and down over the entire length of my tool until she pushed it right down into her throat, her cheeks falling into deep hollows as she sucked me in so far I thought it would end up in her stomach. A storm was gathering in my scrotum and I felt the first rush of sperm into my urethra. Her tongue relayed the message and she plunged up and down with ever increasing speed, gripping me tight between her teeth to heighten the intensity, until jerking violently my dick fired a salvo of steaming seed straight into her gullet. Jet after jet spattered her tonsils and she swallowed greedily to leave room in her mouth to make way for my never-ending ejaculation. Eventually my raging orgasm subsided, and making sure not a drop of sperm escaped, she slipped her lips free of my still twitching penis and lifting her head high to the congregation, triumphantly swallowed all that still swished around in her mouth.

Her performance was rewarded by a resounding round of applause and then, all personal aggression having evaporated, the gendarme dismissed the gathering, which dispersed with supernatural alacrity. I suspect there were half a dozen well-used wives and girlfriends shortly afterwards.

"Magnifique, mon brave," he congratulated me, as Marie-Helene lapped my shaft, removing every last trace of my come, "but perhaps M'sieu could be a little more discreet in future. L'amour, it is a wonderful thing, but maybe not here, au centre de la route, eh?"

I didn't say anything, just tidied myself up but as she swivelled round and settled her bottom back into her seat, I saw his eyes devouring her still very obvious charms. I got out of the car and beckoning to him walked over to his car. I had a very productive little chat with him as I helped get the car back on to the road. Tipping the peak of his kepi, he opened the car door, got in, started the engine and crawled off down the road. I leapt back into the Ferrari in time to stop her re-buttoning her skirt. I flicked it back open and was well pleased to see she had not put her knickers back on. Her sex was still oozing love juice, her pubes were damp and straggly and the magic stockings and suspenders framed it all into a picture of inviting eroticism. It was perfect.

I turned on the ignition, put the car into gear and set off. We had only travelled a couple of K when I saw the police car parked on the grass verge next to a narrow path, almost totally overgrown with ferns, that wound into a thick wood. I pulled up and parked behind it, Marie-Helene cast me a quizzical look as I motioned her to get out of the car. Taking her hand I led her along the trail until right in the middle of the dense timber we came into a clearing. Several huge trees had been felled and their smooth trunks, lopped clear of twigs and branches, lay majestically on the red, cone-covered earth. The gendarme, looking somewhat sheepish, stood behind one of them and, seeing him, Marie-Helene stopped dead in her tracks, she now had some inkling of what I had in mind.

"M'sieu l'agent," I told her, "rated your display so highly that I'm giving you to him, so that he can enjoy your charms first hand."

She didn't like that idea and protested vehemently.

"My authority is never to be questioned," I said sharply, "never, do you understand?"

With a somewhat hangdog look that infuriated me to an irrational degree, she concurred.

"Right," I said, "the skirt, take it off."

She undid the one button at the centre of her waist that still secured the garment and letting it drop to the ground, stood defiantly in all her prick teasing splendour. She may have been feigning displeasure, I just don't know, but she was getting worked up again because her nipples stuck out through the clinging satin of her blouse as rigid as the wheel nuts on the car, and her pubes dripped as if she'd just taken a shower. I ordered her to take off the blouse, and not that it had really hidden anything, with it removed the full magnificence of her lush body was now revealed. Naked splendour's a phrase that comes to mind, and when I say naked, I mean of course apart from the suspender belt, the stockings and the high heels, they're indispensable. In my book, those three items are the only vital weapons a woman needs in her armoury, anything else is a bonus. She was sexier and more alluring than any centrefold and both Thierry, that was his name, and myself twitched in unison.

I unbuckled the thick leather belt holding up my jeans, pulled it through the loops and wound the buckled end around my fist. Standing back to get a good swing I lashed her firmly across her heavy breasts, catching both nipples squarely and leaving a burning two-inch wide welt that glowed like a beacon. A hoarse rasp burst through her lips and stepping forward, Thierry raised his hands in alarm. I, in turn, raised a palm signalling that everything was in order and under control.

"Madame must be reminded that obedience is all," I told him as I lifted my arm once again, "a slave must obey her master at all times without question."

And with that, I gave her a second lash, a full broadside right across her tight stomach, just below the rising mounds of her bosoms. A genuine scream of shocked agony rang through the forest and the resultant strip of abused scarlet flesh gave testament to my determination to bring her fully under my control.

"Besides," I said, turning back to Thierry, "it's her own desire. She wants this, she needs to be dominated and the pain only adds to her pleasure." He seemed doubtful, this was something new to him, as it had been to me, but the pulsing bulge in his trousers showed beyond doubt that he was genuinely inflamed by the action.

"There's no need to take my word for it, ask her yourself," I said.

He did, and with brimming eyes she nodded silent agreement, causing the tears to overflow and roll down her flushed cheeks. Fondling her thighs, the stocking tops and the solid roundness of her buttocks, I could feel the tremors of anticipation tingling through her loins as I guided her over to the tree trunk, on the other side of which Thierry stood salivating. I motioned him to step forward and when he was close up to the giant trunk I pushed her shoulders downwards so that with arms outstretched, she lay arched over it, the rough wood grazing her abdomen and raised pieces of bark digging into her breasts and nipples. I took my stance behind her and with both hands inside her thighs, I pushed her legs wide apart until the whole of her juicy, thatched pudendum lay exposed and available.

"Now Marie-Helene," I said, "make it something he'll always remember."

She reached out over the trunk and on the outside of his trousers she ran her palm over his pulsing member. His over eager, jerking reaction told me that if he was indeed about to have the thrill of a lifetime imprinted into his memory, it certainly wouldn't be because of the duration of the experience.

"You can dispense with the preliminaries," I told her, "you'd better get on with it, and fast."

She could sense the gathering storm in his pants too, and now eager with anticipation she whipped down his zip, delved inside and pulled out his lusting snake. It was hot, rock solid and already had a pool of sticky liquid leaking from its eye. She couldn't quite get her mouth up to it and clasping her hand around his barrel she tugged him closer to her lips, at the same time raising herself on to tip toes in order to push herself further over the tree. Her mouth could devour its prey now alright and she launched her assault by salaciously licking up the salty fluid running over his bell. Her own sex was now dripping and juice trickled down her pubes before falling in droplets to the forest floor. Her long, lovely slit with its pink open lips dared me to get to work on it and my own erection stiffened into concrete.

Gripping the belt I let fly and lashed her smartly across her buttocks. Her mouth opened wide and unable to wait any longer Thierry pushed his glans straight between her lips, stifling the threatened scream. I lashed her again and again and each time the belt struck he pushed in further until her mouth was full of frenzied flesh. Her bottom was red raw when I finally considered she'd had sufficient punishment, both to assuage my anger and to satisfy her need. Although almost delirious with passion, Thierry acceded to my urgent request and managed to pass over his handcuffs. I pulled her arms back over the trunk and with her palms upwards, snapped the cuffs around her wrists. I dropped the belt and unleashing my own demon thrust it straight into her wide-open, welcoming slit. I went in straight up to the hilt, her vaginal muscles dragging my manhood hungrily up to her womb. I was like Thierry, consumed with lust and Marie-Helene was right there with us. With one hand I grasped the handcuffs and leaning back I rode her like a bucking bronco. She pushed back on to me, pleasuring herself unashamedly whilst at the same time working like a suction pump on Thierry's rampant spout. She was crazed with need and all three of us screwed and she ate in a rising tide of frenzy until the crushing spasms of her orgasm sparked my own journey into ecstasy. There were only seconds in it, a trio of earth shattering explosions sent sperm and love juice spurting and squirting everywhere. Surge after surge of my seed propelled itself into her thirsty cavern whilst over on his side of the tree trunk, Thierry had filled her mouth to overflowing, and like the good obedient slave that she now was, in the midst of her spasms, Marie-Helene had dutifully swallowed his entire output.

It was some time before we recovered and managed to pull ourselves together. I was shattered, Marie-Helene had been fucked almost into a seizure and Thierry definitely wasn't ever going to forget that day. That was one of the best pieces of work I've ever done because Thierry became a friend and he's now a highly placed official in the Department of Gendarmerie and as you might imagine, he's a very useful man to know. Oh, and as for the shopping expedition, that had to be cancelled of course. We made it back to the cottage utterly exhausted and after having a good clean up and a change of clothes, we strolled down to the village, indulging ourselves in a simple meal of *steak frites* and rough red *vin de pay*s at the local cafe'. In my elated state it was the equal of any gourmet feast, and as I sat back and poured the last of the wine I remember thinking what a bloody marvellous day it had been.

THREE

We duly completed assembling my wardrobe to her satisfaction the following day, making the trip to Rennes and back without any undue complications. I told her something of my own history on the journey and she was particularly interested in my guitar playing, she seemed to think I was the new Django Reinhardt and I can't say I wasn't flattered, but I explained that the reason I had an acoustic guitar with me was because you can play it anywhere. I was really a rock musician, but you can't get much out of a Les Paul without electricity and a powerful amplifier. I'd been in a band at Manchester University and we'd been doing really well, so well in fact that I'd neglected my studies and was in danger of flunking out. But I determined to make an effort and even took to trying to write my dissertation in the back of the van and in dressing rooms between sets on the gigs. That's why I was so sexually inexperienced, I could have been like the other guys and screwed my bollocks off, but in every spare second that I wasn't studying I practised my guitar. Things came to a head when the band got a record deal and turned pro, they quit straight away but I felt I owed it to my parents, who'd had one hell of a struggle to keep me at university, to try and get my degree, so they found a new lead guitar player and we parted company.

I knew Marie-Helene had found it amusing when she realised that I'd been a virgin up until our first encounter, but she never mentioned it again and I think underneath it all she was justly proud that it was under her tutelage that I had found my true sexual orientation and hardened up my character. I was developing a commanding presence, I could feel it, and neither the Maitre D nor anyone else held any terrors for me now. My sexual experimentation grew ever more exotic yet she never failed to obey a command or deliver complete satisfaction. I indulged myself in a couple more days of orgiastic dominance and then it was time to leave.

I dressed myself in the outfit she'd picked for me to wear for official purposes and she packed the rest of my new gear plus the evening clothes she'd provided me with at the hotel. She also presented me with a pair of cufflinks, very special cufflinks she took care to impress on me. They'd belonged to her husband and featured a design which reminded me somewhat of the mathematical symbol of Pi. I was intrigued because not only had I seen it engraved on the giant standing stone outside the cottage, but on close investigation of her vagina, I'd found it tattooed on the inner surface of her labial lips. She wouldn't answer my questions as to the exact significance of the motif but she told me that it denoted membership of a very ancient exclusive brotherhood to which some of the most powerful men on the planet belonged, and not necessarily those in the public eye but those unseen, unknown people, who regardless of changing governments and political circumstance actually control the world. The Swiss magnate had been one of these persons and there must be no suspicion that she was intimately associating with anyone who was not part of the order, because despite her own wealth and position, they still held total dominion over her; once owned by the Brotherhood, always owned by the Brotherhood, she said. The cufflinks were to signal my right to possess her and whilst I was with her no one would question me, but she stressed that to wear them at any other time would prove dangerous to my health if I was approached by an initiate and found myself unable to respond correctly to the secret signals that members used to establish each others credentials.

She herself donned what she called a working suit, totally in contrast to the dowdy creations I'd seen sported by aspiring British business women. It was an intermediate shade of grey, made from a material that wasn't exactly dull, nor was it bright, it was just right. The skirt was tight and rested two or three inches above her knees, showing off her legs to perfection and the two-buttoned jacket hung to fingertip length. She left the jacket open, her glorious breasts peeping out from beneath a pure white shirt, and she completed the ensemble with a pair of black shoes that like the suit were the epitome of good taste, the heels being neither too high nor too low but just the thing for a business environment.

"What about the stockings?" I demanded.

In reply she put both hands on her thighs and slid the skirt slowly upwards, until the hem ran over the patterned lace tops of a pair of hold ups and came to rest six inches higher, level with her crotch, exposing all that marvellous milky flesh and allowing me just a glimpse of the curly black pubes poking their way from beneath her knickers. She said she knew that no matter what, I'd require her to wear stockings but suspenders would have been visible through the material of the skirt and that wouldn't do in front of her lackeys, so the hold ups were her solution to the problem.

She'd done it again. This lady was turning my life into absolute turmoil. What she considered every day workwear had the effect on me that a whole brigade of gyrating Sunday morning Manchester club strippers had previously failed to manage. We were now off on a serious commercial undertaking and before we'd even got on the road I was stretching my trousers to the limit again. There was no time to do anything about it, we were due to meet the management of her hotel come thalassotherapie centre at Roscoff in an hour, and that was cutting it fine. So with great reluctance, tucking my tail between my legs so to speak, we set off, but this being a business trip we took her Mercedes saloon because she said it made a better impression on the workers if the head of the organisation arrived in a dignified luxury motor.

Well, I don't know about her impressing them, but the establishment certainly impressed the hell out of me. The French are crazy for that seawater therapy, and there, a treatment unit was combined with a five star hotel. Apparently she owned several more like it around the coast, they were only for the very rich and it was this particular segment of her empire that we would be inspecting. Things didn't progress entirely according to plan for me however, her business took all day and for decorum's sake she deemed it wise for us to sleep in separate bedrooms. This happened the following night and the night after that, and by the fourth day we were in Quiberon and I was thoroughly pissed off.

I didn't bother doing the rounds with her; instead I did a

little shopping and then took a walk to the end of the peninsula whilst she took care of business. I'd urged her to try and get through everything as quickly as she could, it was only a couple of hours drive back to the cottage and if we made it back there for the night, I could subject her to some serious correction because she had to answer for my days of deprivation. She was excited at the prospect and in the early afternoon a bellboy she'd despatched to find me, summoned me back to the hotel. She was waiting in the Merc and I slipped straight into the driver's seat and shot off, leaving a trail of burning rubber in my wake.

I took the western coast road out of Quiberon town and slowed my speed considerably as I took in the splendour of the view. It was a beautiful day, the sky was clear and the Atlantic was a delicate shade of deep blue, in stark contrast to the steely grey of its waters around the cliffs near the cottage. She took off her jacket, opened her shirt and eased her skirt higher over her thighs. In no seconds flat I'd got the hots for her again, it was obvious I wasn't going to make it back without relieving my frustrated manhood and so I began to look out for likely spots to sort things out. The landscape was very open and apart from numerous concrete German bunkers, relics of World War Two, I couldn't find an appropriate location. Suddenly, rounding a bend, I came upon an isolated cafe, perched overlooking the sea and like so many buildings in that area, erected right next to a huge standing stone.

I pulled in and we took a table on the terrace, shading ourselves under the parasol. We were the only customers and the waiter strolled leisurely out of the cafe, gave us a cheery greeting, took our order and went back into the cafe. Marie-Helene sat opposite me, her shirt unbuttoned down to her waist and her tight skirt riding up her thighs.

"I want to see your sex," I told her, "right now!"

The sight that greeted the waiter on his return with the drinks almost sent him into a fit of apoplexy, the tray dipped in his hand and he made a valiant attempt to save the drinks, which eluded his clutching hands and smashed on to the tiling of the terrace. Marie-Helene sat with her knickers in her handbag and her skirt hitched up over her bottom, her buttocks sticking to the plastic of the seat. Apologising profusely and hardly able to tear his eyes away from her crotch, he cleared up the debris and went back into the cafe to replace the drinks. Marie-Helene smiled in a self-satisfied sort of way and I was pleased that she'd not baulked at obeying my command in such an open environment.

The waiter returned with fresh drinks and as he set them down on the table, I told her that the view wasn't good enough, I wanted to see more.

"Bring your feet up on to your chair," I ordered, "and open your legs... wide."

She did as I bid, exposing all of her sex, the delicious black pubes and slightly open lips of her vagina arousing me even further. The waiter wasn't slow in following my example and made an immediate marquee out of his pants, but I wasn't going to share her this time, I'd been waiting too long.

"M'sieu," I said, "do you have somewhere private where Madame and myself could spend a little time?"

He said that yes, he had, but I needed a key for the door.

"In that case, M'sieu," I said, "please bring out the key."

It turned out to be a fair sized room set into the side of the building, whose main purpose seemed to be that of a storage area for cleaning implements and the like. It also doubled as the cafe's toilet. The W.C. itself had been plonked up against the far wall and the door opened directly opposite the standing stone. I didn't lock the door but left it wide open as I ordered Marie-Helene inside and rooted around in search of a suitable implement with which to administer a thrashing.

A heap of building materials lay piled in one corner and delving amongst the bags of sand and plaster, I pulled out a bundle of bamboo canes of the type and size usually to be found supporting shrubs or suchlike in plant pots or gardens. Breaking it apart, I sorted through the bundle until I found a cane, that after weighing in my palm for balance and density, seemed eminently suitable for my purpose.

I turned her around to face me and she stood staring at both myself and the cane in nervous anticipation. She had to make amends and she knew it. Not only that, there was a lascivious, hungry look in her eyes that sparked turmoil in my own surging senses. She'd been waiting for something like this. Looking back on it now, I'm certain that if I hadn't asserted my authority at that time, future events may well have progressed very differently.

"Take off your shirt," I ordered.

She responded to my instruction without question, those wonderful breasts falling free once more, her huge nipples hardening and their colour changing from pink to fiery red and on down through the spectrum until they stabilised at the shade of burnt oak. I told her to pull her skirt even higher, which she did until the whole flatness of her stomach was exposed above the forest of her silky bristles, the skirt now nothing but a crushed ring of cloth around her waist. Transferring the bamboo to my left hand, I advanced on her until I was within striking distance, when I smacked her with the full force of my right, open palm on both legs, reddening the tender flesh of her inner thighs. She started leaking love juice there and then and when I twisted her back around, raining blow after blow upon her sumptuous backside the floodgates opened. She'd obviously been lusting for it as much as I had. When I'd finished, the flaring imprints of my palms covered both buttocks, and she was breathing in that spasmodic, intermittent fashion that denotes the onset of arousal.

I glanced back outside and sure enough, just as I knew he would be, the waiter was doing a Peeping Tom, trying to keep out of sight behind the standing stone.

"We've got company," I said.

Twisting to peer over my shoulder Marie-Helene caught a glimpse of him too. A little shiver ran through her body, I think by then she was beginning to find the idea of someone catching her being disciplined in a public place somewhat exciting. Making her bend over and support herself by placing her palms on either side of the toilet seat I took a few steps back in order to admire the scenery. Her qualifications amazed me just as much then as they did on that first night. Her legs were shaped in Heaven, her savaged bottom was a work of art and her vagina was solid gold serviceable sex. I fought a frantic battle with my penis to stop myself plunging into that love nest there and then. I was aroused and throbbing, but I was taking things too quickly, and determined that I would hold myself in check until she'd been punished enough to feel pain that was the equivalent to the level of my previous few days' frustration.

"Stand up straight and turn around," I ordered.

There was a puzzled look in her eyes as she stood facing me.

"You've been an insolent, ungrateful harlot," I said. "On this trip, the days were yours to use in pursuit of your business, but the nights were to be mine."

She'd failed to honour our agreement and must be punished, in full and total retribution for the shaming lack of respect she'd shown to me.

"Isn't that so?" I questioned.

"Yes," she muttered.

In a flash I smacked her hard across her cheeks.

"WHAT?" I roared.

"Yes master," she gasped in shocked tones, tears once more welling up in her eyes.

"And no snivelling," I said, "you cry too easily, worse than a baby, you must learn to take your punishment like the adult you're supposed to be."

I gave her a few seconds to recover some semblance of

composure, and then with the cane now clasped in my right hand, I leant forward and squeezed the giant bud of her left nipple firmly between my thumb and forefinger. All the guitar playing had strengthened my fingers and given me the grip of a vice, so it hurt like the devil. I knew that, before even seeing the confirmation written on her grimacing features. Intensifying my crushing clasp on her nugget, I watched carefully for signs of a reaction until she began to squirm in a sort of delicious appreciation of the pain, then stepping backwards and releasing my grip, I rained a series of strokes across her right breast. A runway of narrow parallel lacerations cut into her flesh as air rushed in and out of her lungs in painful gasps. She bit hard on her lip, savouring the punishment, while striving to obey my orders in respect of not showing weakness as I gave her other breast equal treatment.

I fastened my grip firmly back onto one nipple, slipping my free hand under her crotch and was welcomed by a satisfyingly drenched, red-hot vulva that threatened to snatch my probing fingers deep into its lusting lips. Rolling my wrist close up to her sodden sex I widened the gap between the top of her legs and in response I could feel the nub of her clitoris forcing its way out of its hood and through her ever slackening labia. Removing my hand I raised the cane once again, but instead of striking between her thighs as she was now expecting, I laid it deliberately, but firmly across her rib cage, incising the tender underbellies of her breasts at the same time. She drew in an agonised gasp, and then another, and another as the knotted wood landed firstly, fully across her abdomen in the region of her navel, and then lower down over her pelvic area just above her sprouting thatch. When I'd done she was decorated over the whole front of her body, from breast to vulva with thin raised stripes. I was satisfied.

She was too.

"Now, Madame," I asked her, knowing full well that pain

had the same narcotic effect on her as Spanish fly, "are you truly sorry for your infamous conduct?"

It took her a few moments to gather herself together sufficiently to make a coherent response.

It wasn't agony that delayed her reply.

"Yes Master," she finally managed to reply in a broken sob. .

"Not good enough!" I yelled, although in reality, I was overwhelmed by the carnality she'd injected into those two simple words.

The cane flicked into the archway beneath her pudenda; stinging her vulva and exacting a reaction that was part torture, part ecstasy. This time she screamed aloud and clasping her injured sex pleaded for mercy.

"Take your hands away," I commanded, and the instant she did so I flicked at her pulsing vagina again, immediately dealing out the same treatment to her inner thighs.

"No more, no more Master, please," she begged, "I'm your servant, your slave, I'll never disobey your wishes ever again."

And with that she rushed forward, flung her arms around my neck and sobbed desperately on my shoulder.

"I must have you now," she cried, "now, before I go insane."

Her boobs crushed into my chest, her pussy ground against my pulsating staff and much as I disapproved of the inexcusable forwardness of her action, I was driven over the top myself. Gathering her up in my arms, I carried her out through the doorway, and with her clinging fiercely to me I scooped up one of the wide cafe chairs that were stacked alongside the wall outside. I stomped over to the scrub surrounding the megalith and threw the chair down. The action had been so swift that the waiter was caught unprepared, with a throbbing erection clasped in his hands. He made a hurried attempt to camouflage it and hustle away, but I didn't care.

"M'sieu," I called out to him, "don't leave on my account, enjoy the cabaret."

He stopped, eyeing me in wonder, his penis now revealed as a very serviceable implement. Fleetingly I toyed with the idea of allowing Marie-Helene the pleasure of its company but dismissed the idea in a trice, my own shaft being in dire need of attention, and she herself feverish with desire. I dropped her bottom down onto the hard plastic seat and unleashed my own desperately rampant weapon from its cage. I wasn't shamed by the garcon in any way, my passions were raging and judging by its impressive girth my dick could have been injected with growth hormone.

I tugged her bottom to the edge of the seat so that her vagina was clear of the plastic and her back was as flat as possible. Lifting her legs to guide them over my shoulders, I slipped my palms under her buttocks, raising her backside for easier access, and with her swimming, beaten orifice driving me to distraction, I plunged deep into the well. This was another of those greedy, urgent acts of intercourse, I went at it like a stag in the rutting season and Marie-Helene was only too thankful that I did. She was up and coming before my staff was less than half way on its journey up to her cervix and her vaginal muscles, clamping, sucking and rippling, helped to power its assault on her womb. Once I was fully in I drove up and down her slippery passage with increasing fury, all the time feeling a giant spasm building up in her clutching sheath until shaking, writhing and gasping for breath she exploded in a volcanic orgasm. Her convulsions triggered my own climax and wave after wave of steaming seed surged up my pipe, jetting into her cavity with all the force of a fireman's hose. The resulting lake of my sperm and her love juice filled her well to overflowing; sending rivers of delicious sticky ejaculates flooding down her legs and drenching my own equipment.

Withdrawing my slackening member I glimpsed the waiter. It seemed he'd kept pace with us for he was masturbating furiously, a great gout of solid sperm arching on to the stone; maybe that's what they mean by fertility rites. As his last tremor subsided he reddened in embarrassment, and attempting with great difficulty to sheath his still rampant dick, he threw me an imploring look, as if seeking absolution from a sin.

"M'sieu," I called to him, "I think our little exhibition deserves a drink on the house, n'est ce pas?"

Well of course it did, three or four as a matter of fact, and when we waved goodbye a couple of hours later I thought that, just like Thierry, we'd given another frustrated Breton a day to remember.

## FOUR

Marie-Helene was obliged to complete the tour of inspection dressed in an all-enveloping outfit, a long skirt hanging to her ankles and a tightly buttoned jacket obscuring the wounds to her upper body. When we were finally free of commercial and physical limitations, the weather changed to its usual hurricane intensity and we holed ourselves up in the cottage. I can't pretend I didn't enjoy those days and nights, sheltering behind protective doors, the rain smashing against the closed shutters as we ran the gamut of acceptable perversions. Marie-Helene knew more than I could ever dream of, and when I floundered in search of new horizons, she guided me into pastures new, but with never a trace of condescension because now I most definitely was her master and she was eager to prove herself pliable to my will.

After the weather cleared, one fine morning I was sat on the cliff top with my guitar, trying to finish writing a song that had been running around in my head for days, when she came dashing from the cottage, obviously dying to tell me something. She'd just heard, on the radio, about a concert that was taking place that night and although she wouldn't tell me who was performing or where it was being staged, she desperately wanted to go.

"Can we go, please oh please?" she begged.

Well, if she wanted it that much, I was agreeable, it would make a change if nothing else. I asked her again who was on, but she said it was a surprise and I assumed she didn't want to tell me because it was probably Sacha Distel or maybe something even worse. I dressed myself in jeans and a leather jacket, breathing a sigh of relief when she made no comment on my attire; obviously we weren't about to finish up at some stuffed shirt recital. It was a balmy day and we were out for pleasure and not business, so we took the Ferrari. Marie-Helene asked if she could drive, because she said it would make the surprise more complete if I didn't know where we were going. I was quite happy with that provided that she drove with all her finery on view, and as we set off, without any knickers and her skirt pulled up under her bottom so that her buttocks and vagina pushed down into the leather of the seat, she made an alluring spectacle, her thick bush, thighs, stockings and suspenders merging into an enticing melange of inviting sexuality.

We swept up the steep hill leading into La Clart' and as we hurtled around the sharp bend at the apex of the headland I was absolutely staggered by the view over the Cote de Granit Ros'. I shouted at her to stop and the brakes must have been white hot as we screamed to a halt amid a cloud of smoke. Cars were parked haphazardly along the length of the curve and a small crowd stood taking in the amazing sight, so quite a few other people had obviously had the same first impression as me. Instructing her to stay put I got out of the car for a better look, and when I turned to return to the car I was greeted with much the same sight that had intrigued Thierry in that country lane, because most of the men seemed to have lost interest in the pink rocks and were now ogling the pink of Marie-Helene's private parts, at the same time attempting to placate their womenfolk with the feeble excuse that it was the Ferrari they were admiring.

I vaulted back into the passenger seat and she raced off again, for the next couple of hours or so passing through what was then unfamiliar territory to me, and with her foot flat to the boards we hurtled on until we came to the bay of Mont St. Michel. As we followed the sweep of the bay, the silhouette of the abbey grew increasingly large, until in full view I understood why they call it the marvel of the occident. Slowing down to traverse the causeway, we finally came to a halt close to the only entrance to the inside of the walls. Backed up to the wall, in what's now a car park, a large stage had been erected with, what for the day, was an enormous sound system. Being early for the show, we had time for a bite to eat and a drink and we were soon sitting outside a bar with a dozen oysters each and a bottle of Muscadet in front of us.

"Good for the sex drive," she told me, not that with her I needed any outside assistance to bolster my performance.

The narrow street was thronged with what looked like refugees from the Thin Lizzy fan club, all spandex trousers, leather jackets and chains, so I began to feel a lot better about the show she'd brought me to see. I went inside to use the toilet only to be greeted almost immediately with gleeful shouts of recognition.

"Olly, you great big beautiful bastard, what are you doing here?"

I'd have known that voice anywhere; it was Jet, the singer with my old band. I looked into the gloom, and sure enough there he was leaping to his feet, together with Bugs and Ajax, the other two guys in the band. We'd always got on well together but they were all over me, it was like the second coming of Christ and I soon found out why. Since the last time I'd seen them they'd got pretty big on the continent and were second on the bill at the concert, which was Marie-Helene's big secret, but they'd had a giant bust up with the new lead guitarist and he'd stormed off back to England, leaving them in the lurch. I knew most of their material, Jet had a spare Gibson and so I did the gig. We went down a storm, the top band got totally blown away, we were absolute megastars and Marie-Helene was over the moon because not only was I her master but now I was a celebrity in my own right.

After the show, the lads calmed down enough to give a thought to other things beside getting through the gig and when they finally got round to giving Marie-Helene an in-depth once over, they were gob-smacked. They'd been through a schoolful of girls between them, but none of them had ever even met a classy, sophisticated woman like her and needless to say there were lots of ribald, but envious, comments as we helped the roadies pack the gear. Marie-Helene sat as I'd secretly told her to do, with her legs open enough to display her charms, on a big bass speaker cabinet watching the activity. I can't impress upon you enough what an absolutely glorious woman she was and as we gradually cleared the stage and got closer and closer to her the other guys were working themselves up into a lather. Jet lifted the top cabinet off his Marshall stack which was right next to the one Marie-Helene was sitting on.

"Jesus, what I couldn't do to that," he muttered under his breath, but not quietly enough so that she and I couldn't hear him.

"That's not a very respectful way to talk about my property," I said, "But play your cards right and you might get the chance."

His mouth dropped open "What do you mean, your property?" he gasped.

I told him, and the others, I meant exactly what I said, she was mine to do with as I wished, I owned her body and soul.

"If I decide to share her with you, she'll do exactly as I say, but she's a sophisticated woman, not one of your back street scrubbers and she's got decidedly esoteric tastes, so you'd have to conduct yourself in a proper manner."

Marie-Helene needed to be dominated, to be disciplined, to feel pain and humiliation I told them and, in return, they told me in no uncertain terms that I must have gone loopy. The two roadies, whilst trying to tune into the conversation, were nevertheless still packing gear and I went over to them, gave them a wad of notes and told them to clear off for a couple of hours. All the main lighting had been dismantled, the stage was in relative darkness and the site was deserted apart from ourselves, the crowds having either left or gone into the town for a knees up.

"Come here," I ordered.

She obediently slid off the cabinet, walked straight over and stood meekly in front of me.

"Take off your blouse," I told her. She concurred immediately, slowly unfastening the remaining closed buttons, and slipping the garment from her shoulders, her perfect orbs fell free. Jet and the lads were agog.

"Now, the skirt," I said.

Reaching around to the back of her waist, she unhooked the skirt and wriggled it down over her silky thighs. As it cleared her stocking tops I took a look around and was pleased to see obvious reactions inside all three pairs of jeans; include my own and it made four.

"And the knickers."

That was my final command and once again there she stood, the way I liked to see her best, naked apart from the stockings and high heels.

"Look, but don't touch," I told the band, leaving them inspecting her as minutely as an organism under a microscope whilst I rooted around the stage. There's a lot of interesting gear amongst all the paraphernalia a band carts around with them and I soon came up with a pretty novel idea of how to make use of some of it. Picking up a full reel of broad gaffa tape I went back over to Marie-Helene and taking her firmly by the hand, lead her over to the side of the stage where the scaffolding that had held the lighting rigs was still erected. I told Ajax and Bugs to bring over the long flight case holding all the microphone stands and snapping the lid shut, helped them to push the box up to the base of the scaffolding.

"Get up on there and stand with your back to me with your legs apart," I told her.

She did as I bid, clambering up on to the top of the aluminium case.

"Now, stretch your arms," I ordered, "and keep them there."

I started with her feet, pushing her legs apart to their widest limit and tearing off several long strips of gaffa, I taped firstly one ankle and then the other securely to the scaffolding, taking my time to ensure she endured maximum discomfort to her aching arms. She didn't say a word but I could see her triceps twitching and her arms trembling so I knew she was having to fight the pain. When I considered she'd had enough, I followed the same procedure as with her ankles and taped both her wrists to the scaffold, until finally with the lads' help I pulled the flight case out from underneath her feet, leaving her suspended above the stage.

Now we were ready.

Jet had a broad hand tooled leather guitar strap which I told him to get, together with one of the heavy duty guitar leads he and Bugs both used. Ajax being the drummer had some useful implements on hand, namely his sticks and being a powerful drummer he used the heaviest sticks he could find. So I asked him to give me a pair.

I ran my palm between Marie-Helen's thighs, rubbing along the length of her sex, finding it already damp and expectant. Taking one of the sticks, thickest end uppermost, I thrust it straight up into the depths of her vagina, and after pumping it up and down several times, I left most of it inside her with just several inches sticking out. There was no doubt she'd felt that alright, and when I took the second stick and introduced it into her protesting anus she yelped out loud, wriggling uncomfortably. The guys were stunned, but they were thrown even more when I said it was now their turn.

"You go first," I told Bugs, "give her three lashes anywhere you want."

He was a bit doubtful to say the least, very concerned that he might hurt her.

"She needs to feel the pain," I told him once again, "and the domination. It heightens her passion."

His bulging jeans told me he was well into it. But he was hesitant to strike her. .

"Look at it this way," I said, "in this particular instance she's not being punished, she's being rewarded, it's my little present to her for bringing us all back together."

With some further encouragement, he doubled the guitar lead, clasping the jack plugs firmly in his palm and swinging the rubberised core high, he whipped it down exactly on the spot where you'd expect somebody new to the experience to do so, on one of her buttocks. The cable cut through the air with a satisfying whoosh, a gasp rushing from her lips as it struck home, raising two separate, but distinct elongated U shaped weals. I told him to keep to the same half of her backside and give her two more lashes, and with mounting enthusiasm he did so, leaving a scattered pattern of six burning welts imprinted into her rump. Through the denim, his erection was frightening and he couldn't help but fondle himself as he stepped back to inspect the damage he'd wrought.

The lads couldn't see it, but between the winces, I caught the glow of satisfaction in her face. After giving her a few minutes to compose herself, I then considered who should go next. I plumped for Ajax, who was a big muscular lad. On my instruction he picked up a drumstick and whacked her across the opposite buttock to the one Bugs had abused, but there was no swish through the air this time, drum sticks being so thick and inflexible that unlike the thin stripe left by a cane, the stick made a broadish scarlet impression.

She screamed an almighty yelp of pain, so loud that even though the site was deserted I was afraid that someone might hear and come to investigate. Telling Ajax to hang on for a minute, I tugged the headband from around his forehead and fashioned it into a makeshift gag which I stuffed it into Marie-Helene's mouth. When I'd adjusted it and was certain she could no longer scream, but was able to breathe, I signalled him to carry on. He smacked down a second time, but despite the gag, she let out a muffled cry. I let her rest for a moment and then sanctioned the third strike and he gave her a mighty whack, but there was not even an attempted scream this time, instead she slumped into the scaffolding in a dead faint.

Marie-Helene was out cold for the time being, or so I thought, but when I took the gag from her mouth, she opened her eyes.

She wanted me, she told me. Urgently.

But I'd made a promise that I couldn't break, and adjourning to the truck, we broke open a case of Canterbrau the roadies thought they'd well hidden under a pile of covers. Stu, who was the brainier of the two donkeys, was some kind of electronic genius and in the back of the truck I discovered his latest weird idea. He'd brought along twenty twelve volt car batteries and on gigs he linked them together, in parallel, to produce a two hundred and forty volt output, so they could be used to power an emergency lighting system if the local venue didn't provide one. He's a total lunatic I thought, in absolute agreement with the others, as I joined them in the front of the truck. After a couple of beers I took a look back on stage and seeing Marie-Helene alert and waiting, I called them all back up.

"Your turn Jet," I said, "but leave her backside alone, she's had enough there for the time being."

I held him back just long enough to allow me to give the drumsticks protruding from both her orifices a few thrusts in and out. Nobody but me knew just how much she appreciated that action. His guitar strap was thick heavy leather with his name, Jet Morgan, embossed on the shiny surface and after turning one end around his palm he lashed her with the full length of the strap across her shoulder blades, raising a shudder but not a scream. He was treating her a trifle lightly I thought, although I made no comment. It seemed he caught my unspoken condemnation, striking her once more a little lower down her back, but this time with much more force so that the end of the strap curled around her front and lashed one of her by now enlarged and tender nipples. That certainly provoked a reaction and as the last lash landed across the full width of her rib cage, she gasped and convulsed in what seemed like genuine pain. But then again, through the gritted lips, I detected an undisguisable flash of satisfaction.

The guitar strap left wide swathes of red across her back with 'Jet Morgan' imprinted twice on her tortured flesh. One of her buttocks flared with the marks of the doubled guitar lead and the bruises on the other were threatening to spread and overlap. We couldn't progress any further until she'd endured punishment from me, her master, but it was very obvious that she wouldn't be able to take any further abuse in the thrashing department so I was left in somewhat of a dilemma as to my own course of action. She needed some respite in any case so we took a break back in the truck, to drink some more beer and calm our throbbing senses. Suddenly I had an idea, and grabbing a pair of jump leads from under the driver's seat, I told Jet to disconnect two of the batteries and bring them to me on stage. With help from Bugs and Ajax I ripped the tape from Marie-Helene's wrists and feet and turning her around, re-bound her to the scaffolding so that this time she was facing me.

Being intended for heavy duty use on a truck, the jump leads were hefty affairs with extra large steel crocodile clips fitted to each end. Separating the two leads, I disconnected the clips from one end of each one, leaving an exposed stretch of inner wire. Her nipples were so thoroughly erect by now that it was a simple job to wind the bare wires tightly around them. When Jet and Ajax dumped the two batteries down in front of me, after linking them together to double the power output, I fed the output through the rheostat the roadies had used to control the power to the lights. After clamping the crocodile clips to the battery terminals, I was ready. There wasn't an enormous amount of current and fed through a carefully adjusted rheostat, there was just enough to give her a jolt and gradually pushing up the power, I set her jerking involuntarily on the ends of the leads as I hit her with the electricity. She went rigid against her bonds as the current hit her time and again until she erupted into the most climactically gigantic orgasm I've ever witnessed letting out a prolonged howling ululation. I disconnected the battery in a hurry, scared that she was in danger of spasming into terminal sexual overload. Immediately her body relaxed and she sagged forward, gasping, but held tight to the scaffold by the tape. The guys stood open mouth and hard cocked as I unbound her nipples, whispering to her that it was now her turn to provide us with a similarly satisfying experience. Then, with the lads supporting her weight, I released her from her bonds and set her, staggering uncertainly, back on her high heels.

She took a chestful of deep breaths and gradually regaining her composure she straightened herself up, at the same time shaking her charcoal tresses back into their normal immaculate styling.

"I want you to pleasure us all at the same time," I told her, asking her if she had any ideas as to how she might manage that. After thinking it over for a moment or two, she whispered her solution to me, I thought she had a neat plan and taking her hand I led her to the centre of the stage.

"One of you is going to get a little more than the others," I said to the lads, "so you'd better toss a coin or something to settle who going to be the lucky fella."

Jet had a ten franc coin flicked high in the air before the others could blink an eye, and whether by devious methods or not, contrived to be the winner. They couldn't wait to get at it, they were like dogs around a bitch on heat but after I'd reminded them that Marie-Helene was a lady deserving respect, they managed to contain themselves a little. I fondled her bruised bottom, stroked her inflamed nipples, and finally after kissing her gently on the lips in encouragement I lay down on my back on the rough timbers of the stage, inviting Ajax and Bugs to come and lie full length on either side of me. Marie-Helene waited until they'd settled themselves, then set the ball rolling by setting herself over me, facing my feet, with legs astride my head. Keeping her mile long legs straight she bent over from the waist downwards, giving me a fabulous view of her tortured backside, her straggly dripping pubes and the still wide-open entrance to her vagina. She reached down, and practically ripping open the front of my jeans, freed my pulsating penis. I couldn't help myself, my own inflamed emotions got the better of me and grasping the fronts of her thighs I pulled myself up and sank my face into her soaking, aromatic sex, sucking her sticky vulva and tonguing her projecting clitoris, my nose sinking between her swollen lips. She allowed herself to enjoy this treatment for a short while, bending over even further to plunge her mouth over my throbbing shaft, but after several excruciatingly arousing strokes up and down its entire length she pulled off, and leaning back gently pushed me down to the floor.

"Master, is this not supposed to be for your friends too?" she said, "I think that perhaps you are forgetting them."

She was right, of course, so doing my utmost to suppress my ardour I sank back, allowing her to proceed unhindered. She shuffled forward and then squatting on her haunches she took my penis and guiding it to the gateway to her tunnel, she pushed down until it was buried deep inside her. It was like sliding into a jar of honey and as she finally settled the full weight of her buttocks on my hips I'm sure my bloated bell banged right up against her womb. She wriggled around in an effort to get more comfortable, driving me even crazier in the bargain, and then directed her attention to the guys lying beside me, who along with Jet, who was still standing, had been watching with salivating jaws and throbbing weapons.

Bugs was first in line and leaning over she tugged down the zip to his jeans and after wrestling with his almighty erection, released it from captivity, and after giving it a couple of admiring strokes, she turned to Ajax and repeated the exercise. Testing her plan, she took a pulsing dick in either hand, sliding her clenched fists up and down, whilst at the same time rotating her dripping hole around my own pulsating weapon. Then summoning Jet, she got down to the real nitty gritty.

She positioned him standing, facing her, with one foot on either side of my thighs and his bulging crotch in line with her lips. Letting go of Bugs and Ajax for the moment she slowly opened his jeans, he was shaking with anticipation and I worried that the sexual burn out I'd foreseen for Marie-Helene might overtake him. The moment his manhood was freed it sprang skyward, but hauling it back down she ran her tongue over his glans, flicking it from side to side until she suddenly tugged him forwards, sinking his pulsing penis into her welcoming mouth, his eyes widening as she gripped him tightly with her teeth. Now Jet no longer needed assistance from her hands, she returned them to their former positions on Bugs and Ajax and, after giving each of them an exploratory manipulation, launched into a full four way orgy of sexual adventure.

Juices were bubbling away inside her, flowing out over my own pubes as she very slowly lifted her bottom from its resting place on my stomach, their musky scent seemingly enveloping us all in a heady mist of raging pheromones. She worked her vagina up and down my lusting penis, her hands rising and falling at the same time in perfect synchronisation as she slid the foreskins of two other rampant organs back and forth over their bulbous purple bells, all the while her cheeks sucking and pulling on Jet's violently twitching member. I waited for an upstroke and sliding a hand under her stern thrust two fingers into her anus, increasing her own pleasure greatly. Gasping with delight she slammed her bottom downwards, clamping and unclamping her vaginal muscles until she almost drove me into a delirium. Increasing the length and speed of her strokes, both Bugs and Ajax writhed beneath her manipulating hands and Jet seemed to be disappearing whole into her throat.

It couldn't last long and in no time at all four thrashing, grunting sexual time bombs detonated into a quartet of thermo nuclear orgasms. On either side of me fountains of boiling sperm spurted feet into the air, Jet exploded into her mouth, the eye in my glans opened and stream after stream of my gushing seed pumped into her clutching, climaxing pussy. Gagging a little she swallowed her mouthful of Jet's sperm, and still clutching two softening shafts in her now very sticky hands she sank her fully sated sex back down on to my stomach. We stayed like that for some time, panting and trying to regain our senses until she finally released Bugs and Ajax from her grasp and pulled her lips back from Jet's expended weapon. Sperm was everywhere, in pools on the stage, dripping through her fingers, running down her jaw and as she lifted herself clear of me, my own seed hung from her puffy labials, falling in globules on to my shrinking manhood.

The lads now had something to talk about for years to come, but for the moment they seemed lost for words as I got to my feet and helped Marie-Helene to tidy herself up as best she could.

"That's the power of ownership," I told them. "It doesn't take a platinum credit card, wealth or fame, Marie-Helene is bound to me by my authority over her, she loves me more than life itself."

As if to demonstrate her acquiescence she melted into my arms as I gently enfolded her, kissing her long and sweetly.

FIVE

The lads had booked themselves into a couple of chalets at the motel on the approach road to Mont St. Michel and after the experience we'd given them, they were only too happy to hand one over to us, relegating the roadies to the truck for the night. After a good clean up and a change of clothing for Marie-Helene we went back up to the abbey and toured the bars, drinking far more than was good for us. We were recognised everywhere and feted like true superstars, bottle after bottle of champagne flowing down our necks and huge platters of shellfish appearing from nowhere. That night had been their last gig of the tour and they intended to spend the following couple of days actually seeing something of the country before heading home, but what was really occupying their thoughts was the forthcoming promotional trip to the States their record company had set up for them. They spent just about every second in between eating and drinking, trying to persuade me to rejoin the band full time and do the tour with them, but much as I would have liked to have gone to America, nothing was going to drag me away from Marie-Helene.

After coffee and croissants the following morning, and nursing giant hangovers, we travelled back up the coast with them to the medieval walled City of the Corsairs, St. Malo. Being the home port of the French slave trade I wanted to hang around and discover more of its history, but after nipping off to make a phone call, Marie-Helene came rushing back with the news that there'd been some sort of crisis at the Quiberon hotel and she had to get down there fast. We bade swift farewells to the lads and sped off.

We kept to the Ferrari as we could make better time, and stopped only to change into business clothes but it was still late evening before we got to Quiberon. When we arrived at the hotel she said there wasn't much that could be done that night and so, after settling our luggage into separate rooms, we adjourned to the bar and it wasn't long before I began to get some idea of what the problem might be. The bellhop whom I'd encountered on the previous occasion we were there, had been to the concert at Mont St. Michel and with a mixture of hero worship and scandal mongering, had been telling all and sundry that I was a guitar player, not a business executive and that he'd seen the owner of the hotel and myself, rolling from bar to bar, drunk and unable to keep our hands off each other. Marie-Helene had him sent for and as he entered the bar she sprang from her seat and in a restrained fury took him outside for the dressing down of a lifetime.

I'd noticed an immaculately dressed, distinguished looking middle aged man casting glances our way and as she left the room he came over and addressed me in a totally incomprehensible language, offering me a strange handshake that I wasn't able to properly reciprocate. Looking slightly puzzled he spoke to me again and once more I couldn't understand a word he was saying. A hard light came into his eye, he looked me up and down and started again, this time in French which of course I could understand, on my reply commenting that he could tell by my accent that I was British. Swapping to perfect cultured English he asked me a few seemingly inconsequential questions, such as how long I'd known Marie-Helene and after finally commenting on what a fine establishment she owned, he returned to his seat at the bar.

Marie-Helene herself, her eyes still flashing fire, came back into the room and as she passed his stool he gripped her arm, engaging her for several minutes in an intense conversation, no part of which I was able to hear. Her face drained into white as I watched and when he finally released her she crossed over to me almost in a daze. Of course I asked her straight away what was the matter, but she said it was a business problem, adding that she was very tired and it was time to turn in. There wasn't much point in me hanging around, so I went up to my room as well and I'd not been in there long before a valet came knocking on the door, asking for the evening clothes, Marie-Helene it appeared, had instructed him to collect them and have them pressed. It was only an hour or so later when there was another knock on the door and a messenger handed me a sealed envelope, containing a short, but to the point, note in her handwriting. It was all over, she wrote, and it would be for the better if I left the hotel immediately.

I ran out of my room just in time to see her disappearing into a lift with a young man of almost exactly my height and build, dressed in the white tuxedo. So that was it I thought, she'd already got a toy boy, she'd provided me with his clothes and I'd just been a plaything whilst he'd been away or something, in fact the mysterious man downstairs was probably his father and she'd been caught in the act. The lifts all seemed to be busy and so I raced down flight after flight of stairs intending to confront them, only to make the hotel lobby just as they were pulling away in a chauffeur driven limousine. That finished it for me, in a rage of fury and humiliation I grabbed my belongings from my room, jumped into the Ferrari and thrashed it back northwards, arriving at the ferry port of Roscoff just as the band's truck was about to drive on to the boat. I dumped the car on the quayside, ran to the truck and jumped in.

Needless to say I spent the next few months touring the States with the band, it was pretty gruelling but by the time we came home we were selling out good sized arenas and had an album in the U.S. charts. A mountain of mail was waiting for me, almost all of it bearing French postmarks and tearing them open I discovered that all but one of the letters was from a firm of lawyers in Quimper, asking me to get in touch with them urgently. The odd one out was typed, didn't have a signature and had an unfathomable message. It simply said: The mistake was regrettable, it was meant to be you. However you may now consider all scores settled. There will be no further action.'

What the hell did that mean? I hadn't got a clue, but when I phoned the lawyers I found an answer. Marie-Helene, together with her son, was dead. Their car had been forced off the road by an unidentified vehicle, careering over a clifftop into the sea. My thoughts turned straight away to the Brotherhood and the mystery man at the hotel, we'd all got it wrong it seemed. The Brotherhood had discovered our alliance—I'd been wearing those cuff links—and she was only trying to protect me when she'd told me to leave the hotel, the young man I'd suspected of being her lover was in fact her son who'd turned up unexpectedly, and at a later date, mistaking him for me, the organisation had eliminated them both. I didn't mention any of this to the lawyers, who urged me to go over and see them as soon as possible.

I hired a car the very next day, making it across the channel and to Quimper the same afternoon, and there I sat in the lawyer's office, unable to believe my ears. A few days before she'd met her demise, Marie-Helene had altered her will to include me; her entire empire was now to be divided between her two children and myself. Unfortunately her son had perished in the accident, so there were now just two beneficiaries, and opening a door into a connecting office the lawyer beckoned in my partner. I was thunderstruck, my jaw must have dropped to my feet, it was Marie-Helene, only twenty years younger. She had all the same gorgeous beauty and I fell for her immediately, my penis erupting into a lusting erection just as it had on my first sight of her mother. The lawyer couldn't see my predicament over the top of his desk but she had a clear view and she smiled enticingly as her tongue slid from her lips and ran across her delicately painted lips. Like mother, like daughter I prayed, crossed my fingers and made a wish.

Her name was Veronique and my wish seemed to come true because she took to me right away and resolving to run the empire together, we decided to start back at the hotel at Quiberon. I took the coastal road into the town, where on the trip with Marie-Helene I'd noticed a uniquely different World War Two German bunker. It stood about half a kilometre from the track, in rough open country overlooking the Atlantic, but it wasn't like any of the others, looking from a distance more like a submarine conning tower. I stopped the car and taking Veronique by the hand ushered her through the brambles to the tower, which when we got to it was indeed remarkably similar to that of a U-Boat, the only way in being via iron rungs running up its side. We clambered in through the open top and dropped inside to find it must have been some sort of command post, most of its interior being underground, but with observation slits all round at ground level letting in the light.

Veronique seemed to have no knowledge of the Brotherhood but I resolved to make sure, I didn't want to walk head first into more trouble. The bunker was well equipped with iron rings and grids bolted to the walls and luckily she shared more than looks with her mother. A couple of hours later when we emerged from the tower, she was dishevelled, sore and not a little bruised, but I'd found out what I wanted to know. Now I knew I was safe, there was no tattoo inside Veronique's vagina.

After his tale was ended, Oliver turned to me and said he supposed I'd like to know what actually happened inside the bunker. Did I? You bet I did.

"Ah, well," that's another story he said, although you might get it straight from the horse's mouth, if you're lucky."

He went on to tell me they were still together, twenty years later, in a strong relationship that had stood the test of time, and at that moment the door opened and in walked the most sensuous creature I've ever encountered. I had no idea how old she was, I thought thirty five, maybe forty, but whatever, she was one very tasty lady. My own weapon boggled and I flushed scarlet as it sprang into life, stretching my trousers to the limit. She couldn't help but notice, neither could Oliver and looking questioningly towards him, she received an immediate affirmative nod.

Taking my hand, she spoke in a voice as liquid as virgin olive oil.

"Perhaps you'd like to take a drink," she said, "and then we'll see if there isn't some way to resolve your little personal problem."

AFTERWORD
I have seen Oliver's cufflinks and the design exactly matches the one Lolli described. Against his advice I intend to research further.

# BRAT

*by Sean O'Kane*

It is very seldom that an author gets to meet a character from one of his own books, in the flesh.

'Taming the Brat' had all been written from Alan Masterson's accounts of his adventures with Laura Andreotti—the Brat—or just plain Brat—as she became known. But one night when I felt that I had had all I could take of staring at a monitor screen and had decided to pack up, I checked my e-mail before shutting down. There was a message from Alan inviting me to dinner the following evening, he felt that he might have someone new for me to interview at The Lodge. I hoped it was Madame because the truth was that I needed her. But I doubted that she was willing yet.

Kathy, my girlfriend, had proved quite amenable to having her backside warmed with my belt. The first time I had used it on her she had made a great show of outraged indignation and struggled furiously as I held her face down over my knees and gave her four or five vigorous smacks with it. I only used a fairly short length so there wasn't a great deal of force, but she had only just got used to being spanked as a prelude to sex and it came as a bit of a shock to her. When I let her up she flew at me, trying to claw at my face and calling me all sorts of names. We had quite a struggle which gradually resolved itself into a tussle of quite a different nature. She was half undressed to start with and the feel of her body pressed hard against mine, together with the memory of how deliciously her buttocks had rippled and wobbled under the leather of the belt, had their inevitable effect on me. I overpowered her very easily and held her wrists so that she couldn't do anything except writhe and wriggle against me. At last she ran out of insults and I bent to kiss her. She looked lovely with her face flushed and her long hair dishevelled, and even I was surprised by how eagerly she returned the kiss. Her lips were warm and soft and her tongue darted swiftly between my own lips. After some moments I let her wrists go and her arms went round me immediately, pressing me even closer to her body so that she could rub her pelvis against the straining bulge of my erection. When we at last pulled apart she gripped her hands hard in my hair.

"You bastard!" she whispered, before pulling me to her again.

From then on, although we hadn't spoken about it, a quick session with the belt had become a regular feature of our foreplay. I knew she was having trouble coming to terms with her own willingness to allow herself to be put over my knee and beaten, albeit lightly and I didn't feel that I could move on to anything more severe just yet. But I was determined that I would. I was certain that she would respond to more open domination but having decided that if she hadn't liked the belt I would have broken with her, now that she was on the path towards submissiveness I was anxious not to alienate her by going too fast.

I needed to speak to Madame, but I knew she wasn't ready to speak to me.

The following evening I rolled up at the address in Soho which Alan had given me and got the first shock of the evening. The maitre d' introduced himself as Henri once he knew I was meeting Alan and I suddenly realised I was in the restaurant where Laura had so embarrassed Alan when they first met. And it was the same restaurant to which they had returned for Brat to make amends for her behaviour as Laura.

He led me over to a small bar where I could enjoy a drink and wait for my host. A large Scotch was served on the house; Henri told me that he had strict instructions that I was not to pay for anything. As an impecunious writer I was not about to waste such hospitality and I was halfway through my second drink when I caught a whiff of expensive perfume and received the main shock of the evening.

A woman's voice at my side, speaking with a slight American accent ordered a glass of wine. I turned slightly and there she was.

There was no mistaking her.

The large sea-grey eyes, the glorious mane of blonde hair, the strong intelligent face, the perfect figure. It was all there, just as Alan had told me, and just as I had faithfully described it to the readers. I must have stared for quite a few seconds. Brat was indeed an exceptionally beautiful woman but I retained enough professional pride to realise that I had done a good job describing her. She smiled at me and the full reality of her suddenly burst over me. Not only did she exude the extraordinary allure that Alan had told me about, a kind of sexual energy which seemed to radiate from her, but also it dawned on me that here was the woman whose every beating, every humiliation and every sexual exploit I had written down, described in loving detail, and then published. I blushed to the roots of my hair.

"Mr O'Kane I presume." She said.

I nodded, still not able to trust my voice. I was riveted by her. She wore a simple short, sheath dress of deep blue. Spaghetti straps over her naked shoulders supported a low cut bodice which showed off to perfection the full swells of her breasts and a single large pearl on a thick gold chain hung at the start of her cleavage just in case the breasts themselves didn't draw the eye of the beholder adequately. The dress ended at mid-thigh with short splits on each side to allow for movement within the figure-hugging cut of the outfit. As she hoisted herself up onto her stool the dress rode up to a height which revealed an expanse of thigh with skin so smooth it seemed to have a sheen all of its own, without stockings being needed. And the dress rode up enough for me to be quite sure that she wasn't wearing any.

She took her time about settling herself and taking a sip

of her drink, and I realised that she was enjoying my discomfort. I simply didn't know what to say to someone who had stepped right out of my own pages, and who, within those pages had been revealed in every physical and mental detail for the delectation of my readers.

"You did quite a job Mr O'Kane," she said at last. "I read the book and it was pretty good. That's just about how it all happened."

"Thank you…er…Laura…Brat?"

"Brat," she said firmly. "I've got a letter here from my master, I've got to give it to you after dinner. He had to go abroad and asked me to meet you."

How very convenient, I thought. Now the initial shock of actually meeting her was wearing off I could see that there was something on her mind. I remembered how Alan had described Laura, before she became Brat, as frequently having a harsh, challenging air about her, and I thought I could detect something of that about her now. And what was Alan playing at? He had set me up, I was quite sure of that but to what end?

My thoughts were interrupted by Henri who came to tell us that our table was ready.

"Mr Masterson has reserved our private dining room for you both," he told us. "As I said you are not to pay for anything…especially not service." He glanced significantly at Brat. "Is that not so Brat?"

"Bet your ass Henri," she said and they both laughed.

We dined splendidly and in splendid isolation. Brat acted as waitress and I had to admit she had learned to do it very well, but we hardly exchanged a word as we ate. Apart from still having trouble coming to terms with her reality, I was also mesmerised by her body; the length and gracefulness of her legs, the curves of her buttocks under the tight silk of her dress and of course the expanse of breast flesh she revealed every time she bent to serve me. She was efficient but didn't give me the impression that she was enjoying herself. I wondered just how sternly Alan had had to order her here tonight, and what did he intend? At last, over coffee Brat seemed to reach some kind of decision.

"My master wanted me to make it plain that I was to serve you in any way you required," she said. I looked hard at her and she returned my stare levelly. So, I thought, was this yet another test? Was Alan setting me up to see whether I could command her? If he was then it was one test I was definitely going to pass. I could see how it would be very easy to feel intimidated by her overwhelming sex appeal and beauty, but my time at The Lodge had not been wasted.

As calmly as I could I sat back and continued to meet her gaze. "Then get over here Brat, I want to use your mouth," I told her.

She was sitting with her hands steepled under her chin, and was there just the hint of an approving nod before she pushed her chair back and came over to kneel between my spread knees? Her thick hair hid her face and hands from my view, but I could feel her fingers working expertly at my flies and soon her soft little tongue made tingling contact with the still engorging head of my member. She licked round the sheath of foreskin until I was fully erect and then I felt her lips slide slowly over my helm and her tongue explore the slit. Reaching down with both hands I pulled her hair back so that I could see as well as feel. Immediately she pulled her head back a little and put her tongue out so that I had a clear view of it lapping at the plum coloured helm and then trailing slowly down the shaft. She circled one hand round the base of my throbbing erection and gently moved it up and down while her mouth closed over me once again and she began to suck eagerly, moving her head from side to side as well as up and down, sometimes greedy sucking noises escaped her. Slowly she moved further and further down, taking in more and more of my shaft until I could feel the exquisite constriction of her throat around me. Convulsively I gripped my hands harder in her hair and pushed her head down while I bucked my hips up urgently at her. She never flinched, just stayed as she was and let the rod of my sex slide further down her throat. I pulled back and then thrust again, once more pulling her down onto me. Three more such thrusts and I felt the irresistible tides of my orgasm begin to flood. My penis tensed and swelled, Brat felt it and her hand gripped me tighter, moving up and down faster and faster. With a groan of pure delight I let my body take over completely and felt the sperm pump deep into her throat while I rammed her head down brutally hard. She took it all, swallowing long and slow while I thrust into her mouth and erupted time and again. It was a superb blow job, the best I had ever experienced and I spent a long time savouring every last discharge, Brat for her part kept me deep in her mouth and swirled her tongue around the slit from which my seed had splashed, making sure that she had got it all. At last she tucked my softening length back into my clothes and resumed her seat, running one elegant finger around her chin and then sucking it to gather in an errant drop of semen. Just watching her do that had me hardening again, but she reached into her bag and produced the promised letter for me. It was in Alan's handwriting and addressed to me; in it he explained that he had been called abroad at short notice. I was still suspicious but read on. 'I had planned to take Brat down to The Lodge this weekend, but can you do the honours instead? I've contacted John and he's okay about it. You'll be a sort of honorary, short stay member, everyone's very pleased with you and Falconer, so relax and enjoy! I've been busy recently so Brat may be feeling a bit left out of things. She likes a lot of attention.'

When I had read it, my pulse racing at the thought of a weekend as a member of The Lodge—and with Brat at my disposal, I told her the main drift of the contents.

"I figured," she said. "I'm staying at the penthouse so you can pick me up there."

So quickly had she switched from obedient submissive to rich and commanding heiress that I was nearly caught napping.

"Right. Be ready for ten tomorrow morning." I managed to snap back.

"Sure." She smiled an annoyingly secretive little smile and stood up to leave.

The next morning I took the lift up to Alan's penthouse dead on time. I hadn't got much sleep after dropping Brat off back there the previous night. I had read Alan's note again and again and replayed the evening's events in my mind. It seemed as though from the first time I had set foot in The Lodge I had undergone a series of tests. And this looked like it was another one, but the potential for pleasure this time was enormous. There was really only one thing to do; relax, go with the flow and just see what transpired.

Brat was waiting for me in the white room. This was the gymnasium-like room which Alan had set up in which to indulge his and his women's tastes. Brat and the girls in the office were its usual guests. She was leaning casually against a thick stake of smoothly polished wood, which rose to a height of about eight feet. Chains and rings hung from its top. It was, I knew, one of Alan's favourite whipping posts. I couldn't help wondering if she had deliberately posed against it, after all she must have enjoyed many a good thrashing while chained naked to it. And yet here she was fully clothed and quite unconcerned by the touch of that same wood. When she saw me she gave a lazy sort of smile, pushed herself away from the post and sauntered towards me, her heels clicking on the plain, polished wood floor. She brushed casually past other chains which hung from the ceiling and, in a gesture which was surely calculated to excite me, she stepped over a whipping stool and allowed her short skirt to ride up the long thighs as she did so.

I realised that she was making a statement. She was a proud and willing submissive, quite at ease in the room where her master took his pleasure with her. But now her master had turned her over to another man, and she wanted that man to be in no doubt as to what she was and what she was used to.

There was no mistaking the cool challenge in her eyes that morning. I had to retain my composure at all costs, treat all this as completely normal. If I gave in to my overwhelming lust for her or looked in any way flustered or uncertain, I would earn her contempt.

"Come on or we'll be late," I managed before turning on my heel and preceding her back to the lift.

For most of the way we drove in silence. Brat had looked round my car disdainfully when she had taken her seat but had not commented on its shortcomings compared to Alan's Bentley. It was she who broke the silence in the end.

"Going down to The Lodge always gets me horny. My master usually lets me jack off, any objections?"

"No, go ahead," I replied as calmly as I could.

She squirmed around for a few seconds, tried to get one long leg up onto the dashboard and gave up.

"Look, no offence Mr O'Kane, but it is kind of cramped in here. Can you stop off somewhere quiet and I'll do it outside."

I shrugged casually and began to take small side turnings until at last we found a narrow road which ran alongside some woods. There was a pull-off into some kind of forestry track and I took that, stopping a few yards along when we were out of sight of the road.

"Thanks," Brat said. "Do you want to watch?"

"If it's going to be a good show, then okay, I'll watch." Somehow I kept my voice under control while my mind filled with images of that glorious body being openly displayed in the act of onanistic pleasure.

"Oh I think you'll like it," Brat replied with a chuckle and got out of the car. She had taken her jacket off during the drive and was wearing only a light pullover with the mini skirt. I watched her hips and buttocks sway as she walked a little way in front of the car and then turned to face it with her back against a large tree. In one breathtaking movement she reached down to the hem of the skirt with both hands and worked it up until it was bunched at her hips. She hadn't bothered with any knickers and as she settled her legs well apart my eyes drank in the sight of the long, well-muscled line of her thighs leading up to the tight fleece of blonde curls at their junction. She ran her hands up and down the fronts of her thighs, letting me feast my eyes on her, then the hands moved to rub up and down the inner thighs. I could see her fingernails leave faint white traces on the soft skin as she teased herself. Gradually each rub up the thighs went higher and higher until her hands cupped her labia and her fingers trailed along the length of their crease. She tilted her pelvis forward as she did so, so that I could get a good view of their plump perfection. At first she made no attempt to part the lips and I could just imagine her nails scraping lightly along the soft and eager flesh but then suddenly she pressed harder and ran her hands back towards the other crease, her buttock crease and then pulled them forward again. This time she bucked her hips as the fingers separated the labia and ran forward along the pink inner flesh of her vulva. When they got right to the front she pulled her labia up and apart so that I could clearly see the convolutions of her soft inner lips and the clitoral hood. I tore my gaze away momentarily and looked at her face. Her eyes were closed and she was lost in her own world of pleasure, part of which I realised lay in knowing that she was being watched. Suddenly I recalled Alan telling me how keen she had been on masturbating, even when she had only just begun to be tamed.

I looked back down and now the fingers of one hand were delving deep up into her vagina while the spread fingers of the other held her lips open and rubbed at her clitoris. Her hips undulated and rotated more and more urgently, her head came forward so that she could watch her fingers at work. They moved faster and faster, I couldn't see how many she had managed to get up her but suddenly her head went back and she let out a cry which rang through the woods. Her body locked rigid for a second and then thrust against her hands which were now clenched hard on her sex flesh, a series of short stabbing spasms followed and then she slumped against the tree, spent and satisfied for the moment.

She stayed motionless for a while before straightening up and running one hand through her thick hair, tossing it casually back and shaking her head to settle it. Then she bent and retrieved her bag to take out a tissue and wipe herself before lowering her skirt and returning to the car. She slipped back into her seat as if nothing had happened and I played along; making no comment but just turning the car and continuing the journey. The only difference now was that over-laying the scent of her perfume was the spicy trace of the juices which had lubricated her.

When we rejoined the main road we found ourselves only a few miles from The Lodge and quite soon we had driven down the long drive, parked up and were standing in the main hall. But this time I was here as a guest rather than as a writer.

A pretty brunette was seated behind the reception desk but before I could approach her, Madame came out of the lounge and greeted us.

She was dressed in her usual simple style but as ever her natural height was emphasised by the high-heeled boots.

"Ah, Mr O'Kane," she said. "A pleasure to welcome you once again."

She flashed her brief smile at me and we locked gazes while shaking hands. I flattered myself that while she might not like or trust me yet, there was just slightly more respect in her manner than before. But then she turned to Brat and I was surprised by the sudden coldness in her manner. She made no attempt to greet her but reached out and took Brat's chin between finger and thumb, staring hard at her.

"You look flushed child. Did Mr O'Kane take his pleasure with you on the way down or did you... I wonder... did you ask him for permission to indulge in your habit of frigging yourself at every opportunity?"

Brat shifted uncomfortably under the relentless stare from Madame's dark eyes, but made no reply. The finger and thumb clamped into a vice-tight grip. Brat tried to cry out but suddenly Madame's free hand darted out and shot up Brat's skirt. It was done so fast that she never had time to try and avoid it. In a fraction of a second she was pinned by Madame's hands at both ends. I watched as Brat balanced on tiptoes, her hands pawing vainly at Madame's steel-hard grip on her face while the Russian woman's other hand explored between her legs.

Just as suddenly as she'd seized her, Madame released her. Brat staggered a bit and massaged her face. Madame lifted her fingers to her nose and smiled grimly.

"Your master would not have allowed that Brat, you little slut. What did you tell Mr O'Kane?"

Brat looked down sullenly and made no reply. Again with blinding speed Madame's hand shot out and delivered a stinging blow to Brat's cheek which made her stagger again.

"Answer me!"

"I told him he let me," she muttered.

Madame turned to me. "To my mind this little minx was never properly trained. She needs thrashing nearly every day. But her master is too much in love I think. However, you are not—so don't be fooled."

She turned on her heel and left. I was furious beyond words at this humiliation in front of the woman whose respect, above everyone else's at The Lodge, I wanted to gain.

I glared at Brat. She tossed her head back proudly and stared at me defiantly. Madame was right, as far as I could see Laura was back, sullen and rebellious. Maybe Alan had indeed tamed her, but in his absence she still seemed capable of setting her own terms. Well, Alan wasn't here; I was and he'd given her to me for the weekend. So be it, even if I wasn't a full member of The Lodge, I could damn well behave like one.

I turned to the girl at reception.

"Give me my room disc," I told her curtly.

She pushed it over with a trembling hand, her breasts rising and falling with her nervous breathing. Madame ruled all the girls with an absolute authority, and although they worshipped her, her anger—even if not directed at them personally—inspired terror. I took the disc and flung it at Brat so hard that she had no chance of catching it.

"That's another punishment I owe you," I told her as she bent to retrieve it. "Put it on and keep it on till I tell you different."

She did as she was told, avoiding my eyes. "Now go and get changed and get to work!" I snapped again. She left the hall via one of the doors at the back to make her way to the girls' dormitories. I turned back to the girl on reception duty and leaned over the desk to reach into the low-cut bodice of the satin uniform she wore. I grasped a warm handful of breast and pulled her roughly to her feet, she gasped a little as I yanked on her breast again to pull her closer.

"I want her in harness straight after breakfast tomorrow and the next day, understand?" I tweaked hard on the rubbery nipple.

"Yes Master! I'll see to it!" she squeaked, and I released her.

I stormed up to my room still furious with Brat and everyone else. Maybe it wasn't just Alan or Brat who had thrown down some kind of gauntlet, maybe the whole of The Lodge had. Perhaps I was just 'one of those writer chaps' who couldn't bring themselves to chastise a willing submissive; and they would let the girls have some fun with him.

I calmed down a bit by going for a swim and then sweating in the sauna before dressing for dinner. In the dining room Brat was on waitress duty, dressed in a scarlet gown and looking at her best. Even amongst the group of beautiful girls she was working with, she stood out. I heard several of the men comment on their disappointment that she was already booked for the night. I saw Brat frequently glance over towards me when she told them who had reserved her and there were some raised eyebrows and meaningful glances exchanged. My determination to have my revenge on Brat grew in proportion to my paranoia and I hardly tasted the superb meal she served me.

At last Brat brought my coffee and as she bent to place it in front of me, I reached round behind her and found the hidden slit at the back of her gown. I plunged my hand into it and felt the soft warmth of her thighs just below the buttocks, but they were too closely pressed together to allow me to reach between them.

"Open them," I told her.

"It's against the rules!" she protested.

I knew perfectly well it was, technically, but I also knew that she and all the other waitresses would have been fondled and probed throughout the meal.

"Don't give me that. Do as you're told!"

She opened for me and I was able to slip my fingers along her sex and put my forefinger up into her vagina. She was rather dry and tight and I had to work on her for a while, rubbing hard at her clitoris until I felt it begin to harden and then getting two fingers up and twisting them before she began to respond and I felt the vaginal channel moisten. I looked up at her face. She was glancing round nervously to see if Yuri or Ivan were about, but I took my time and had an effect as well. Brat's breathing was noticeably deeper, her face was flushed and her labia were engorged and soft beneath my fingers. I gripped them hard and squeezed. Brat gasped and jerked upright.

"You like the whip Brat," I deliberately made it a plain statement of fact. She whimpered and looked round again, either for help or retribution, but there was none of either. I increased the pressure.

"Yes! Yes!" she panted quickly, "I like my master... masters to whip me."

"Good, then you're in for a treat tonight."

I released her and sat back. She took a breath and recovered her composure then looked down at me, for the first time a little nervously.

"Whatever you say master."

Before I dismissed her I told her I wanted her to go to the common room when she had finished her domestic duties. I could see that that surprised her. She was probably thinking that I would be so desperate to have her that I would order her to my room, take her and then release her for the other guests. And under their more experienced hands she could enjoy herself. She left my table without a word.

I didn't hurry up to the common room, I knew it would be an hour or so before her domestic duties were finished and I wanted to savour the experience of The Lodge. I went to the bar and was served by a charming girl who could well have been the Marietta who Alan described in 'Taming the Brat'. She had the slender figure, jet-black hair and pale skin alright, and was certainly very responsive. As soon as my hand found its way into her dress she opened her legs and allowed me to roam freely. In contrast to the resentful Brat in the dining room, this girl moistened at almost the first touch, and squirmed in delight when I felt her clitoris and ran the tip of a finger round its thrusting little peak. Reluctantly I let her go as I could see that there were other members waiting to be served.

In fact there were four girls serving in the bar and they were almost constantly handled and fondled, not just under their dresses but also their breasts were frequently stroked and sometimes pulled clear of the bodices for caressing and teasing. It was all done quite casually and the girls kept their pleasure under control so as not to interfere with their duties, although after a while I could see that the repeated handling was having its effect and little moans and gasps began to accompany the fondling. Eventually, just as I was wondering why the rule about not interfering with girls on domestic duties was even bothered with, Ivan strolled by. One rather chubby little blonde had a guest's hand right up her and was having real trouble controlling her pleasure at being so casually handled while he ignored her and talked to his friends.

Immediately he saw her, Ivan unslung the multi thonged whip which hung from his belt and approached the group. The man removed his hand from the girl's skirt and she stood back, looking nervous.

"Just give her ten please Ivan. I'll have her for the night anyway," the man said. Ivan favoured him with one of his rare smiles while the girl reached behind her and, using the slit pulled her dress round to the front of her thighs and bunched it there. Then she bent over the arms of one of the chairs beside the group, offering pale but ample buttocks and thighs to the whip.

And while the men drank and talked, commenting on how charmingly the plump flesh rippled under the lashing and how the girl confined herself to soft gasps and cries, Ivan laid on the ten strokes. I could see that he wasn't using anything like the full extent of his awesome strength; he was plying the whip just to make an enjoyable spectacle and leave a pleasing pattern of criss-crossing welts on the soft skin. As soon as he had carried out the sentence he left. The girl stood up and adjusted her dress, looking flushed and excited while the man whose handling of her had resulted in her flogging took a bank note from his wallet and stuffed it into her cleavage. She bobbed a little curtsy, thanked him and resumed her duties.

I could see how it worked now. Madame didn't want her

domestic routines too badly disrupted by the girls being put to hard use too soon. But John wanted them available enough to provide an hors d'oeuvre for later activities. So the official disapproval made the casual handling of the girls a forbidden, and therefore greater pleasure all round. A judicious whipping provided enjoyable punishment for any girl caught being handled, but didn't leave her too badly marked for any guest who really wanted her later on. Everyone got what they wanted; it was very neat.

\*\*\*

The common room was in full swing when I entered, a stark contrast from the restrained club-like atmosphere of the bar. The huge room with its opulent furnishings was occupied by about twenty or thirty of the guests and almost the same number of girls. Yuri stood by the door keeping an impassive eye on things.

This was the heart of The Lodge. This was where the strange contrast between ordered luxury and sexual excess came into sharp focus. In this room were the masters and their slaves. No-one had noticed me enter and I had time to look around me and get used to what was going on. The air was thick with cigar smoke, and most of the seats were occupied by dinner-suited men who were being served by the girls. But up here the girls were fully available for use. It was this that they were trained for and obviously embraced their roles enthusiastically. This aspect of The Lodge, above all others fascinated me. The girls who were serving were making their way around the room quite unperturbed by the sound of whips being applied to their colleagues all round them. Right at the far end of the room I could see one girl tied to the marble fireplace, with her arms spread out along it. She had been stripped down to her stockings and shoes. Beside and just behind her a tall man in his early forties was standing and giving her a thorough working over with a scourge. She was writhing under repeated lashes to her shoulders and back, which sported an impressive mesh of red weals. But as soon as she was released she fell to her knees and reached for the man's bulging trousers, with obvious eagerness and was soon sucking hungrily on his rigidly aroused sex.

In the middle of the room two girls were suspended by their wrists from a chain which hung from a chandelier. These two had been stripped completely naked. Their feet dangled a foot clear of the floor and they had been suspended back to back. A thick leather strap bound their ankles together and to each other's, another performed the same function at their knees. Their tautly stretched arms accentuated the thrusting breasts, which provided the targets for the two men handling the whips. They stood in front of each girl and laid on lashes from breast to thigh while the girls' bodies shook and swayed like a living pendulum under the whips. A cheer went up from the spectators when one girl broke and achieved a shuddering climax, her companion followed suit soon after and they were hauled down, only to be replaced by two more, who stripped off with not the slightest show of reluctance.

Under one of the windows, just opposite me, there were two trestles. Over these two more naked girls were tied, face down. Their ankles had been pulled well apart before being tied to the legs of the trestles so that the coral-pink gashes of their sexes were displayed as well as the brown buds of their anuses between their inviting buttocks. In fact that was all that was visible of them and they made a stunning display. Obviously I wasn't the first to find them attractive. From both sexes and one of the anuses displayed, the milky residue of semen was seeping down their thighs. At the end of each trestle hung a three-tongued tawse and these had obviously been well used as both sets of buttocks and upper thighs were liberally marked with broad red swathes.

For a moment I was sorely tempted to indulge myself

immediately, but I had business to attend to first. I looked round for Brat and was glad to see that she hadn't been put to use yet. Even though a girl wears a disc, if she is sent to the common room, then while she is there she is common property, so any man in the room could do what he liked with her. Quickly I scanned the room for an item of bondage furniture or restraint that wasn't in use, and my eye lighted on an arrangement of bars mounted on short wooden posts which stood beside one of the sofas. One bar was set at hip height, but the one beyond it was set slightly higher. Leather straps were set at the bases of the posts supporting the first bar, while a series of holes in the second pair of posts seemed to allow the straps passed through them to be moved up or down. My imagination immediately supplied the form of a girl bent forward and tied so that the first bar prevented her hips from moving forward under punishment, while the second supported her chest and immobilised her arms and torso. But what if…?

Before anyone could commandeer Brat I strode forward and summoned her. She finished serving a drink and then came to stand in front of me.

"Can I get you something master?" In front of these men, experienced in casually dealing with submissive female flesh, she managed to load the words with almost outright contempt. From the corner of my eye I saw conversations halted at a couple of tables and men turn to look at us.

"Strip naked and stand by those bars," I told her.

She made no verbal response, but simply did as I had said, stepping out of her dress and even using one of the bars to balance herself against while she unrolled her stockings. When she stood up straight and now completely nude she was a superb sight, and I heard behind me the whips begin to fall silent as men turned to look and appreciate. Alan had clearly not beaten her recently, her skin was flawless and sun-tanned to a soft golden hue, even the full, firm mounds of the breasts were tanned the same colour. There was just the narrowest strip of white flesh at her crotch which set of the small bush of blonde pubes to perfection. She was well aware of the effect her body had on men and opened her legs slightly while joining her hands behind her back. The slight shifting of her body set the breasts swaying just a little. She knew what she was doing alright and looked straight at me with an 'okay, what next big man?' sort of challenge in her eye.

"Over the bars Brat," I said.

She turned to face them and bent over. It became immediately apparent why she had been allowed to retain a G-string while sunbathing. The generous curves of her buttocks stood out starkly pale against the gold of the rest of her body, any marks of whip, crop or cane would stand out superbly on them. I heard some of the men rise from their seats and come over to watch. I guessed they wanted to see what I was capable of doing with such a superb body to work on. Well they were going to find out.

"I didn't say bend over forwards Brat. Stand up, turn away from the bars and lean back."

As she stood up I was delighted to see the sudden uncertainty in her eyes. I took charge then, positioning her ankles by the straps in the front posts and buckling them tight. As I straightened up a silver haired man in his early fifties addressed me.

"You're using the toast rack then?" he asked, and then continued when I looked puzzled. "It's most commonly used to toast the buttocks you see."

"Not this time it isn't," I told him grimly. "Lean back Brat."

Cautiously she did as she was told, groping behind her for the second bar and then spreading her arms apart as she let herself down. Once her arms were fully spread and she had no choice but to let her head fall back so that her hair trailed on the floor, I joined in the general admiration of the effect I had created. If Brat had looked inviting before, she looked a picture of submissive display now. Her legs were tied open and the first bar, just behind her hips pushed her mons forward so the soft purse of her sex was clearly visible. Her flat stomach, now beginning to heave with nervous breathing stretched up to the full depth of her rib cage which supported the straining breasts. Despite their bulk they hardly flattened to the sides, but retained their magnificent shape almost perfectly, pushing up eagerly it seemed to receive whatever was coming.

I moved round to the second bar and shifted the straps down by three holes. Brat, her head upside down and her throat stretched, stared nervously at me as I worked. Once I thought I had got it about right I grasped her left wrist and pulled it down to buckle one strap tightly around it. She couldn't help gasping at the strictness of the bondage as her other arm was wrenched down and back, and the wrist tightly fastened. Then I stood up to admire my handiwork, and I realised I wasn't alone. More or less the whole room, girls as well as men had gathered to see what I would do with Brat, and I could see growing respect on the men's faces.

Brat was now tautly bowed backwards over the bars, the tensioning of her pectorals when her arms had been stretched back had served to pull the breasts even tighter and it would serve, I saw, to steady them under the whip. But the best feature of her bondage was that as you stood in front of her legs and let your eye roam up her body, from the straining muscles in the long thighs, up over the now open sex, up the torso and finally to her breasts, her head was quite invisible. She had simply become a body to be used for a master's pleasure. And something like this thought had obviously gone through her mind as well, because the perfectly profiled breasts now sported hard, deep-red nipples. I couldn't resist just reaching out with one finger and running it up along the exposed flesh of her vulva. As I had thought, it was moist and the clitoris was a hard little nub which I barely touched, but even that was enough to elicit a moan from her. And as we all watched a tiny dewdrop appeared at her vaginal opening. She was ready to go now.

From somewhere I was handed a short flail with seven or eight flat leather lashes, about a foot long. Not too heavy and ideal for the area I was intending to work over. I swished it in the air a couple of times to get its feel and then struck without warning. I struck across her mons and even in that position Brat's body managed a jump as the leather smacked home.

"Come now Brat," I chided. "Of all people I know you've taken worse than that."

If she made a response it was lost in the smacking of the second lash landing. Her stomach heaved and clenched. I was standing by her left thigh and began to work on that next, and at each impact Brat twisted and writhed on her rack. Then I slowly moved up her body, enjoying the most intoxicating rush of excitement I had ever experienced. The lovely body was so helpless and vulnerable. It was crying out be taken possession of, to be mastered, and tonight I was going to be the master. I stopped for a moment when I got to the left breast, and watched as she gulped for breath. For a second she managed to crane her head up to look at me and then whispered a word that could have been 'yes', when she saw where I was poised. Her head fell back and I struck, making the mound of the breast shudder. From somewhere she found the leeway to arch herself even more than she was already forced to and a cry escaped her. I gave it four more, keeping myself firmly in check and not giving in to the temptation to strike with my full strength. She heaved and sobbed all the time, her head thrashing from side to side, but when I stopped again I reached down and plunged my hand into her sex. She was desperate for me and I was able to thrust three fingers easily into the vagina, turning and twisting them as the heel of my palm rubbed at her clitoris. She exploded. Shrill cries of ecstasy broke from her as her stretched body arched and spasmed in blatant delight at her treatment. And I felt her internal muscles twitch and clamp onto my fingers. I let her have her climax and then went back to work.

I moved to her right side and began again.

Brat was shouting and moaning constantly now, disconnected words pouring from her between cries as the whip drove her relentlessly onwards to another shattering climax. It arrived again just as I gave her right breast the same treatment and revelled in the way the vulnerable softness of it absorbed the lashes and rippled just as her entire body did as she orgasmed with no help from my fingers this time. It was pure joy in her own submission to someone who was prepared to drive her to her limits.

As I stood back, suddenly aware of the fact that I was panting and hot from my own exertions, there was a spontaneous round of applause from the onlookers, and male hands clapped me on the back.

The silver haired man appeared at my side again. "Twenty five! A good thrashing indeed. Well done Mr O'Kane!"

Someone handed me a drink and it was all I could do before I was led away, to remember to detail off one of the girls to let Brat up and then bring her to me. I just had time to glance back once more and admire the taut and crimson striped body tied over the bars, before I was welcomed into The Lodge.

Brat was brought to me when she had dressed again and I spared her the time only to tell her to go to my room and wait for me there. She was flushed, sweating and bedraggled, so I told her to smarten herself up before I got there. Her replies were properly respectful now, and there was no defiance.

I passed an enjoyable hour or so in conversation with various men, one or two of whom Falconer had already interviewed. I even availed myself of one of the girls on the trestles. Brat's beating had left me with a throbbing erection, and it was sheer delight to plunge it into an utterly anonymous sex which was displayed so slavishly and concentrate purely on my own pleasure as I rammed into it and withdrew, then plunged in again to pause and just appreciate the twitchings of the internal muscles around my shaft. The girl being nameless and faceless in that position, only made it easier to concentrate on the uncomplicated delight of bringing oneself to ejaculation in the churning moisture of a female's excited body.

By the time I decided I was ready to take Brat on again and took my leave of the common room, I knew I was 'one of them'. I had proved myself. But I was still angry with Brat. Madame hadn't seen me deliver that beating, but she had witnessed my humiliation earlier.

When I entered my room Brat, who had been sitting on the edge of the bed stood up immediately, and I was pleased to note that she put her hands behind her back and looked down as I approached. Maybe it was that she respected me as a master now, or maybe it was because she had seen the cane that I carried. I had borrowed it from the common room and exited with the encouragement of the members ringing in my ears.

I told her I was going to cane her backside till it was raw.

"The beating in the common room was purely for appearances' sake. I am now going to punish you for tricking me earlier today."

Once again I watched her strip, and this time noticed a tremor in her hands as she did so. She knew now that I wouldn't stop a beating until she had absorbed so much pain that it transformed itself into that strange pleasure I had seen so often at The Lodge. It wouldn't be a mildly pleasant paddling or spanking; it would take her on the long climb through the whole scale of pain before she found pleasure. And as I had seen with other girls, she was both terrified and thrilled at the prospect.

I had her kneel on the floor and bend forward to put her

forehead on it, then I took straps from the posts of the bed and made her reach back through her legs and grasp her ankles. It was a position I had seen in one of Alan's prints at the penthouse and rather liked the utter humiliation it involved. I tied her wrists to her ankles and then undressed myself while she waited. Her back and buttocks were of course unmarked by the earlier beating. I would attend to her back in due course, and for now I addressed her buttocks.

They were pushed up very nicely for me and her shoulders were pushed so far down that really all I could see was the wide expanse of her bottom, her sex lips nestling in their hollow at the tops of the thighs, the thighs themselves and her feet and wrists bound together. Although the same sense of exhilarating power which had swept through me in the common room, swept through me again and had my sex throbbing up into full erection again, I knew that this time what I really wanted was to get her into bed, wild with all the passion that another beating would arouse in her.

But still the beating itself was something to be savoured in its own right, and I swished the cane behind her before I started. Then I stood over her and laid it across the crown of the buttocks, she shivered at its touch and I could see her tense herself, but leave her buttocks relaxed—Alan had taught her well. I lifted the cane away and brought it down in a short scything arc.

It made a deeply satisfying contact with an exciting Crack! as it landed. The twin pillows of soft, tightly stretched flesh rippled as the shock ran through them. Brat cried out and squirmed desperately. All of a sudden the need to get inside her body swamped me completely. I wanted to finish her punishment and then take the possession of her body which I had earned. I cracked in five or six strokes more, not keeping any real count, not taking my time but just loving the way her body writhed and she moaned and screamed under the fusillade of slicing cuts which left her buttocks lividly striped. I had fully intended to take her to orgasm but I was too impatient, I threw down the cane and fumbled with her bonds in my haste to get at her.

As soon as she was free she rolled onto her back, opened her legs wide and reached for me. For just a second I knelt between her legs and then sank down onto her, feeling the soft lips of her sex open easily for me as I slid up into her. She groaned with pleasure as she felt my rod slide into her depths and then she wrapped her legs round my hips to hold me in. Her need was as great as mine and she was gasping and panting with the onset of orgasm. I rammed myself into her time after time, not caring for anything but the frantic bucking of her body under me as she propelled both herself and me to our climaxes. And when she felt my penis swell and tense before it began pumping, she practically screamed at me to fill her with my spend, flood her until she could take no more. She wanted to be taken as totally as she had been under the whip and the cane.

For a long time afterwards we lay where we were and let the storms abate. Eventually I rolled off her and after a moment or two she propped herself up on one elbow and looked down at me seriously.

"It was worth tricking you on the way down here," she said. "But I never thought it would be. I thought you were just some kind of voyeur with a pen—no guts to do it yourself. But I was wrong."

She moved more of her weight onto me and slowly began to move down my body, licking and kissing. Taking her time. And when at last she reached the thatch of coarse pubic hair at my crotch, I felt myself respond again and she chuckled throatily as she felt me begin to pulse towards erection again.

And while she buried her head deep between my legs and I felt her tongue swirl as far back as my anus, I told her what I had planned for her the next day. She purred in contentment as she worked and listened to what I was going to do to her. Only when I had finished did she at last hold my shaft at the base and gently slip her lips over the gleaming helm.

"I'll take it that you're happy with that then Brat," I said, and lay back to enjoy the rest of the blowjob. Her head bobbed up and down on my sex in reply.

The next morning after breakfast I walked round to the stable yard and found that my instructions had been carried out. Brat stood harnessed to a trap, waiting patiently, her reins tied to a ring on the stable wall. I inspected her carefully, never having had a pony girl at my disposal before. She had a thick bit in her mouth which I liked as it kept it well open. The bridle had been carefully buckled around her head to leave a good mane of blonde hair free at the back. The wrist restraints, which were clipped to the shafts of the cart, were beautifully tooled leather, and in deference to her skittish nature she had leather blinkers on, again in crafted leather. I remembered Alan's description of the harness she wore at home in Suffolk and regretted that she wasn't more restricted. I would have liked some constriction on the large breasts and it crossed my mind to wonder why Alan hadn't had her pierced and ringed there. It would have allowed far greater possibilities, and I decided I would mention it to him. For the time being I ran my hands down her torso, savouring the feel of the breasts, the flat stomach and the neat little fleece of blonde pubic hair at her crotch. She moaned through her bit and pranced a little at my touch, but a quick slap to her breasts quietened her down. I moved to stand behind her and admired the dark ridges the cane had embossed on her buttocks before I swung up into the seat and whipped her up with a light touch to her shoulder.

Just as Alan and Sam Andreotti had about a year before, I headed due south, down towards the lake. There was something there which I knew suited my purposes. And sure enough when I found the copse of trees that Alan had mentioned, I could see they were perfect.

I pulled Brat over onto the grass and encouraged her with

the whip until I reined her in just under a young but mature enough tree. I unclipped her restraints from the shafts and led her over to the tree, passing the reins round the trunk and tying them off before clipping her wrists together behind her back. Then I returned to the trap and wheeled it a little way until it stood under a branch which looked solid enough to take Brat's weight. I returned to her and led her by her reins to the trap and helped her up onto the seat which was sloping forward, down to where the shafts now met the ground. She balanced precariously so I unbuckled her reins from her bridle and bound her wrists in front of her with them and then hurriedly slung them over the branch. I jumped down, went to the other side of the branch and hauled down as hard as I could. Brat's body rose clear of the trap to hang with her feet just a couple of inches clear of the seat, a muffled cry came from behind her bit as her arms took the strain. I passed the reins around the tree trunk again and once more tied them off, very firmly this time. Then all I had to do was pull the trap clear and Brat dangled enticingly, spinning slowly on her reins, her feet and legs kicking around for some purchase. I used my belt to tie her ankles together and that stopped any wriggling detracting from the wonderful sight she made. Her suspension did truly amazing things to her breasts and I reached up to fondle them and tease the already hardening nipples into full erection. I almost regretted the beating I had given her in the common room, which had left dull red weals across them. And I had to admit that a further beating wouldn't enhance their appearance; so it was her back which was next for the whip.

This time I was much more relaxed. I took my time and enjoyed the Swish! Smack! of the leather across her broad shoulders and upper back. She grunted and moaned at each lash and I left her plenty of time between strokes so that she could really soak up the bite of the whip. I was so bound up in watching her sway and spin at the end of her reins that I nearly jumped out of my skin when a hand tapped me on the shoulder.

It was Madame.

She gave me her quick smile and walked past me to grip Brat's ankles and spin her around slowly, examining her.

"Not yet a full day, and already you have done breasts, abdomen, thighs, back and buttocks, Mr O'Kane. I'm impressed. Come."

She walked over to stand by the trap and I followed her.

"You know, I think, that I did not like the idea of you and your friend writing your book. But I am persuaded that you are both to be trusted. Alan did well appointing you to look after Brat. You understand slaves."

I thanked her profusely. Not only did it look as though I would get her story, but I would be able to ask her advice about Kathy. She accepted my thanks and then pointed out that maybe I should think about taking Brat down now. I did so and put her back between the shafts of the trap to wait by the tree while we talked.

"When you have written up your latest experiences here and shown them to Mr Masterson—and I know he is very keen to read them—then I will phone you and we will talk. I think you will find my story interesting."

Again I expressed my gratitude for her trust and then tentatively introduced the subject of Kathy, telling her where I had got to so far.

"She sounds as if she might have possibilities," Madame said thoughtfully when I had finished. "Do nothing more with her until we have spoken again. And now I must ask you to return our dear Brat to the house. She is required in the dining room at lunchtime."

I suggested that Madame might like to drive Brat back herself. I was in a good mood and fancied a walk to work up an appetite for lunch.

I watched as Brat swung the trap round and set off back to the house, a couple of stinging cracks across the shoulders serving to get her pulling strongly up the slight incline. I strolled along after the two women, enjoying the fine morning and looking forward to interviewing Madame at last.

And as the sound of the trap rattling along ahead of me faded, I felt that perhaps, just perhaps, one day I might enjoy driving Kathy along this same road.

*The End*

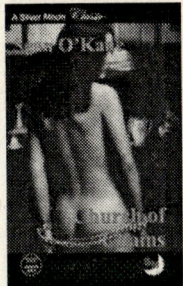

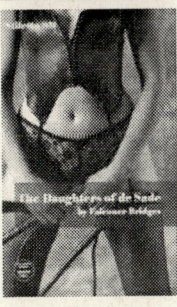

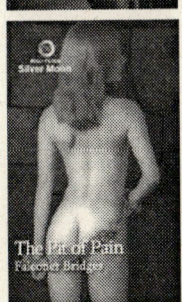

| | | |
|---|---|---|
| **Churchof ?ams** — Sean O'Kane | **Taming the Brat** Sean O'Kane | **Lu...** Sean O'Kane |
| **The Gladiator** Sean O'Kane | **The Prize** An Arena Novel Sean O'Kane | **Slave's Honour** An Arena Novel Sean O'Kane |
| **Last Slave Standing** Sean O'Kane | **Slavemaker** Sean O'Kane | **The Brotherhood** by Falconer Bridges |
| **The Daughters of de Sade** by Falconer Bridges | **The Pit of Pain** Falconer Bridges | **Slaves of the Bloodline** Falconer Bridges |

There are over 100 stunningly erotic novels of domination and submission in the Silver Moon catalogue. You can see the full range, including Club and Illustrated editions by writing to:

Silver Moon Reader Services
Shadowline Publishing Ltd,
No 2 Granary House
Ropery Road,
Gainsborough,
Lincs. DH21 2NS

You will receive a copy of the latest issue of the Readers' Club magazine, with articles, features, reviews, adverts and news plus a full list of our publications and an order form.